FALLING FOR THE WINGMAN
Shannon Stults

www.BOROUGHSPUBLISHINGGROUP.com

FALLING FOR THE WINGMAN
Copyright © 2021 Shannon Stults

ISBN: 978-1-953810-91-5

To Emory who reminds me when given the choice between ice cream and froyo one should always go for the ice cream.
Love you, pal

FALLING FOR THE WINGMAN

Chapter 1

"Come on, Bentley. You're telling me you didn't do *anything* over winter break?" Aubrey stared at me as she leaned back against the blue metal of her closed locker, her arms crossed in front of her.

I shrugged. "Dad had to get ready for the new soccer season. And Mom stayed in the basement writing most of the time, which means I was on babysitting duty."

"Boring. You'd think with all the money your mom makes on her health and fitness books she'd take the time to enjoy it every once in a while."

"It's not so bad. My mom already travels so much for work anyway. She likes to relax at home when she can." I grabbed the chemistry book from my locker and shoved it in the small messenger bag hanging from my shoulder. "What about you? Do anything exciting?"

She picked at the dark red polish on her nails. "Oh, you know. Christmas up north with my mom's family, then New Year's with the rest of the Miller clan in LA."

I tried not to be jealous as she described her winter break outside our small town of Oakcrest, South Carolina.

"Oh, and did I mention my parents let me go skiing with Beth and her family at their condo for a week?" she added, perking up for the first time all morning.

"You finally told your parents about your girlfriend, and they let you stay at her place?"

Despite Aubrey's painfully tight skinny jeans, low-cut purple top, and face full of dark, smoky makeup, her parents were uber religious and conservative. They'd met each other on a Christian dating website, went to church every Sunday, and made Aubrey pray with them each night before bed. A complete stranger would be terrified to come out to Aubrey's parents.

Aubrey laughed. "Please. Do you honestly think I'd still be allowed out of the house if my parents found out?" She shook her head. "As far as they know, Beth is a friend." She ruffled her short, black hair.

"Did you two," I leaned in closer, lowering my voice to a whisper, "*do* anything?"

"Your sexual innocence is so amusing."

"What would you know about it?" It wasn't like I was some doe-eyed little girl. I was seventeen. I'd had my fair share of heavy make-out sessions. Well, fair-*ish*.

"Relax. Nothing happened. She slept in her bed, and I had an air mattress on the floor. We're still taking things slow."

I wasn't sure how staying a week at her girlfriend's vacation house was considered taking it slow. Then again, I knew a few people who probably thought a sexy sleepover was moving at an agonizing snail's pace.

I took a step back and shut my locker door with a clang, internally groaning at the guy with green eyes watching me.

"What's up, Bentley?"

Cooper Bradshaw leaned against the locker next to mine, mirroring Aubrey's posture to a T. His dirty blond hair was a few inches shorter than it'd been before the break, and his eyes shone with the type of renewed energy that usually resulted from a much-needed break from the oppression of high school. In his case, that break most likely involved copious amounts of partying and drinking at the University of South Carolina campus.

There was an ease to him, a carelessness I'd never been able to understand and I envied sometimes. And then there was his charm that made most girls swoon. Crossed in front of him, his arms pulled his red sweatshirt tightly across his broad shoulders.

I had no idea how long he'd been there, but the grin spreading across his face as his gaze shifted between me and Aubrey told me he'd at least heard some of our conversation.

"Miller." He gave Aubrey a wink and a once-over. "Always a pleasure."

I had to keep myself from rolling my eyes. I figured he'd assume his charm would work on our school's partially out lesbian. He must not have gotten the memo there were, in fact, women in the world even he couldn't attract.

"Bradshaw." Aubrey didn't smile back, offering him zero chance to interpret her greeting as flirtation. The last thing she needed was him crying "bi" to get one more girl's attention.

"What do you want?" I asked before either of them could say more.

He straightened, the grin on his face dimming some as he looked at me. "Lovely to see you too. I'm fine today, thanks for asking. Why yes, I did have fun over the holidays. How was your break?"

I couldn't remember the last time Cooper Bradshaw sought me out for conversation, casual or otherwise. Which made me almost certain he had more than catching up on his mind. I stared at him without saying a word. I didn't have to wait long.

"I need a favor," he finally said, the false pleasantries forgotten.

"I'll see you later, Aubrey," I told her before turning on my heel and heading down the hall. As expected, Cooper was at my side. "Does this favor involve me tutoring you or something?" That was the kind of favor I was used to. In the last two years, I'd somehow become the go-to person when anyone needed help with their grades, especially when it came to the school's varsity athletes. Probably because of all the times I'd helped my older brothers and their friends before they graduated. And because I was currently tied for the top spot in our junior class.

Cooper laughed, throwing his arm over my shoulders. "You insult me, Bentley. You and I both know we have the same GPA."

I grimaced at his arm on my shoulders and at the truth in his words. It so happened Cooper was the guy I was tied with GPA-wise.

By some cruel joke, he'd been gifted with looks, athleticism, *and* brains. It was unfair, to say the least. A trifecta like that, he was an instant hit with the female student population, as well as a few guys, no doubt. The rest of the males in our class were torn between jealousy and hero worship. He was literally everything they wished they could be: nerd or jock. He was the complete package, and he knew it.

I shrugged his arm off my shoulders, turning sharply around a corner and down another hall.

"Hey, Cooper," Ashley Morales practically purred as she and half of the cheerleading squad passed us, making her interest blatantly clear. Not that it mattered.

Sure, Cooper was a flirt. But it was universally understood—at least at Oakcrest High—Cooper Bradshaw only dated college girls.

Only his version of dating consisted of partying all night with a girl, sleeping with her, and the next morning, promptly forgetting about her existence. As far as I knew, Cooper had never had a serious relationship in his life.

"Ladies," he said, giving them an appreciative glance, but nothing more.

A few of them giggled, and I shook my head at how sad it all was. "What do you want?"

He grinned. "Have I mentioned how much I like your hair?" He reached out, twirling one of the dark brown and hot-pink curls around his finger. "It looks incredibly badass."

I slapped his hand away. "I'm bored, Coop. Get to the point."

"You may have heard about what happened to my car…"

Here we go. "You mean when you were having so much *fun* over the break you failed to notice the large telephone pole you were swerving into? Pretty sure the whole school heard about that one."

It had been the biggest piece of gossip to blow up my phone all break. Everyone was talking about New Year's Eve when Cooper partied a little too hard at the University of South Carolina and totaled his precious Maserati.

"So, when do you get a new one?"

"If my dad gets his way, never. He says I need to learn some responsibility."

"Gasp. Cooper Bradshaw learn to be responsible? The horror."

He shook his head like he was completely mystified by the thought. Cooper had never been one to earn anything. His parents were loaded, and for as long as I could remember, everything in his life had been handed to him on a platter.

"What does this have to do with me?" I asked. The first bell of the morning hadn't even rung yet, and already it felt like this day would last forever.

He shoved his hands in his pockets. "I need a ride to school." He rushed on when I opened my mouth to object. "It's only until my dad comes to his senses. I had to ride the bus this morning, and it was the worst hour of my life. Even you don't have the heart to make me suffer through that again."

Wanna bet? "Why me?" We turned another corner into the science hall.

"Because you live next door," he answered like it should be obvious.

"Surely there's someone else you'd rather ride with?"

He shook his head. "Not who's willing to get up early enough to come to our neck of the woods every morning."

"I don't think so." Truth be told, he was probably the last person I wanted to see first thing in the morning. I much preferred our current arrangement where we tried to ignore only thirty yards separated our houses.

"Come on, please. I promised Liam I'd give him a ride, and now that the Maserati is out of commission, he's stuck taking a bus too."

"Liam who?" There was only one Liam I knew, and considering he lived several hours away, I was pretty sure it wasn't him.

He gave me a look, a long crease forming between his eyebrows. "Liam Haynes."

A soft thud echoed through the hall as I tripped over my own foot. I'd managed to right myself midstride, but not before drawing the attention of several people in the hall.

"You okay?" he asked through tight lips as he clearly tried not to laugh.

"I'm fine," I said, shaking it off. "Why would Liam Haynes need a ride? I thought he was in Charleston."

"He came back at the end of the break. He and his mom moved in with his Aunt Claire. He's still unpacking and getting settled in. Tomorrow's his first day at school."

My stomach somersaulted. Liam Haynes was back in town. And even better, he needed me to give him a ride.

Cooper batted his long eyelashes, his bottom lip poking out slightly. "It'll be like old times. The three of us, hanging out. Please," he added softly.

"Fine." I stopped at the chemistry lab door. "I'll give you guys a ride, but only for tomorrow. Then you can sucker someone else into being your chauffeur."

The warning bell for first period rang, and he grinned. "You're amazing, you know that?" He grabbed me by the shoulders and planted an obnoxiously loud peck on my cheek.

I groaned, and he took off down the hall without a look back. "That may have been cute when we were five," I yelled after him, wiping at my cheek. "Now it's gross."

I heard him laughing as he reached the end of the hall and turned the corner.

***

I'm home. My heavy bag hit the wood floor of our foyer with a loud, echoing *thunk* as I rolled the stress and tension of the first day back at school from my shoulders.

"Benny." My favorite three-year-old came racing down the hall and slammed into my legs, so I threw her up in the air to a fit of giggles before settling her on my hip. Two moderately deep voices yelled at each other off in the distance.

"What are they fighting about now?" I asked Addie, hugging her tight and spinning us around.

She screamed in delight, her dark pigtails bouncing high on her head. "PlayStation."

What else was new?

Much to her dismay, I set my baby sister on her feet and made my way into the oversize den at the back of the house. Noah and Caden stood in the middle, wrestling over a controller. Noah's shirt was wrinkled and his face red, making it clear they'd been at it for a while. From the looks of it, Caden was winning, probably due to the two years and four inches he had on our twelve-year-old brother.

I cleared my throat, and the two pulled apart. Caden fixed his glasses hanging askew over his nose, and Noah pointed a finger at him. "He's been playing for half an hour, and he won't let me have a turn."

"The idiot turned the game off before I could save it. I was on my highest—"

"Homework."

Noah's mouth fell open. "But I didn't get a turn on the PlayStation."

I shook my head. "Homework, or you won't *have* a PlayStation anymore."

They looked at each other before marching with heavy stomps out of the den. Addie grinned at my side. "Good job, Benny."

"Thanks. Where's Mom?"

"Office." She held up one pudgy little finger. "Said she had one more chapter," she explained, the Rs of the last two words sounding more like Ws.

One more chapter. Meaning she'd be holed up writing in her basement office for another few hours at least. It also meant I was left in charge of my three siblings until then, not to mention the mountain of homework my teachers had piled on me my first day back.

I studied Addie. "Want to make cookies?"

"Ooh, ooh, ooh, ooh," she squealed, nodding frantically as she jumped up and down.

"Good. I'll race you to the kitchen."

She took off without hesitation.

An hour and a half later, I stood at the kitchen island while I carefully moved yet another dozen double-chocolate cookies from the pan to the cooling racks. Addie had abandoned me as soon as the first batch came out, waiting only long enough for one to cool before she snatched it from the rack, catapulted from her stepstool, and shot out of the kitchen. From the sounds of her innocently out-of-tune singing filling the house, she was now in the den, watching one of her favorite TV shows.

Noah and Caden had left their homework on the kitchen table for inspection before running off with their own plate of cookies. They were likely kicking the soccer ball around out back or watching TV up in their room, which left me alone to finish up the cookies and do the dishes.

"Hey, honey."

I looked up from the mixing bowl I was rinsing off in the island sink. Mom came in wearing cotton shorts and a thin, black sweater. She raised her arms up over her head in her usual post-writing stretch.

"Hey, Mom." I smiled. "So Theo and Xander finally left this morning?"

My two older brothers had been staying with us over their break from Coastal Carolina University. Judging from the fully stocked fridge and the lack of dirty clothes strewn around the house, I assumed they packed up and headed back to Myrtle Beach to start their semester.

"Don't sound so pleased. You know you miss them when they're gone."

"Them, sure. Their piles of stinky laundry, not so much."

"Did you pick Samantha and Sebastian up from school today?" she asked, glancing out the window to the twins' house across the cul-de-sac.

"Nah. Dr. Caldwell took the day off so she could take them to a movie after school. But I'm watching them tomorrow."

Mom lifted her hands to her hair and pulled it from its messy bun, running her fingers through it a few times. Then she took in the dirty dishes and the several dozen cookies cooling on the counter behind me.

"Oh no. What's wrong?"

I shrugged. "I'm fine."

Her eyes narrowed. "Honey, you're baking," she said slowly. She fell onto one of the island's barstools. "Tell me what happened."

Curse my tendency for stress-baking. Ever since my obsession with *Cupcake Wars* back in sixth grade, I had a habit of turning to baked goods whenever something was wrong. Now anytime I got in the mood to bake, Mom felt the need to sit me down for a quick heart-to-heart.

"Do you remember Liam Haynes?"

"Of course. You, Cooper, and Liam were nearly inseparable all through middle school. Why?"

I put the large mixing bowl into the dishwasher. "He and his mom moved back into town over the break."

"Really? In the middle of the year? I wonder why they'd do that." She watched as I loaded dish after dish. "You nervous about seeing him again?"

"A little." I hadn't been able to think about anything else all day. "I don't know if we'll get along like we used to. What if he's totally different from the kid I knew?"

She nodded. "A lot can change about a person in three years."

"What if I'm not the same girl he was friends with? What if I'm not what he expects?" What if, after all this time, the girl I am now disappoints him?

"I guess you won't know until you see him. Some friendships don't last forever. But I promise, true friends stay close no matter how far or how long they're apart."

Mom grabbed a cookie from the counter and bit into it. "You two will get back in the swing of things. Give it time," she said through a mouthful of cookie. She took another bite and stood. "These are amazing, by the way."

"Thanks." Mom smiled before she left the kitchen to go find Addie. With the dirty dishes sitting in the dishwasher, I grabbed some Tupperware containers from the cabinet and separated all the cookies evenly between them.

Mom was right. No need to stress about Liam. We were friends.

Once upon a time, I'd thought maybe there could be more, but Liam moved to Charleston, and I was left to wonder what could've been. I was sure of one thing: Liam and I had been best friends once, and we'd be able to find our way back.

Of course, Cooper had been my best friend too. Yet, up until today, we'd barely spoken in the last three years. Mom must be right about that as well.

Some friendships weren't meant to last.

Chapter 2

The next morning, Cooper waited by my white Camry his thumbs speedily tapping away at his phone screen. He had on thick jeans and a black coat impossibly accentuating his lean and muscular build. He looked up as I approached, and a radiant smile spread across his face.

"Morning, Erikson." He sounded painfully chipper and awake. Apparently, Cooper—known for his late-night partying—was a morning person.

Unfortunately, I wasn't. "Any luck finding a ride for tomorrow?" My warm breath was visible in the icy air. I walked around the front of the car, juggling two travel coffee mugs in one hand while I grabbed the door handle with my other.

"Straight to business, I see." He opened the passenger door and fell into the seat beside me before adjusting it to accommodate his long legs. "Not yet, though I can ask around some more today if that makes you feel better."

"Much." I set one of the coffee mugs in a cup-holder before starting the car and taking a long, delicious drag from the other. Turning the heat up to full blast, I could already feel the warmth and caffeine heating my insides and spreading renewed life through my veins. Some people crawled out of bed with smiles on their faces and a song in their hearts. Others needed coffee.

Lots and lots of coffee.

Cooper reached for the other mug. "This for me?"

I tore it from his hand and shoved it back in the cupholder. "No."

One of his eyebrows lifted. "You know, some would consider that addictive behavior. I think you might have a problem."

"Bite me."

"I think I enjoy seeing this side of you, Bentley."

"And I'm going to enjoy seeing you *walk* your perky ass to school."

"Perky, huh?" He waggled his brows. "That mean you've been checking out my butt?"

"I was calling you perky, not your... You know, maybe it would be safer for you if you stopped talking." Once the car was warm enough, I threw it into reverse and backed it down the driveway. "Tell me how to get to Liam's house. That's it."

Liam lived on the other side of town, which meant a good fifteen minutes of riding in virtual silence aside from the occasional direction. Coop had turned on the radio and turned up the volume as soon as we left my driveway. I didn't care. My brain was too busy freaking out to notice what song was playing, and my fingers practically tingled with nervous energy.

This was it. The moment I would see Liam again. There was a time I thought we'd be perfect together: that he and I were meant to be someday. Who knew? Maybe Liam was exactly as I'd imagined him all these years. Handsome, smart, kind. Everything I always wanted. Or he could be something different and unexpected, and completely irresistible.

Either way, it would be a cute story to tell the kids someday.

"What are you smiling about?"

"Nothing." I forced my daydream and its accompanying grin away.

He pointed to a small house on the right. "This is it."

I pulled into the narrow driveway and up to a house with light blue paneling and black shutters. My gaze shifted to the front door as it swung open, and my heart took a galloping leap as Liam stepped outside.

Bundled in a thick gray coat with a backpack slung over one shoulder, he jogged down a small set of concrete steps and over to the car, his shaggy light blond hair flopping over his eyes. No doubt about it: he was still as gorgeous as I remembered.

He reached Cooper's side of the car and yanked the back door open, then fell in with a huff before he slammed the door shut. "Jesus, it's cold out there."

Cooper spoke without turning to look at him. "Liam, you remember Bentley."

Not knowing what to say or if I could even say anything at all, I turned and offered a small wave.

Liam's eyes widened as he took me in. "Bentley Erikson? Holy shit. You look amazing."

"Thank you," I forced out, my cheeks flooding with heat. His smile was enough to turn my insides into complete mush. "You look…really good too."

His gaze traveled over me. "I mean, look at you. You're all grown up."

Cooper rolled his eyes at the windshield.

"Three years will do that," I said.

Liam shook his head. "Wow."

"Hey, I uh…I had some coffee left over this morning." I grabbed the second travel mug, avoiding Cooper's glare. "If you want it."

Instead of reaching for the mug, he sat back and started buckling his seat belt. "Ah, thanks, but I'm good."

"Oh, okay," I muttered, trying not to sound as disappointed as I felt.

He smiled. "Coop can have it, though. He loves coffee. Can't get out of bed without it."

Cooper looked excessively pleased with himself as he attempted to take the mug. This time I let him.

"Don't mind if I do." He made a show of taking a long, indulgent sip.

Jerk.

I pulled back out onto the road. "So why the move back? I mean, not that we're not happy to have you back," I stammered. "I…it's weird to come back in the middle of the year, isn't it?"

"My mom really missed it here. I don't think she ever felt at home in Charleston, and she'd had enough. And then there's the soccer season. We wanted to get out here in time for me to play my junior year, maybe catch the eye of a few college scouts. Hey, does your dad still coach?"

I nodded. "Almost ten years now."

"Man, you're so lucky. Matt Erikson, Clemson alum and soccer legend, is your dad. Not to mention his three championships coaching at Florence and, what, like three more at Oakcrest?"

"Four," Cooper corrected, his chest puffed and shoulders back. It was widely understood those two championships probably wouldn't have been possible without Cooper.

"What about you, Bentley? You play?"

"Oh no. I'm afraid neither of my parents saw fit to give me their athletic gene." Every one of my brothers had the strength and coordination to dominate pretty much any sport they attempted. I was lucky not to strike out at T-ball.

"So, what about you two? Are you guys a thing now?"

A bark of laughter escaped my throat as I pulled into the school parking lot. "Definitely not. I agreed to give him a ride since he totaled his car like a complete moron."

Cooper glared at me, but Liam chuckled. "Yeah, I heard *all* about that." Once I'd parked in my usual spot, he put a hand on Cooper's shoulder and squeezed, the humor leaving his eyes as his brows drew together. "All kidding aside, you really should be more careful, you know. You could have seriously hurt yourself."

Cooper's knuckles whitened as he gripped the travel mug. "I'll see you guys later." His voice was low, not at all matching the light and playful mood he'd been in for most of the drive. Without another word, he opened the car door and climbed out, not looking back as he threw his bag over his shoulder and walked away.

I killed the engine and opened the door as Liam hopped out of the back. "That was weird."

Across the parking lot, Cooper threw the school door open and disappeared inside.

Liam sighed. "He's still sensitive about the accident." He walked around the car, backpack in hand. "I'd told him not to drive after I saw how much he drank at the party. But he didn't listen. I think he resents me a little for it now."

"Coop was drinking when he wrecked the car?" Of all the stupid, idiotic, selfish... "He could have killed someone."

"Trust me, he's been beating himself up pretty hard about it since."

All the times I'd heard the story, yet no one had mentioned that detail. "How has nobody said anything about the alcohol?"

"No doubt Mr. Bradshaw had the whole thing kept quiet. The perks of having a rich dad." The last sentence sounded like it had been dipped in acid, and I couldn't really blame him.

"You were there? I didn't realize you went to those parties."

"Every weekend since Coop got his license. I guess you could call it a tradition of ours."

"Oh." I knew the stories of Coop going to Columbia most Friday nights, renting a room downtown and then partying with college students the whole weekend. I hadn't realized Liam took part in those weekends too. "You guys must have a lot of fun."

He shrugged. "Not really. I don't do much at those parties. I'm more of a wingman for Coop. You know, the Goose to his Maverick. I help him land a girl while keeping an eye on him. Then I make sure he and whatever girl he's hooked up with have a sober ride home."

Relief flooded my body, and I had to look down to keep from grinning like an idiot. Could he be any more perfect?

"So, I'll see you later?" I could have cringed at the sound of desperation in my voice.

"Yeah, sure."

He smiled and started the trek across the parking lot.

"What about after school? Will you need a ride home?"

He turned to face me, taking small steps backwards toward the doors. "Nah. Soccer tryouts start today. I can get a ride from one of the guys."

"Oh, right."

"Thanks again," he called out before jogging to the doors.

"Any time."

***

"So what's the deal with this Liam guy?" Aubrey asked when we settled in at our usual lunch table. "All day, all anyone has talked about is Liam Haynes. Is he a god or something?"

I shook my head and swallowed a bite of my sandwich. It was easy to forget she'd moved to Oakcrest only two years ago. "Not a god. He's got a complicated history."

Aubrey's smoky eyes lit up. "That means drama. Tell me."

"Liam used to go to middle school with us. Actually, he lived right next door to Cooper and me."

Her eyebrows waggled. "I've seen your neighborhood. That means he's loaded."

"He used to be. His dad worked for this big corporation and raked in tons of money. But then it got out that he was embezzling, and there was this huge trial. Liam's dad went to prison and all the money he'd taken was seized. Not to mention what they lost in legal fees. Liam's mom didn't work, and she couldn't afford to stay here anymore. So they packed up and moved in with Liam's grandparents in Charleston."

"Wow, you weren't kidding."

"Watching Liam's family fall from grace was a big deal in Oakcrest. He's a really nice guy. He was the most popular kid in our school. Well, he and Cooper both were," I amended. "The three of us were friends. Always together at school, running around the neighborhood, playing games and stuff."

Aubrey's brow furrowed. "You and Cooper Bradshaw were friends?"

"Technically, Coop and I were best friends before Liam moved in next door. We did everything together." I took another bite of my turkey and cheese.

"But now you can't stand him. What changed?"

"Honestly, I don't know. Everything was fine until the day Liam left town. Then as soon as Liam and his mom drove off, it was like Cooper wanted nothing to do with me. I think it was \ too hard for him, and he didn't know how to cope. I tried to talk to him, but he gave me the cold shoulder. I never heard from Liam again until today."

"But the two of them managed to stay friends?" Aubrey nodded to the table across the cafeteria where Liam and Cooper sat laughing and eating with some of last year's soccer team.

I tossed the turkey sandwich onto my plate with a little more force than necessary. "Guess so," I muttered.

"Well, at least that explains why everyone's talking about him." Aubrey sat back in her chair. "I thought it was because he's hot."

"*You* think he's hot?"

Aubrey laughed. "Geez, Bentley. Relax. Just because I prefer hamburgers doesn't mean I can't appreciate a good hot dog—" She froze mid-sentence, and we both burst out in a fit of laughter.

"Sorry." She gasped between laughs. "That did not sound as perverted in my head."

"I think you said it right."

"I meant that while I'm not personally attracted to Liam, I can see how he is attractive to others. And clearly you think he is too, or you wouldn't have freaked out on me. Did you guys date or something?"

"No, we were good friends, nothing more. I mean, he *was* my first kiss but—"

"Spill," Aubrey demanded, sitting up straight.

"There's really not much to tell. It was the morning Coop and I said good-bye to him. Liam hugged me, and then right before he was about to turn away, he kissed me. Right there in front of everyone. And then they drove away."

Aubrey grinned. "Was it hot? Was there tongue?"

"We were in eighth grade, and our parents were watching." She gave me a look that told me she'd been doing a lot worse in eighth grade. "It was nice," I said quietly. "Perfect."

More than perfect. In only a few seconds, he'd taken my breath away and opened my heart to things I'd never felt before. And then he left.

I'd learned what it felt like to have loved and lost, all in a matter of minutes.

"You guys didn't get together after that?"

"He didn't even call me. I guess he knew it wouldn't've worked out. You can't start a real relationship with four hours between you. It would've been too hard and too painful. Maybe the kiss was a way to acknowledge there was something between us before he left forever."

Aubrey gave me a knowing smirk. "Maybe, but now he's back."

"Yeah." I fought my own grin and glanced over at the table where he sat. "Now he's back."

And I was going to do whatever it took to keep him from slipping through my fingers again.

Chapter 3

"See ya, Bent."

I looked up to see Corey Hill, one of the jocks I tutored regularly, pass me with a smile on his face. "Bye."

With my messenger bag hanging over my shoulder and my thick coat draped over my arm, I made my escape through the school's main doors. The sun was shining, warming me in my black sweater, jeans, and boots.

The parking lot was like a ghost town. I spotted my white Camry effortlessly, then almost stopped when I registered the tall figure leaning against it.

"What are you doing here?"

Cooper's arms were crossed, the sleeves of his navy-blue shirt pushed up to his elbows despite the cold. "I told you I needed a ride today." He stood straight, grabbing his bag and coat from where they sat on the trunk. "And before you ask, no, I didn't find someone else to get me to school tomorrow."

"I assumed you'd be at soccer tryouts right now."

"I probably would be if I were playing this year."

I was prepared to say something snarky, but I stopped myself when I saw his face. "But you love soccer. Why aren't you playing?"

He shrugged, not looking at me. "Don't feel like it this year. Figure there's better things I could be doing with my time."

"Like partying with random college girls?"

He gave me a mocking smile. "You know me so well." He tapped the hood of my car. "You going to give me a ride or not?"

"Fine, get in."

Neither of us spoke, and soon we were pulling out onto the main road. He'd taken control of the radio again, but this time I turned it down to low. "So, how does Liam like being back?"

"Fine, I guess."

"Does he miss his old school?"

"I don't know. We haven't really talked about it." He leaned forward to turn the volume up, but I turned it back down.

"What about a girlfriend? Does he have a girlfriend back home?"

"Ugh." Cooper's head fell back against the headrest.

"What?"

"I almost forgot you had a huge crush on him before he left."

"I did not," I shot back, and it was technically true. I hadn't thought of Liam in that way until *after* he'd kissed me. It was like the act of putting his lips on mine had awoken a set of feelings up until then that had lain dormant.

"Whatever."

I waited, but he said nothing else. "Well, does he? Have a girlfriend, I mean."

"No."

"What about at the South Carolina campus? Does he have a girlfriend there?" As often as they'd visited in the last two years, it wasn't so unbelievable to think that he might've met a girl he was interested in.

"Trust me. Liam doesn't have a girlfriend in Charleston or Columbia or anywhere else."

"Good." The word slipped out before I could stop it.

"Good? What does that mean?"

I shrugged. "It means I like him, and I want to get to know him better. I think he and I could be a good fit."

"I think you're wrong."

"Why?"

He stared at me. "You don't know him like you used to. You don't even know what kind of girl he'd be interested in."

"If only there was someone who could help me figure out what he likes. Someone who knows him better than anyone else. Like a best friend or something," I mused.

"You want *me* to help you? Why would I do that?"

"We could make a deal. I drive you to and from school, you help me figure out how to get Liam's interest."

"You're serious?"

I nodded. *Whatever it took,* I'd vowed. Even if it meant making a deal with the devil himself. My own personal, arrogant, annoyingly attractive devil. "Come on. You could be my goat."

"Your what?"

"You know, like in that eighties movie. Liam mentioned it this morning. Goat and Maverick. You'd be my wingman."

Are you talking about *Top Gun?*"

"Yeah." At least I thought I was, since I'd never actually seen it.

"First, it's Goose. *Goose* and Maverick. Second, you're insane."

"At least help me find some stuff we have in common to get the ball rolling. Then if it's meant to be and he asks me out and we live happily ever after, great. If not, no big deal. At least I won't have to wonder anymore."

"I don't think this is going to end the way you want it to."

"Good thing I didn't ask what you think."

He stared out the window. "Where are we going?" he asked. We weren't taking the usual route to our neighborhood.

"You aren't the only one who needs a ride in the afternoon." I turned right onto a small street and then left, pulling up under an awning behind the short line of cars waiting in front of a massive brick building. The sign out front read *Oakcrest Academy.*

The town's small, yet exceptionally exclusive and expensive private school provided an elite, highly respected curriculum for ages two all the way up to eighth grade. There weren't many who had the money or connections to get into the prestigious school, and I knew only two kids who went there.

"Oh great," Coop muttered.

The line moved fast, and almost as soon as I'd stopped at the front, two uniform-clad thirteen-year-olds scooted into the backseat.

Sebastian Caldwell slid in first with curly red hair and freckles splattered across his nose and forehead. His twin sister's hair, also red, was tied in a long braid over her shoulder. Samantha shut the door behind her, took one look at Cooper in the front seat, and sneered.

"What's the mouth-breather doing here?"

I gave Samantha a quick warning look. "Cooper's going to need a ride home for a while, so we're going to give him one."

"Whatever. As long as he doesn't try to talk to us. I'd hate for my IQ to drop ten points from having to listen to him." She pulled an apple out of her backpack as I focused on the road.

"Hey," Samantha yelled from the backseat.

Cooper held her apple in his hand, the bite he'd taken out of it crunching in his mouth.

"You stole my apple."

"So astute, Captain Obvious. Maybe now you'll learn to respect your elders." He turned to me. "Since when do you drive the Wonder Twins around?"

"We're not the Wonder Twins." In my rearview mirror, Sebastian stared out the window, avoiding eye contact with Cooper. "The Wonder Twins are superheroes and can change into water or animals. We can't do that. So we couldn't be the Wonder Twins."

"Ladies and gentlemen, her trusty sidekick, Literal Boy," Coop murmured for only me to hear.

I smacked his shoulder. "Be nice." It was no secret Cooper and the Caldwell twins didn't get along. I speculated it had something to do with Dr. Caldwell and her family taking up residence in Liam's old house soon after he moved away.

But then it could also have started with Sebastian's 6:00 a.m. saxophone practices three summers ago. Even for a morning person like Cooper, there seemed to be only so much of the screeching a man could take before sunrise. One morning, he'd run out of his house, shirtless and groggy, raced over to the Caldwells' to bang on the door, and then stole the saxophone right out of Sebastian's hands.

"And if I were a superhero, I wouldn't want to be one of the Wonder Twins anyway. Turning into different animals wouldn't be so bad, I guess, but turning into water? I'd rather be Superman. He has so many more powers than Zan and Jayna. Plus, he can fly," Sebastian went on, barely taking a breath in between sentences.

If Samantha's thing was rude bluntness, Sebastian's was nervous rambling.

"Of course that's if I was a DC superhero. If I was a Marvel hero, I'd want to be Doctor Strange, what with—"

"You really don't have to explain."

Sebastian fell silent.

"I expect you to replace that apple," Samantha declared.

"Here." I reached around the back of my seat and pulled a small Tupperware container from my messenger bag. Sebastian's attention shot to the container of cookies as I handed them to his sister. "You can each have two."

Cooper's face fell. "You were holding on to that all day, and you didn't tell me?"

"Eat your fruit."

He stared at the half-eaten apple in his hand, clearly not as interested in it anymore, then looked at me with sad, blinking eyes. "Don't I get one?"

"No."

Samantha leaned forward and grinned wickedly over his shoulder. "Maybe now you'll learn to respect your superiors." She waved a cookie in front of his face, then shot back in her seat when he tried to snatch it from her. He failed.

"Do you pick them up every day?" Cooper asked between not-so-satisfying bites of Samantha's apple.

I nodded. "Their mom doesn't get off until five, so I pick them up and hang out at their house with them for a couple hours."

"So, you babysit them." He flinched when something hard thumped against the back of his seat. Samantha glared daggers at him.

"I don't babysit. It's more like tutoring. I help them with their homework, that's all."

Before long we were in our neighborhood and pulling up to the cul-de-sac where three large houses sat, each similar in size and style, but unique in their own ways. Cooper's sat in the middle directly at the end of the street, my house to the right, and the twins' house on the left. I pulled up my driveway and parked. Samantha and Sebastian threw their doors open and raced each other to their front door on the opposite side of the cul-de-sac.

Cooper was out just as quickly, yanking the back door open and grabbing the almost empty container of cookies before taking a frantic bite of one. He moaned, his body visibly relaxing as he chewed. "Damn, you sure know how to make a cookie."

I grabbed my bag from the backseat as the twins unlocked their front door and darted inside Liam's old house. "So," I said, turning to Cooper. He was still shoveling cookies into his mouth. "Will you help me with Liam? Be my wingman?"

His forehead creased. "Depends. You said you pick the twins up from school every day?"

I nodded.

"Do you bring them cookies every day?"

"Not every day. I only had these because I made a ton of them last night and needed to get rid of them."

Cooper's face fell.

"But if you help me, I'll make you all the cookies you want."

He closed the container of cookies and moved to grab his bag from the floor of the passenger seat. "Fine. But I can't make any promises it'll work out the way you want it to."

"Really? You'll help me?" My smile grew until it was almost painful. Not only was he going to help me get the guy of my dreams, but he was willing to endure car rides with the twins to do it. "I think you overestimate my baking skills."

"I think you underestimate how much I don't want to take the bus."

Chapter 4

Hours later, I settled in at our breakfast table to knock out my homework when Dad finally got home.

"Hey, sweetie." He set his bag and coat on the table, followed by the Oakcrest Soccer cap he wore every day. He untucked his polo shirt before stretching his arms out and scratching his milk-white belly. With a mammoth-size yawn, he placed a kiss on the top of my head. "How was school?"

"Fine," I said, carefully writing out a list of numbers. "The boys finished their homework and did their chores. Addie's had a bath and been put down for the night. I made spaghetti for everyone, and there's some leftovers in the fridge if you want them."

"Didn't Mom tell you?" He ran a hand through his short, chestnut brown hair. "I took the assistant coaches and athletic director out for dinner to kick off the season. I already ate."

At least that explained why he was home so late. "No, she didn't tell me. She's been down in the office, working all day."

Dad kissed my head again. "Your mom is so lucky to have a daughter as wonderful and supportive as you. We both are."

"Thanks." I smiled up at him, and he squeezed my shoulders in return.

"So, what are you working on?"

"Matrices and quadratic equations."

He looked at the paper over my shoulder filled with random boxes, letters, and numbers. "I have no idea what you just said, but it looks hard." He laughed.

"Not really that hard once you get the hang of it. But it's time consuming."

He grimaced.

"How was your day?"

"It was interesting." He opened one of the topmost cabinets and grabbed a can of Coke. Mom didn't approve of soda and junk food in the house, so Dad kept his own not-so-secret stash up out of Mom's reach. He rested his elbows on the island counter and popped the top on his drink. "Guess who showed up at tryouts today."

The list would be long—my dad had made soccer one of Oakcrest's highest-earning sports, and therefore one of the most popular. But I also knew the one guy at tryouts Dad would be so interested in. "Liam Haynes."

His eyes narrowed. "Okay, but I bet you can't tell me who *didn't* show up at tryouts."

Another long list, but still only one who would get the coach's attention for not showing. "Cooper."

Dad stood up straight. "You remember the days when I would come home and you'd say *Hey, Dad. How was your day?* and I'd go on and on about my classes and soccer, and you'd sit there pretending to listen but not really knowing what I was talking about?" he asked. "Why isn't today one of those days?"

"I gave Liam and Cooper a ride to school this morning. The subject came up."

"You did? Why? And how did you know Liam was back before I did?"

I put my pencil down. "Cooper told me yesterday Liam moved back over break. He also asked me for a ride to school because Liam shares a car with his mom, and Coop's Maserati is out of commission after the accident."

Dad scowled. "Right, I heard about that." He glanced out the kitchen window and over at the dark gray house next door. It was pitch black outside, making the lights from inside Coop's house stand out against the night. "I have half a mind to go over there and give him a good talking-to."

"I don't think you need to. His car is totaled, and his dad is refusing to get him a new one until he can be more responsible."

"Good. It's about time that man started paying attention to his kid. Maybe if he spent some time at home with him instead of flying off across the world every chance he gets, his son wouldn't be in this mess in the first place."

"It's not like he does it for fun, Dad. It's his job." Cooper's dad was a commercial pilot, earning the big bucks by flying internationally for one of the world's largest airlines. His dad was rarely around when we were kids, and even less now that we were older.

Dad shook his head. "I'm not sure how the man sleeps at night knowing the kind of stuff his son is off doing while he's forgetting to be a father."

Apparently, Dad was aware of the gossip too. It wasn't like my dad didn't like Cooper. Since we were kids, he'd loved him like one of his own sons, and I was sure that was what made him so protective of Cooper when it came to his own father. But I bet it also made it harder for him to sit by and watch while Cooper made stupid mistakes.

"Did he tell you why he wasn't playing this year?" he asked.

"He said he didn't feel like it anymore."

"That's bullshit."

"Dad," I warned. The boys were down the hall, and it wasn't hard to hear his raised voice when he got upset.

"I'm sorry, honey. But that boy has got more heart for the game than I've ever seen. I don't believe he'd give it all up because he doesn't feel like it." He downed the last of his Coke and threw the can in the trash. "Something else is going on here."

***

The next morning, Cooper was waiting by my car. I was running a few minutes late after I'd decided to take the time to straighten my hair. I'd also thrown on a little extra makeup around the eyes, thinking it might help catch a certain someone's attention.

I ran out the door ten minutes later than I'd told Cooper, but he didn't say anything. He was bundled in his coat, leaning against the car while looking at his phone. I hurried down the porch steps, carrying the same two mugs of coffee I'd brought the day before. I set one on the roof of the car before I pulled open the back door and threw my bag into the backseat.

I slid into the front, placing both travel mugs into the cupholders, and started the car. Cooper and I sat in silence while we waited for it to warm up, and I rubbed my hands together to warm my stiff fingers.

Cooper hadn't said anything, which was a complete one-eighty from his good mood yesterday morning. Instead, he laid his head back against the seat and closed his eyes.

"Tell me about Liam," I said when the silence became unnerving.

"Too early." His eyes were puffy and dark underneath, and I knew he'd much rather be in his warm bed right now.

I grabbed my mug and took a sip. "Think how much earlier it will be when you have to ride the bus tomorrow."

Cooper peeked at me through one eye. It traveled to the mug in my hand, and then to the one in the cupholder. He moved to get it, but I swatted his hand away. "That's not for you. Now tell me about Liam."

"For starters, he likes it when you're nice to his friends," he said pointedly. "He also hates coffee."

My eyes narrowed. "He didn't say that yesterday when I offered it to him."

"He also didn't say he secretly listens to Beyoncé, but that doesn't change the fact he does."

I hesitated a minute before I finally gave in and handed him the mug.

"Thank you." He pushed back the lid and took a sip, sighing with contentment.

I put the car in reverse and backed down the driveway. "Why are you so grumpy this morning?"

"Didn't sleep well." He took another sip from his coffee. "Needs less sugar next time."

Like there was going to be a next time. "Liam hates coffee and loves Beyoncé. What else?"

"Let's see..." Coop thought for a minute. "He likes soccer."

"No kidding."

"He got held back in the fifth grade."

I frowned. "How about a few things I don't already know?"

"His favorite color is orange. He listens to rap."

"None of this is helpful."

Cooper sighed. "Well, what do you want me to say?"

"What stuff does he look for? What kind of girl does he like?"

"The kind with female sex organs."

I glared at him. "Be serious."

"I mean he's not picky." He took a sip of coffee. "I've never noticed him having a certain type."

So yesterday when he said he didn't think I was Liam's type, he really meant he didn't think Liam would like *me*. "I've got to say, you're not off to a great start with this whole wingman thing."

He watched me, his expression turning sour. "Look, if you want my advice, be yourself. Don't try to make yourself into the kind of girl he would like because then it's not real. If he likes you for who you are, that's fine. If he doesn't, then he's not the guy for you."

I slowed as we reached Liam's driveway. "That's easy for you to say. You're literally turning girls away left and right."

"That's because I know they're not the right girls for me."

"How can you know that when you don't give any of them a chance?"

Liam came through his front door and down the steps, and I hadn't realized I was grinning until I turned back to Cooper.

His eyes had turned to slits and his lip curled like the question disgusted him.

"Trust me. I know."

Chapter 5

"Heads up," Aubrey said. "There's a pop quiz in history, and I'm pretty sure I failed it." She turned the dial on her locker forcefully, messing up the combination a few times before she finally got it.

"Okay, thanks." I went back switching out books for my next two classes.

"Hey, so I was talking to Beth last night, and we're thinking about catching a movie Friday night. You want to come?"

"As much as I love being the awkward third wheel on your dates, I already told my mom I'd watch the kids while she and Dad have their own date night."

"Fine, not this Friday. But next time. Beth hasn't seen you in weeks, and I'm going to get a complex if she keeps asking me how you are in the middle of our make-out sessions."

"Deal."

"Hey, Bentley."

I whirled to face the source of the deep voice, my gaze landing directly on Liam's dark brown eyes. "Hey, Liam." *Okay, whoa. Take it down a few notches, Bentley.* I cleared my throat. "What's up?"

He grinned. "Nothing. I, uh, wanted to ask you something."

My stomach fluttered. Aubrey stared into her locker, unmoving and clearly pretending not to listen. "Okay. Shoot."

He ran a hand through his hair. "This may seem kind of random, and you can always say no…"

"Yeah?" My heart beat a nervous rhythm in my chest.

"Do you think you could help me out with some of my classes?"

My shoulders sagged. "Oh."

"I didn't have the best grades in Charleston. The teachers here are ahead on the curriculum, so I'm going to have to play catch-up. Your dad told me to get my grades up if I want a spot on the team. Cooper said you were the smartest person in school, so I thought—"

"Cooper said that?"

"Yeah. So, I thought maybe you could help me out. I heard you're a good tutor, and I could pay you if you want."

"Of course, I'll help you. You don't have to pay me. We're friends."

"Awesome. You have no idea how relieved I am to hear that."

I shut my locker door and leaned against it. "What classes do you need help with?"

"Mostly algebra and chemistry."

"Great, those are my best subjects. When do you want to start?"

"Is tomorrow okay?" he asked.

"Yeah," I said with a smile. "Tomorrow's perfect."

***

"Cooper Bradshaw, you are a genius." I ran up behind him before he reached the main door leading out to the parking lot. He stopped, spun, and then my arms were wrapped around him in a bear hug before I could stop myself. Suddenly I was nine years old again and he bought me a fudgesicle from the ice cream man.

"Uh, thanks." He patted my back mechanically, but when I pulled away, the corners of his mouth turned up. "Care to tell me why?"

"Your plan worked."

He reached for the door and held it open for me. "Which plan is that?"

I stepped outside, cringing as the bitterly cold wind clawed at my face and hair, then shoved my hands in my pockets. "Liam came by my locker after third period. He asked me to help him study."

Coop's eyebrows rose. "Oh yeah? Good for you." We reached the car, and I climbed in as fast as I could, started the engine, and blasted the heat.

Coop rubbed his hands together and set them in front of one of the vents. "When and where is this *studying*," he used air quotes, "thing happening?"

"Tomorrow at lunch."

He frowned. "Your first date's in the middle of the school day?"

"It's not a date. He asked me to tutor him tomorrow at lunch."

He said nothing until we were on the road. "How exactly am I the genius responsible for this turn of events?"

"You told Liam to ask me to tutor him. It's brilliant. This way I can spend time with him and get to know him, and then he'll realize what a great girlfriend I'd be. Nice job, Goat."

"For the second time, it's Goose. Stop referencing movies you don't understand." Cooper shook his head. "I didn't tell him to do anything. I may have told him you were smart or something, but that's it."

Technically, he'd told Liam I was the smartest person in our school, but if I mentioned that now, he'd only deny it. "All that matters is thanks to you, I'm one step closer to getting the boy of my dreams."

"And then what? Have you really thought this through? You've never even had a boyfriend before. What makes you think you can handle Liam?"

"I have too had a boyfriend, thank you very much."

His gaze shot to mine. "What? When?"

"Don't sound so shocked. Guys are capable of finding me attractive and wanting to be my boyfriend."

"That's not what I meant. I...I never knew." He went silent, staring out the passenger-side window.

"Not that it's your business, but his name was Louis. I met him the summer before tenth grade." The reason Cooper hadn't known was because he'd stopped talking to me by then.

"Sorry. I don't know why I assumed you hadn't dated anyone yet."

"Like you're the only one who can go around having relations with the opposite sex." Granted, my relations had never gone beyond second base. But still, it wasn't like I'd never had any action at all.

"I said I'm sorry. Let's drop it."

We made our way to Oakcrest Academy in silence. I'd half expected Cooper to turn the radio up to fill the void, but he seemed preoccupied while staring out the window.

"Do you know what you two are going to talk about tomorrow?" he asked.

"You mean aside from chemical formulas and quadratics? I didn't realize I needed to prepare any other topics of conversation."

"You want to talk about more than schoolwork. You need to find some common ground and show him that you're interested in knowing more about him." He tapped his fingers on his knee. "He likes working on cars. He's been fixing his mom's for years whenever it messes up. You could try talking to him about that if you know anything about cars and stuff."

I didn't, but it didn't mean I couldn't do a quick Internet search session on cars before I went to bed tonight. "Thanks."

The pickup line at Oakcrest Academy moved even faster than yesterday, and as soon as I'd reached the front, the back door opened, and Samantha and Sebastian slid in.

"Oh great, it's the apple-thieving Neanderthal again." Samantha glared at Cooper.

He glanced back at her, taking in her shiny purple headband and perfectly braided red hair. "Well if it isn't Prepubescent Barbie. Tell me, does your kind automatically come with the lackluster insults or do accessories cost extra? If I were your parents, I'd try to get my money back."

Samantha's mouth fell open. I didn't think she was used to having someone talk back to her. Sebastian usually kept quiet when his sister was in a mood, and I'd learned to let her comments roll off a long time ago.

"Stick a sock in it, booger breath," she finally said.

"Booger breath, really? That one of those fancy SAT words your ten-thousand-dollar-a-semester education is teaching you? Seriously, your parents are probably due for a refund."

A muffled chuckle. In the rearview mirror, Samantha smacked Sebastian's shoulder. "What are you laughing at?"

"Relax," Cooper said. "It's not his fault he was the only twin born with a sense of humor." Coop looked over his shoulder and gave Sebastian a conspiratorial wink.

"*Bentley*," Samantha yelled.

I reached for my messenger bag, and the Tupperware container I'd packed as a last resort. "Who wants cookies?"

***

"You always need to have the same on each side." Liam and I had been going over his chemistry homework for the last fifteen minutes, and I was still struggling to explain chemical equations to him. For some reason, I was having trouble getting it to click in his mind.

"If you have six hydrogen atoms on this side of the equation," I pointed to the left side of my paper, then the right, "you should have six hydrogen atoms on this side. Get it?"

"Uh-huh." He stared at something on his phone, the same thing he'd been doing for the last several minutes.

Lunch had started off great. Aubrey offered to sit with some other friends today so Liam and I could have time alone. He'd shown up at my table, looking incredibly handsome with his shaggy blond hair, green sweater, and jeans. He smiled as he sat down next to me, pulling his book out with enthusiasm. But after only a few minutes of trying to get him to understand the chemistry work, his attention was slipping.

My phone buzzed in my pocket with a text from Cooper.

How's the "studying?"

I looked up. Cooper smirked at me from across the cafeteria at the table he and his soccer friends usually occupied.

Everything's great. Thanks for asking.

My phone vibrated in my hand almost instantly.

Then why does he look like he's about to fall asleep?

At some point Liam had laid his head in his hand as he stared down at the paper filled with chemical equations. His eyelids drooped.

Ass.

When I looked up again, Cooper's head was back as his body shook with laughter.

I turned my attention back to my tutor-ee. "Hey, Liam."

"Yeah?"

"Cooper told me you're really into fixing cars."

He perked up instantly. "Yeah. Ever since I started taking auto repair in ninth grade." He dropped the hand his head had rested in and sat up straighter, his brown eyes looking more vibrant. "They don't offer it here, but I can still work on my mom's car whenever I want."

"Well, think of this formula as all the parts under the hood of the car." I waited to see if the word *formula* led him to zone out again, but he managed to stay focused.

"You can take everything out, clean it up, rearrange it, but in the end, you still have to have all those parts inside the car to make it work. The car won't run without the engine or transmission. Or the same number of hoses and screws that were holding everything together to start with. Just like these equations won't work unless you have all the same parts on both sides."

He studied the paper. "Okay, yeah. I see what you're saying. So think of it like trying to get all the pieces to fit back together under the hood." He looked up and placed his hand gently on my arm. "Thanks. You're really good at this."

And just like that, Liam was bent over the paper and attempting to work through the problems again. I grabbed my phone once more, sending Cooper an emoji with its tongue sticking out. But when I looked up, prepared with my best smirk, he was gone.

Chapter 6

"*I want my purple princess dress.*"

I took a deep breath, doing my best not to scream back at Addie like I desperately wanted to. "I told you. Your purple princess dress is in the washer right now. You're going to have to wait until I can get the laundry done. But until then, you can wear one of your other princess dresses." She had about a thousand of them in her closet.

"But I want my *purple* one." From the second she woke up this morning I knew it was going to be a rough day. She'd been up late last night, and thanks to Noah and Caden's screaming match over a game of one-on-one basketball out in the driveway this morning, Addie hadn't been able to sleep in.

All day she'd found things to cry about. First it was her juice tasted funny, then her eggs were too scrambled. Then her tablet died in the middle of her favorite show, and she screamed for four minutes straight while I worked to pull it up on the den TV.

Mom had been working in the basement since six in the morning, and Dad was out for the day with some old college buddies. I'd managed to get breakfast made for all the kids, but was struggling to get the chores done and the house cleaned up with Addie having a fit every ten minutes. I'd given the boys some chores to do, but they were no help.

Low snickers carried down the hall from the kitchen, and I groaned. They were up to something. I'd bet my entire life's savings on it.

I grabbed the basket full of clean clothes from the top of the dryer and followed the damning sounds, Addie screaming and tugging on the bottom of my blue and white flannel shirt in the process.

I whirled around, gently prying her hand from my shirt. "Addie, sweetie," I said in the softest voice I could manage. "Why don't we go up to your room, put on a movie, and you can lie down for a bit?"

She scrunched up her red, tear-streaked face, and the waterworks started flowing again. "But I don't wanna take a nap," she cried miserably. I struggled not to roll my eyes. Life was so hard for a three-year-old.

"I know you don't. But you'll feel so much better once you do. I promise." I shifted the heavy basket to my other hip. "It's only for a little while. Just lie down long enough to see if you fall asleep." As exhausted as she was, she'd be out in three minutes, tops.

She shook her head, this time grabbing my jeans. They were my comfiest pair, the ones I wore only when I was hanging around the house all day. They weren't flattering at all, but at least they were loose enough for Addie to get a good grip without pinching my skin underneath. "I'm not tired."

"That's fine. If you don't fall asleep in ten minutes, I'll come up and get you. How about that?"

"I don't wanna nap, and you can't make me." Addie spun and darted off, probably to go make a mess of the den I'd just finished cleaning. With a huff, I turned and carried the basket toward the kitchen, tripping over one of Noah's shoes lying in the middle of the hallway.

"*I've already told you guys twenty times to pick your crap up off the floor.*" I swung around the corner and into the kitchen, but my gaze caught on my two younger brothers, and I almost dropped the basket.

"What are you two doing?" They stood at the island, haphazardly filling a large mixing bowl with random amounts of junk food from Dad's stash. Empty food boxes and bits of Doritos, Pop-Tarts, and a combination of other nutritionally deficient foods had fallen all over the counter and floor.

Caden shrugged as he poured in about two cups of Frosted Flakes. "We got hungry, so we thought we'd whip up a snack."

I glanced at the clock on the microwave. It was a bit after four in the afternoon. "That's going to make you guys sick." Had they even eaten a proper lunch? I couldn't remember.

Noah shook his head. "No worries. We can handle it."

"Like how you *handled* chugging giant homemade milkshakes two weeks ago?" Right before they both puked their guts up all over their bedroom floor.

"Exactly." He scooped up the bowl, and the two of them rounded the island.

"You didn't clean up your mess, and I want your bathroom cleaned today. I know for a fact it's not supposed to smell like that."

"We'll get to it."

I dropped the basket on the floor and swung around. "Or you could do it now, like I asked."

Caden gave me a hard look. "Chill out, Bentley. You're not Mom."

I stood in silence as the two walked out, having no words to say that wouldn't come out a screaming, enraged jumble. Instead, I took three deep breaths. Why had I agreed to spend my Saturday watching after my three younger siblings?

It wouldn't have been so bad if it weren't for the fact that Mom had spent almost every evening of the last week down in the basement, writing, while Dad ran soccer practices, leaving me to handle Addie, dinner, and the boys' homework and chores the last several days. Not to mention how Friday night—the night I was supposed to get the house to relax—had turned into me watching the kids so Mom could take a long call with her editor. I was nearing my wit's end, and if I didn't get a break soon, there was a good chance I'd either explode or break down in sobs.

I picked up the basket of clothes and put it on the breakfast table, then grabbed the broom from the pantry and started sweeping up the bits of food the boys had left behind. If it were anything else, I'd leave it until they finally decided to clean up their own mess. But I couldn't bring myself to ignore it knowing a colony of ants would get to it before they did.

I made quick work of sweeping up the food and tossed the debris in the trash, followed by the five or so boxes they'd left empty on the counter. My stress level had already eased some.

Over at the table, I got to work folding the laundry. I'd managed to get through three shirts when my phone rang. I glanced at the name on the screen before gladly swiping to answer.

"Hey, Aubrey. What's up?" I set the phone between my ear and shoulder as I went back to folding.

"Hey, Erikson. Listen, Beth canceled our date tonight because her cousin Maya is visiting. So now my night's wide open. You want to do something?"

"I wish I could. My mom's on this crazy writing roll, and she's been in the office since before dawn. Until she comes out, I have to watch my brothers and sister."

She sighed. "That sucks. You don't think she'd come out if you told her you needed to spend time with a friend? Especially after you already had to ditch movie night with me and Beth a couple weeks ago?"

Of course she would. But my mom was the kind of writer who was either extremely focused or not at all. I could tell her I wanted to go out, and she'd step away from her computer and watch the kids. But then her mind would still be in writing mode. And when she was in writing mode but unable to jot down any of her thoughts, she got cranky. Ultimately, I was doing my siblings a favor by leaving Mom where she was.

"I'm sorry. We'll do something tomorrow, though, I promise."

"Yeah, okay. So, anything new with you and Liam? Has he asked you out yet?"

She asked the same question every day, and so far my answer was always the same. "I don't get it. I've been tutoring him for over three weeks. We've spent ten lunches together, three days a week, and still nothing." Sure, he flirted sometimes, but that was as far as it ever went. "I'm starting to think he isn't interested in me."

"Give him time. Some guys are shy and need a little prodding. Maybe *you* should ask *him* out."

"And risk getting brutally rejected right before I quiz him on the quadratic formula. Yeah, that's not happening."

A piercing scream filled the house, sending an electric shock down my already frazzled nerves. "Aubrey, I have to go."

I dropped the pair of shorts and the phone and ran to the den, careful not to trip over Caden's shin guard and face plant on the floor. When I reached the den, Addie was crying her eyes out while the boys stared wide-eyed at the TV. Blood and guts spewed everywhere on the screen.

Addie looked at me. "I was watching *PAW Patrol*, and they changed it," she screamed.

"Put it back," I told them.

"No way. She's been watching TV all day. It's our turn." Noah never took his eyes off the tablet he held.

"I *want* PAW Patrol."

"You're not even watching it," I yelled to Noah over Addie's piercing cry. "Let her watch her show while you two play whatever stupid games you've got going on those."

"PAAAAAWWWWWWW Paaaaaatrooooooolllllll."

I clenched my fists, fighting the urge to hit something. Hard. "Or better yet, how about you two get up off your asses and clean up your shit. Or I will personally take all your phones and your tablets and your PlayStation outside and smash them out in the road and leave them for cars to run over."

Caden's eyes went wide behind his glasses. "Geez, Bentley, are you on the rag this week or something?"

"That's it."

I flew across the room, ripping the tablet from Noah's hands flinging it to the ground. "Hey, that's mine. *Ow.*" I grabbed him by the arm and wrenched him up off the sofa, then did the same with Caden.

"Out." I shoved them toward the back door while ignoring the sounds of their protests. "If you're not going to help me clean up your goddamn messes, the least you can do is stop making them and get the hell outside."

The boys said nothing as I threw the doors to the back porch open. Once they were out, I yanked the doors shut and spun around.

Addie's mouth gaped, and the tears came pouring again. I reached to pick her up, and she nestled her face into my shoulder and started soaking my ratty flannel button-up with tears and snot.

"It's okay, honey," I told her in a soothing voice. "I'm sorry I screamed like that."

"You…said a…b-bad word," she cried between sobs.

"I know, I'm sorry." I patted her back. "What do you say we go up to your room and you and me can watch a movie together?"

The tears came harder as she jerked her head from side to side. "*I don't want a nap,*" she screamed in my ear, trying to wrestle her way out of my arms.

"What on Earth is going on in here?" Mom stood in the den, her hair a greasy mess and her face shiny like she hadn't washed it in days. Her eyes were bloodshot from staring at the computer screen nonstop for hours. "I'm downstairs trying to work, and all of a sudden I hear screaming and doors slamming like I'm living in one of the *Real World* houses." She looked around the den at the random items scattered around the floor I'd told the boys to pick up. "This place is a mess."

"I was trying to clean it up—"

"*Mommy*," Addie cried, and she reached out for Mom, who walked over to grab her from my hands. "Benny said bad words."

Mom's eyes narrowed on mine. "Bentley."

"Well, if Noah and Caden would do what I've been asking them to instead of ignoring me all day—"

"Okay." She held her hand up to quiet me. "I'll talk to the boys and take Addie up for a nap." Instead of screaming, my little sister hugged her tighter. "Why don't you go for a walk or something. Get some fresh air. I think that would be best for everyone involved."

I stared at her. How was it that she could be AWOL all day, leaving me with two teenage boys and a grumpy three-year-old, then come in when everything blows up and make it sound like I was the one with the problem?

I clenched my fists tighter, not saying anything as I stomped past, down the hall, and out the front door. The door slammed behind me, and I sank down onto the porch steps.

I dropped my head in my hands and took several slow breaths. Most days I didn't mind being the girl with five brothers and a sister, and a somewhat lacking parental unit.

But then some days it really, really sucked.

"Everything okay?"

My head snapped up. I'd been so wrapped up in my thoughts I hadn't even heard Cooper approach.

He stood at the bottom of the steps, taking advantage of the unusually warm February temperature by wearing a short-sleeved T-shirt and jeans. His chin had some blond stubble, like he hadn't bothered to shave this morning.

"Everything's fine. What are you doing here?"

He nodded to the trashcan at the top of his driveway. "I was taking out some stuff when I heard your door slam."

"I mean what are you doing in Oakcrest? It's the weekend. Shouldn't you be in Columbia?"

"It's kind of hard to get to Columbia without a car."

I considered that. "True. But if you really wanted to go, I'm sure you'd find a way."

"Touché." The corners of his eyes softened. "You sure you're okay?"

I nodded. "It's really loud in there, and I needed a little peace and quiet."

As if on cue, the front door flew open. Noah raced across the porch and down the steps, nearly trampling me as Caden yelled obscenities and chased after him.

I dragged my hands down my face. So much for getting some peace. I doubted there was anywhere in this house that would be far enough away right now.

"You know, my place is usually pretty quiet. You're welcome to come over if you need to get away from here for a bit." He shoved his hands in his pockets. "We could put on a movie, or sit in silence and ignore each other for an hour or two. Your call."

I snorted. Normally I wouldn't dream of spending the afternoon hanging out with Cooper. But then again, the only thing I wanted even less at this point was going back inside. "You know what? A movie sounds great."

Chapter 7

Walking into Cooper's house for the first time in years was...weird. For the most part, everything was the same. Same layout with the open floor plan, high ceilings, and curved staircase sweeping down into the foyer. But everything else was different from the mint green walls to the brand-new-looking furniture, even the small decorative touches.

"You guys redecorated?" I caught my reflection in the hall mirror. I wore zero makeup, and my hair looked like a bird's nest with bits of brown and pink falling out of the messy bun. If I were with anyone other than Cooper, I might've cared.

"Only about four times. My sister has her own interior design thing now. It's small, but she's really good, so business is picking up fast." Cooper led the way down the hall and back to the kitchen.

"How is Caitlyn? I haven't seen her in years." I let my fingertips trace the white chair rail as I followed him down the hall and into the kitchen.

He went around the wide, white granite island. "She's good. Living in Greenville with her boyfriend. He's one of those boring stiffs who sits behind a desk all day pushing papers." He opened the fridge and turned to me. "Want a drink or something?"

I nodded, and he pulled out two Coke cans, handing one over. "You don't like her boyfriend?"

"Nah, Owen's fine. I like ragging on him. He's actually a really good guy."

I cracked open the top of my drink and took a sip. "What about your parents? Do they like him?"

"I'm not sure they've spent enough time with him to know."

"Do they still fight a lot?" His parents had been pleasant to each other in public or when they had guests over when we were growing up, but I'd overheard my fair share of screaming matches when they hadn't realized I was in the house. Back then, Cooper and Caitlyn tended to spend more time at my house than their own.

"Not really." He took a sip of his drink and walked over to the family room off the kitchen. "Then again, it's hard to fight when you never see each other. One of the perks of not coming home, I guess."

"They don't come home? Like, ever?"

"I see them every once in a while. Mom was here a few hours to celebrate Christmas with me, Caitlyn, and Owen. Dad managed to make an appearance after my Maserati got totaled." He plopped down on the sectional sofa in the center of the room, setting his feet to rest on the dark wood coffee table.

"I'm sorry."

"Don't feel bad for me. I'm living the dream, right? I get the house to myself, and I can do anything I want." He drummed his fingers against his Coke can, and I got the impression it wasn't that simple.

I was tempted to push the subject. Maybe I would've three years ago, but despite the morning rides and the invitation to use his empty house as a quiet sanctuary, he and I weren't friends. Not really. I had no business forcing him to bare his soul like that.

I walked around the sofa and came to stop in front of the long rows of DVDs and Blu-ray cases. "Impressive collection. I don't think I remember it being even half this size."

"I consider myself quite the film connoisseur. I've been steadily adding to it for the last few years."

I scanned the titles, mystified when I recognized only a few, and the ones I knew hardly screamed *Cooper Bradshaw*. "They're all so old. You really watch all these?"

"The old ones are the best ones. The movies they make now are all gimmicky bull. People don't make them like they used to."

I stared at him over my shoulder. "You're being serious?"

He placed his hands behind his head, relaxing back into the sofa cushions. "I like the simplicity of them. Back before all the CGI and crap they do to movies now. Back when movies were real."

I shook my head. "Knowing you the way I do, I wouldn't've guessed that at all."

"Maybe you don't know me as well as you think."

I smiled. "Touché." I turned back to the wide selection of old movies. "So, which one do you want to watch?"

"You pick."

I ran my fingers over the spines of the cases. "Oh, I wouldn't know where to start. I don't think I've seen any of these."

"You're kidding." In a flash, Cooper was off the sofa and standing in front of me. "You've never seen *Citizen Kane*? *Psycho*? Not even *Gone with the Wind*?"

"I have a three-year-old sister. I rarely get the chance to watch anything that isn't animated. Let alone black and white or without some sort of talking animal."

"Okay." He turned to the movies and had to look for only a moment before he found what he wanted. "Let's start with an easy one."

He snatched the case off the shelf before I could see what it was and put the disc into the player. Then he returned to his spot on the sofa, patting the cushion next to him. Coke still in hand, I sat with a good two feet between us.

"Prepare yourself." His eyes were wide, and he practically bounced in his seat, like he was waiting for me to open a present he'd spent hours of thought picking out instead of a movie he'd taken three seconds to decide on. "This will ruin those cheesy rom-coms for you for the rest of your life."

He pressed a button on the remote, and the TV came to life. There was a blast of trumpet music as the screen showed a gray Warner Bros. logo. In the next shot, a black-and-white map of Africa. Three names in white letters popped up on the screen, then were quickly replaced by one word.

Casablanca.

***

Forty-five minutes later, we sat slouched back on the sofa cushions, my legs crossed in front of me and Coop's stretched out. His feet rested on the coffee table and our eyes were glued to the screen. It was the part where Rick was drinking in the dark, looking back at an almost dreamy montage of him and Ilsa in Paris together when they'd first fallen in love.

It was beautiful and heartbreaking reminiscing with him over the love he'd once had, but eventually lost. And as Rick read Ilsa's note in the pouring rain at the train station, a small tear slipped down my cheek.

Riiiiing.

I was pulled instantly back into reality, and I swiped at my cheek as Cooper paused the movie, then pulled his phone from his jeans pocket. At some point, we'd both started leaning on the throw pillow between us, and I barely had to glance over now to see Liam's name pop up on his screen.

"Go ahead." I stretched my arms over my head and my legs out in front of me. "I need to get a refill anyway." I grabbed the empty Coke can and made the short trek over to the fridge.

"Get me one too," Cooper called before answering his phone. "Hey, man. What's up?"

I opened the fridge and gawked at the distinct lack of fresh groceries. Instead, the shelves were filled to the brim with containers from various takeout restaurants. Pizza, Chinese, Italian, seafood. Pretty much every place that delivered to our neighborhood.

Poor Coop. Was this really what he ate every night?

I grabbed two Cokes from the door of the fridge, then walked back over and sat next to him, placing both drinks on the coffee table.

"Yeah. That's cool," Coop muttered. Liam's muffled response was too quiet for me to hear. Coop shook his head. "Nothing. We're watching a movie."

A pause, then I swore I heard the voice ask, *Who's we?*

Cooper glanced over at me. "Me and Bentley. She's never seen *Casablanca.*"

There was another pause before Liam said something, and Cooper looked at me again. "Uh…yeah, sure." He held the phone out to me, watching it with narrowed eyes. "He wants to talk to you."

"He does?" I whispered. "Why?"

Coop shrugged, and I took the phone from him. "Hello?"

"Hey. What's going on?"

I hesitated. "Um, nothing. What are you doing?" I felt like a ten-year-old who finally got up the nerve to call her crush and then had no idea what to say. Only this time my crush had called me. Sort of.

"Nothing much. I wanted to ask you something."

My heart sped up. "Yeah?"

"I was wondering… Do you want to go out with me sometime?"

I threw a hand over my mouth to keep from screaming, then jumped up off the sofa and hopped in place, not caring Coop was watching me. "Yeah, sure. When?"

"How about tonight? I've got my mom's car for the evening, so I can pick you up at seven."

I checked the clock on Coop's phone. That was a little over an hour away, barely enough time to get ready. "Okay, great. I'll see you then. Bye." I hung up and tossed the phone to Cooper.

His eyebrows rose. "I take it that was good news."

"He asked me out." I squealed, dancing around in place again. "He wants to go out…with me…tonight."

"Really? Tonight?" His brow furrowed. "That's kind of short notice."

"If I had any other plans, I might care. But now that my mom has emerged from her writing den, I don't. So I don't." I danced over to him. "Your tutoring plan worked, and now I'm going on a date with Liam Haynes."

I took his unshaved cheeks in my hands. "You're amazing, you know that?" I repeated his words from the first day back at school before giving his cheek a quick peck like we used to do when we were little kids. And like when we were little, he couldn't hold back his grin.

I stood straight, looking down at my baggy jeans and ratty flannel shirt. "I have to go get ready." I spun on the spot, catching a glimpse of Humphrey Bogart and Ingrid Bergman frozen on the TV screen. "Okay if we finish this another time?"

He waved a hand in the air. "Sure. No problem. Go have fun tonight."

Oh, I intended to.

Chapter 8

Liam showed up in his mom's Honda three minutes early. I checked my hair and makeup in the mirror one last time, then darted down the stairs. My blue flats tapped with each step, and I smoothed my hands over the teal sweater and flowy black skirt I'd settled on.

Mom watched Liam through the front window.

"It's hard to believe that's the same boy who kissed you in his driveway only a few years ago." She gave me a quick once-over before nodding her approval. "Don't stay out too late, okay?"

"You sure this is okay? I know you still have a ton of writing to do, and if you stop now—"

She put her hands on my shoulders. "I'm sure, and I'm sorry about snapping at you earlier. You're so good to me, and sometimes I forget how lucky I am to have you. You and Liam have fun tonight. You deserve it." She smiled. "Love you."

I grabbed my jean jacket from the table by the door and put it on, shoving my phone and small wallet in the pocket. "Thanks. Love you too." Out the window, Liam had already started his way to the front door. I hurried to open it, not looking forward to the scene the boys would make if he came inside.

"Hey, you ready?" he asked as I met him at the bottom of the porch steps. "Have you eaten? I was thinking we could go to my favorite Mexican place."

"Sounds great."

Instead of conversation, the car ride into town consisted of a series of rap songs by some guy I'd never heard of, which proved Cooper's intel to be pretty spot-on. Not that I ever really doubted him. It was loud to the point of painful, but I didn't care, too busy gawking as Liam's lips moved like lightning, matching the rapper's lyrics word for word. It was mesmerizing.

He wore dark jeans and a red polo under a black leather jacket. His shaggy blond hair curled around his ears, accentuating his sharp cheekbones. I couldn't count the number of times I'd dreamed of that face in the weeks after he'd put his lips on mine and awakened my body to feelings of electricity and butterflies.

Now I was going on a date with him.

We parked outside the small Mexican restaurant in downtown Oakcrest, and Liam led me inside. *Casa Queso* was busier than usual, but the hostess was able to put us at one of the tall tables right in the middle.

"Sorry this was so last minute," Liam said after our waiter had taken our drink orders. "I didn't know what I'd be doing tonight, but when Coop said you two were hanging out, I thought, *why not?*"

"I guess it's a good thing I was over there."

"You and Coop hang out a lot?"

I pulled at the hem of my sweater. "Not really. Actually, we've hardly even spoken the last couple years."

"What happened? You two used to be best friends."

"I don't know. After you left, I guess we moved on." I certainly wasn't going to admit Cooper had completely ditched me. Not to Liam, of all people.

"So then why the movie tonight?"

"Oh, that was sort of last minute too. Coop could tell I was having a rough day, and I think he was trying to cheer me up. My mom was working in her office all day, and I was in charge of watching Addie, Noah, and Caden, and trying to clean the house. They were being less than cooperative."

"That sucks."

I waited for him to say more, but he must've been as nervous as I was because we ended up sitting in awkward silence until our drinks came. The waiter took our dinner orders with a kind smile and set us up with some chips and salsa to tide us over before he left.

Come on, Bentley. Say something. I tried to come up with some question about cars or the rapper we'd listened to on the way over, or a random, off-the-wall comment on the color orange.

My brain was a complete and total blank.

"It's a shame he didn't pick a better one," he finally said.

I stared at him for a beat too long. *Crap.* Had I been so focused on coming up with a conversation starter that I'd totally missed something? "Sorry, who?"

He smiled as he scooped salsa onto a chip. "Cooper. If he was trying to make you feel better, he could have picked something better than *Casablanca*. That movie's like ancient."

"Oh, right." I laughed, but it came out breathy and weak. "Actually, the movie wasn't so bad. Or at least, what I saw of it. You called right in the middle, so we didn't get to finish. You don't like *Casablanca*?"

"Never seen it."

"Oh. Then how do you know it's not good?"

He shrugged. "Old and boring never is. Give me an action flick with awesome special effects, and I'm game."

"Oh, cool." God, what was the last action movie I saw? *Ninja Turtles*? The one with the Vikings and their pet dragons? Something told me neither of those were the type of movie he was talking about.

We sat through another bout of silence, Liam's gaze wandering aimlessly around the restaurant while I tried desperately to come up with something to say. Then an idea hit me.

I pulled my phone from the pocket of my jean jacket, pulling up my texts.

Quick. What's Liam's favorite movie?

I waited for what felt like forever with no response. Geez, shouldn't he have his phone glued to his hand just like everyone else? I tried again.

Coop?

My phone vibrated in my hand.

Ask him.

PLEASE….

I followed up with a pouting emoji.

I could almost hear his eyes roll as the next one slowly came in.

Fast and Furious.

I'd barely finished reading the text before words began tumbling out of my mouth. "You know what movie I love?"

Liam's attention came back to me, and it took him a second to realize what I'd said. "What movie?"

"*The Fast and the Furious*."

Liam's smile seemed genuine, maybe even a little surprised, as he leaned in closer. "No way. I love those movies. Which one's your favorite?"

Shoot. I'd nearly forgotten it was a series. I tried to remember what I could of the ones I'd seen years and years ago, which admittedly hadn't been many. "The one with Vin Diesel?"

He let out a chuckle that made my insides melt, then leaned in even closer and put his arms on the table. "Good one. And you're right. *2 Fast 2 Furious* wasn't great, and *Tokyo Drift* is easily the worst."

Was that really what I'd said? I sure as hell had no idea.

"For real, though, which is your favorite?"

I smiled to hide my panic. "Wow, that's a hard one. I mean, can you ever really pick a favorite from such a good lineup?" Liam's expression didn't change, and it was clear I'd given the wrong answer.

Oh God, how many were there again? I took a stab in the dark. "The fourth one?"

"Nice. Mine too," he said, and I couldn't believe my luck. Maybe destiny really was on my side. "What's your favorite part?"

Or maybe not. "Umm…" I looked down at my phone, my thumbs flying over the keyboard.

What's fourth one about?

"It's so hard to pick one thing about it." I waited. "Let's see…"

Buzz.

Original cast back together to take down drug lord.

"I think mostly I liked how they brought all the original characters back. It really brought the franchise full circle."

Liam nodded his agreement and ran a hand through his hair. "Ever since I saw that first one, I told myself I was going to get a 1970 Dodge Charger like Dom had. O'Conner's Nissan Skyline was nice too, but there's nothing like the roar of that nine-hundred horsepower engine…"

His eyes lit up as he went on about the different types of cars in the movies, comparing and contrasting them while giving his own experienced opinion on each one.

I hadn't heard him talk half this much in our tutoring sessions, but apparently with the right topic, he was quite the chatterbox. He barely paused as the waiter brought out our orders ten minutes later, he still waxing poetic about makes, models, and horsepower in between bites of his *carne asada* burrito.

I smiled as he talked, showing I was interested in what he said even though I only understood about half of it. I knew virtually nothing about cars, and it never came up since Liam did most of the talking. Which meant I got to sit back, eat my fish tacos, and admire the way he kept having to brush his hair out of his eyes each time his enthusiasm shined through.

"I mean, if you knew the kind of time and money it takes to build up your own car from nothing, especially one of the classics. And then that feeling you get when it's finally done?" Liam relaxed back into his seat with a sigh.

I smiled up at him. "I can imagine." But when I tried to, all I saw was a shirtless Liam standing in front of a fancy sports car with grease smudges and a sexy smile.

I grabbed my phone again while Liam went into great detail about all the work he'd done on his mom's car.

Thanks, Goat. I owe you one.

First for the movie escape at his house, now for helping me out on my date. This day had gone from one of the worst to easily one of the best I'd had in…a *long* time. And it was all thanks to Cooper.

In some ways, it'd felt like I was hanging out and conspiring with the old Cooper. The one who always made me laugh, the one who didn't care about parties or girls as long as whatever we did, we did it together.

I hadn't realized how much I missed that guy until now.

Buzz. I smiled to myself as I glanced down at my phone.

All just part of the deal.

My stomach sank. None of that mattered, though. This wasn't the old Cooper, and any resemblance I saw was nothing more than wishful thinking. We weren't friends anymore. His choice. The sooner I remembered that, the better.

I shoved my phone back in my pocket and smiled across the table at Liam, giving all my attention to someone who actually deserved it.

***

As I stepped out of the house Monday morning, I said flatly, "Good morning."

Cooper's eyes shot up to me, one eyebrow raised. If he was questioning the stilted, formal greeting, he'd have to get over it.

Despite my best efforts over the last two days, his little dig Saturday night had gotten to me. To the point where I almost couldn't enjoy the victory that'd been my date with Liam. Almost. But I'd decided this morning enough was enough.

What did I care if Cooper was helping me with Liam only because of our deal? I'd gotten along fine without him the last three years, and I would again when Liam and I were officially together and there was nothing to link Coop and me anymore.

But deal or not, I owed him for offering me sanctuary at his place Saturday afternoon.

I took the porch steps two at a time and handed him one of the two travel mugs of coffee I grabbed minutes ago, this one with considerably less sugar than the other.

His gaze zeroed in on the mug, eyes narrowing, and the corners of his lips curled slightly. "For me?"

"It's the least I can do after Saturday."

His small smile fell into a hard line. "Oh right. Your *date*."

I would have corrected him if it weren't for his obvious disdain. Was he really so disgusted he was helping me get a guy? Like he didn't understand how he could possibly have sunk so low?

God, he really was an ass.

I rounded the car, pretending not to notice his blatant lack of enthusiasm. "It went great, by the way. Once I got him talking about movies and cars, it was smooth sailing. Did you know he's saving up to buy parts and rebuild a car?"

Cooper got in, I started the car, and cold air blasted through the vents, taking its sweet, precious time to heat up. I really should start warming up the car *before* it was time to go. "*And* we talked about some of his favorite places in Charleston for me to check out if I ever visit."

"You got all that from talking about his favorite movie?"

I nodded. "Thanks to you, I was able to get the ball rolling." And once I had, talking with Liam had only gotten easier as the night went on.

"You know it's not normal to text another guy when you're on a date, right?" He eyed the bag I'd tossed in the back. "You hiding cookies in there?"

"I'll make some more tonight if you want, as an extra thank you," I offered as we finally headed out. "Or would you prefer some other baked good? I can do cakes, pies, breads. And I've been known to make a pretty mean brownie."

He thought for a second, taking a sip from his coffee. "Cupcakes. Like the ones you made me for my thirteenth birthday."

I laughed. "Silly-eyed monster faces and everything?"

"Of course," he scoffed. "What's a cupcake if it's not decorated like a brightly colored monster head?"

"Extra icing?"

He looked at me with mock sentiment. "Aw, you remembered."

"All right, monster cupcakes it is. But on one condition."

"What?"

I looked at him. "You have to be nicer to the twins."

"You want *me* to be nicer? I'm pretty sure Samantha called me a knuckle-dragging ape in Latin the other day."

"Samantha uses her intellect as a defense mechanism, and Sebastian doesn't say anything because he thinks you don't like him."

"It's not that I don't like him. I don't know him. Other than he likes to play instruments at obscenely early hours of the morning."

"He's really into comic books."

"I've noticed."

"And he plays a lot of video games."

He shook his head. "Doesn't he know those things rot your brain?"

"He's also trying out for soccer at school," I offered. "His dad used to play in college, and he wants Sebastian to learn. He has Seb practicing at least an hour in the backyard every day. Unfortunately, Mr. Caldwell works a lot and doesn't have time to teach him. He doesn't spend much time with the twins at all, actually."

"Not all of our dads can be like yours, Bent." He ran a hand through his hair. "Look, I can't make any promises, but I'll *try* to be nicer. Okay?"

"That's all I ask."

We pulled into Liam's driveway, waiting only a minute or two before he was out the door.

"Good morning, Bentley." He settled into the car with a particularly cute grin.

"Hey." I'd hoped the weird nervousness I'd felt around him the last few weeks would be gone after our date, but after a Sunday of reliving all the usual romantic daydreams—and creating a few new ones—my heart beat as wildly as ever.

"Cooper." Liam nodded to him.

"Liam."

Liam sat back in his seat, and I half expected the two of them to fall into their usual morning silence. "How was your weekend, Coop?" he asked instead.

"Peachy," Coop muttered back.

"My weekend was fantastic. Especially Saturday, huh, Bentley?"

I nodded, biting down on the smile trying to take over my face while simultaneously wondering where this early morning cheer had come from. If I didn't already know better, I would've thought he'd drunk an entire pot of coffee on his way out the door. "Saturday was fun."

He leaned forward in his seat, patting Cooper on the shoulder. "Oh yeah, sorry to mess up y'all's movie plan. No hard feelings?"

"None at all." Coop's voice was back to the flat, uninterested tone he had before. "And there were no plans. I felt bad for Bent, so I offered her a quiet place to hang out. That's all."

I tried—and failed—to ignore the familiar sting.

All part of the deal.

The offer to watch a movie and hang out hadn't been genuine either. A pity invite to ease his conscience. I should've known better.

I *should*'ve spat in his stupid, sugar-free coffee.

Liam patted Cooper's shoulder again. "That was awfully nice of you. Then again, what else were you going to do all day, am I right? Can't really get up to your usual wild weekend ways with the Maserati out of commission, can you?"

To that, Cooper said nothing.

"Still," Liam went on, "I'm relieved to know your *whole* weekend wasn't ruined because of me." While he sounded as cheerful and upbeat as ever, that last sentence sounded almost like a taunt.

Only that made absolutely zero sense. For one thing, Liam wasn't that kind of guy. And for another, what would Liam even have to taunt Cooper over? And for what reason?

No. Most likely, I'd imagined the entire thing.

Just as I was probably imagining the thick, almost suffocating tension filling the car as we drove the rest of the way to school in silence.

***

Aubrey closed her locker and turned to me. "How are the morning car rides going? The three of you best friends yet?"

"Hardly." I stared at the chemistry book I needed for my next class, not really focusing on it. "It's kind of weird actually."

"What is?"

"The way Liam and Cooper act with each other. I feel like the more time I spend with them, the less they seem like they're actually best friends. Or that they even like each other."

Aubrey seemed to think about it for a moment. "They look like they get along at lunch."

"I know but... Okay, so when Coop and I are in the car in the mornings, everything seems totally normal. We're laughing and joking for the most part." It was even kind of nice, not that I'd ever admit it out loud after what he'd said about Saturday.

Pity invite, indeed.

"But then as soon as Liam gets in the car, it's like the two of them will barely even acknowledge the other is there. And don't get me started on the weirdness this morning." I sucked in a breath. "They're best friends, have been for years. Everyone knows it. But if you saw them in my car each morning, you'd swear they barely know each other."

"I see."

"See what? 'Cause I'm feeling pretty blind right now."

She bit her lip, the skin between her brows creasing. "Do you think maybe it's possible—"

"Hey, Bentley."

Over my shoulder, Liam smiled that same cute grin he'd worn as he got in the car this morning, as if the awkward tension between him and Coop had never happened.

"Hey, Liam." I grabbed the book from my locker and closed the door. "What's up?"

"I was wondering if you're doing anything tomorrow night. We could get dinner again or see a movie or something."

Butterflies took flight in my stomach. "I'd really like that."

"Awesome. Do you mind driving? My mom's scheduled for an extra shift, so I won't have the car."

"Sure, no problem." This was the boy I'd been dreaming about for three years. I'd walk to his house barefoot in a snowstorm if it meant going on a second date with him. "I can be there at seven."

"Cool," he said.

"Cool."

Liam adjusted the strap of his backpack on his shoulder. "So, I'll see you at lunch, right? We've got that test in Algebra II coming up, and I really need your help."

"Yeah, I'll see you then." Liam smiled, and after he walked away I turned to Aubrey, a huge grin spreading across my face. "Sorry, what were you saying?"

She shook her head. "Nothing. It doesn't matter."

Chapter 9

"He's not getting any better, is he?" Samantha asked.

We stood at one of the many wide windows at the back of her house, watching Sebastian kick the soccer ball around the backyard while bundled up in a hoodie and sweatpants. Even on a frigid, windy day like this he was determined to complete the hour of practice a day his dad required of him after school.

He dribbled the ball with his feet back and forth across the lawn, awkwardly stumbling every few steps.

"Not really, no."

Samantha sighed. "I don't get why Dad has to be so hard on him about soccer. Seb doesn't even like it that much. It's not fair."

"Your dad played, and he loved it. I think he wants that kind of experience for your brother."

"Well, he's wasting his time." Samantha turned away from the window and returned to her open math book on the island bar. "Just like this stupid homework is wasting my Friday afternoon. Why do I have to know the formula for these things when I can put it in a calculator?"

"Because you won't always have a calculator on you."

"No one goes anywhere without their phone. I can Google the equation or plug the problem into an app. Done." She sat on the barstool and glared down at her homework.

"What if you got stranded on a desert island and your phone died?" I suggested. "You wouldn't have a calculator then."

"True. But if I was stuck on a desert island, finding the area of a trapezoid would be the least of my worries."

Well, she had me there. "Just get it done."

Samantha rolled her eyes, grabbed her pencil, and set to work on her math problems, letting out the occasional grunt and groan as I got to work on the dishes. Ten minutes later, she shoved the book away with a muttered "Thank god" and ran up the stairs to go call one of her friends.

A muffled laugh caught my ear, and I glanced out the window where Sebastian had been alone only minutes ago.

Beside him, bouncing a soccer ball in the air from one knee to the other, was Cooper. He grinned as he expertly maneuvered the ball as effortlessly and fluidly as a pro. Sebastian watched him in amazement, counting higher each time the ball hit anywhere other than the ground.

After a last maneuver, Cooper gave the ball one last bounce with the top of his head before he caught it. He talked animatedly to Sebastian as he dropped the ball and dribbled it around the yard with laser-like focus, yet somehow he made it look as natural as walking or breathing. He said something that made Sebastian laugh, and Coop's lips spread into a wide grin lighting up his face.

It was the happiest I'd seen him in years.

Sebastian listened attentively, even mirroring some of Coop's movements. Finally, Cooper snatched up the ball and handed it over to Sebastian. He asked him something, pointing at the house, and Sebastian nodded.

I returned my attention to the dishes as the back door opened.

"How's it going, Bent?" Cooper asked when he saw me.

"You mean since I last saw you an hour ago?"

He shrugged with a lazy grin on his face.

"It's going fine." I set the last plate in the dishwasher and closed it, then crossed my arms and leaned against the counter. "Was that male bonding I saw happening out there? Didn't you call him Satan's even more evil sidekick yesterday?"

"I was talking about Samantha. And I wouldn't call it bonding. I was coming back from a run and saw him kicking the ball around, so I thought I'd show the kid some moves to help him out."

"Since when do you care about helping Sebastian?"

Cooper sat at the bar across from me. "Have you seen him play? The kid is rough. The least I could do was give him a few pointers."

He tapped his fingers on the granite countertop, a sign I'd come to recognize meant there was more to it than he was letting on. I felt my lips curve before I could stop them.

"What?"

"Nothing," I said, still smiling.

"You're the one who told me to be nicer to them."

"That doesn't mean I actually expected you to do it."

"Yeah, well. What choice did I have after you put my cupcakes on the line?" He winked, and for a moment I could see exactly what it was that drew Ashley Morales and the rest of those girls to him. Especially when it mixed with that same joyful grin I'd seen while he was kicking the ball around outside.

That boy has got more heart for the game than I've ever seen. I don't believe he'd give it all up because he doesn't feel like it.

"Can I ask you something?"

His fingers stilled. "Sure."

"Why aren't you playing soccer this year?"

"I already told you. I don't feel like it."

"I remember. But I also saw how happy you were playing out back with Seb."

"So?"

I rested my elbows on the counter between us. "So, I can't figure out why someone who loves the game that much would lie and say he suddenly doesn't want to play this year."

He rolled his eyes, and his fingers started tapping again. "I didn't lie. I really don't want to."

"Coop, I'm not buying your story and neither is my dad, so why don't you tell me what's really going on."

He sat for a minute, then asked. "The honest truth?"

"No, I prefer the dishonest one," I teased. "Yes. Obviously."

Cooper looked down at his hands, now splayed out on the countertop. "I'm not playing soccer this year because of Liam."

"Liam? What does he have to do with whether you play?"

"He's a good player. A great one actually. But—and I'm simply stating a fact here, not trying to boost my own ego—he's not as good as me."

"Okay. So you can't play because you're better than Liam?"

"Exactly. Like I said, he's a great player. Maybe even good enough to get a scholarship to play in college somewhere. But scouts don't hand those things out to just anybody. They give them to the best, and Liam's chances of catching a scout's eye are much better if I'm not there."

"But what about you? Wouldn't you want a scholarship to play somewhere?"

"Want? Sure. But I don't need a scholarship. Not like Liam does. I've got the highest GPA in our class—"

"Second highest."

He smirked. "I'm tied for the highest GPA in our class. I live in the wealthiest neighborhood in Oakcrest, and my dad is raking in a couple hundred thousand a year along with my mom's inheritance money. Liam's dad is in prison, his mom works extra shifts whenever she can, and they live with his aunt." He shook his head. "I can go to school wherever I want, but Liam needs a scholarship."

"Wow." I hadn't thought of it like that. "I've got to admit, that was probably the last thing I expected to hear." Especially coming from the guy who up until recently was dragging his best friend to parties every weekend to have a sober ride back to the hotel. "It doesn't seem fair, though. There's still no guarantee Liam would even get a scholarship. Why should you have to put aside your dreams so Liam can have a somewhat better chance?"

"Why not?" His eyes met mine. "He gets everything else."

"What does that mean?"

He stared down at his hands again. "Let's just say I'm used to letting Liam get what he wants."

"Could you say that again? I'm not sure it was cryptic enough the first time."

"Forget it. It doesn't matter." He rubbed his hands together, his mood shifting instantly. "So, big plans tonight? I'm sensing you're the type that really likes to go wild and reckless on a Friday night. Let me guess. Maybe an exciting game of Pictionary with the family? Or perhaps you and Aubrey have a *Downton Abbey* marathon?"

"As a matter of fact, my parents are taking us all ice skating in Greenville before the season ends. If you remember anything about my skating ability, you know what a daredevil that makes me."

"Talk about life on the edge." He laughed, then his fingers started tapping again. "What about tomorrow? We still haven't finished *Casablanca*, you know."

"Oh." Neither of us had mentioned Saturday or the unfinished movie in days. Not since Cooper had admitted to Liam he only invited me over because he felt bad for me. But the way he looked at me now, that wasn't pity in his eyes.

They were soft, sincere. Hopeful. But why?

"Liam and I are hanging out at his aunt's place tomorrow."

He sat back in his seat. "What is that now, three dates in one week? I guess your plan is working, then."

"Maybe, I don't know. We're taking things slow." So slow, in fact, that sometimes it felt more like we were hanging out as friends as opposed to being on an actual date. Case in point, Liam still hadn't even *tried* to kiss me. Not once. "Right now, it's hard to tell if he even really likes me."

"Maybe that's because you're too busy texting me during your dates to notice." His playful smirk reappeared, but the light in his eyes didn't shine quite as bright.

"How else was I going to find out which team won the last World Cup?"

Coop shook his head. "First of all, you're the daughter of the high school soccer coach. You of all people should know these things. And second, there is a thing called Google. It's great. You can even get to it on your phone now."

"But it's so much easier to ask you." Coop always knew the answer, and he always seemed to find a way to make me laugh when he sent it. And thanks to him, each date had ended feeling like a massive victory. Minus the no kissing part. Coop was single-handedly the best wingman ever.

Which made it all the more annoying whenever that cold shoulder of his reemerged.

He stood from his seat and came around the island to stand next to me. "I'm just saying, you're going to have to get to a point where you trust him not to run away if you don't like the same music he does or you don't know who the highest-earning soccer player in the world is."

"But dating him is so much easier when you know all the right answers." I grabbed a nearby dishtowel and wiped the counter vigorously. "Until I know for sure he really does like me, I intend to have all the right answers."

He set his hand gently on mine to still it, and he stared down at them, his eyes hard and focused, like he was choosing his words carefully. "Slow is good," he said, finally looking up at me again. "Not a lot of guys would take their time if they didn't think it was worth it."

I tried to picture Liam, the way he was whenever we were together, wondering if maybe there would be something in his eyes that revealed a hidden depth of emotion for me. That said he *was* taking his time because he *did* think I was worth it.

But I couldn't think of anything beyond the bright green eyes staring into mine.

"Sunday?" I asked quietly, the word spilling out without much forethought.

He tilted his head slightly. "What about Sunday?"

"The movie. We could finish it Sunday if you really want to. If you aren't already busy, I mean."

He grinned, taking his hand from mine, and suddenly I could breathe again. I hadn't even realized I'd stopped.

"I think I can fit you into my busy schedule," he said, answering the second of my two implied questions and ignoring the first altogether. "Come over around five?"

"Sure, sounds good."

He nodded. "Okay. I'll see you then." He turned and went for the back door he'd come through, gently closing it behind him as he left. I looked down to where I clutched the dishtowel, a small smile spreading across my face, and went back to wiping the counter.

***

I sat staring through blurry eyes as the end credits popped up on the screen.

"You okay?" Cooper asked from beside me.

I didn't answer right away, taking a minute to compose myself. I wiped at my tear-streaked face. "You could've told me." My nose was stuffy, making the words come out deeper and slightly muffled.

"Told you what?"

I whipped around to face him. "That they don't end up together in the end. That Rick sacrifices his love for Ilsa so she'll get on that plane and out of Africa." Against all sanity, the tears started flowing again thinking about it.

Coop had decided despite my having seen the first half of the movie already, I couldn't possibly get the full effect of the film by starting it in the middle where we left off. We'd agreed to watch the whole thing over from the beginning, which had clearly been a bad idea since the full effect of the movie left me a red-faced, runny-nosed, teary-eyed mess.

He handed me a tissue, and I used it to wipe my eyes and cheeks before blowing my nose into it with reckless abandon. I saw him grimace a little at the harsh sound, but when I turned, there was a smile on his face. "This is not funny."

"Actually, it kind of is."

"You should have told me it was a sad ending."

Another reason I tended to avoid movies not made for kids. I was a crier. And not in the cute, single tear kind of way. In the loud, blubbering way making it impossible to see a tear-jerker in the movie theater without making everyone else super uncomfortable. It never failed. My throat got tight and my eyes shot off tears like geysers. I'd sniff and moan, and in the end my face looked puffy like I'd been stung by twenty bees.

Cooper, on the other hand, had spent the last several minutes struggling not to laugh at me.

"I wouldn't've agreed to watch this with you if I knew."

He scooted closer, putting his arm around my shoulders. "Come on, where's your appreciation for the tragic ending?"

"It died along with my heart and soul three minutes ago," I said, throwing his arm off. He laughed some more. I wiped at my face again before taking several deep, calming breaths.

He watched me with a smile plastered on his face. "What?" *God, please don't let there be snot all over me.*

"Nothing." He sat back into the sofa cushion. "I missed this."

"Me crying like a complete idiot in front of you?"

"No, though I certainly found that enjoyable. I guess I missed hanging out with you. Like when we were kids."

Then why had he said all that stuff about it being part of the deal and feeling bad for me? Even a week later, I still felt that same sting remembering the way he'd brushed me off. Especially since I was getting used to having him around again. Enjoying it even.

Which was stupid since it was only a matter of time before he inevitably got another car and found something better to do than hang out with me. And then he'd disappear yet again.

"Me too," I admitted. "But I wasn't the one who decided to completely ignore my best friend of eight years out of the blue."

His smile fell. "Right. Is it too late to say I'm sorry about that? It was a douche move on my part."

"So why did you do it?"

Coop looked back at the TV screen where names still rolled, and music continued to play. "It's complicated."

"I'm as smart as you are," I said. "I could probably keep up."

He grabbed the remote from the coffee table and turned off the TV. "Didn't you have a date yesterday?" He got up and headed into the kitchen, grabbing a bag of chips and setting it out on the counter along with two drinks from the fridge. "How was it?"

"Great, if you like watching a bunch of car movies back-to-back for several hours."

"I take it you don't." He set the drinks on the table and then held the chip bag out to me.

I reached in and grabbed a handful. "It was my own fault. On our first date, I told him I liked the Fast and Furious movies, so he thought it would be fun if we watched all of them together, marathon style."

"You remember what I told you about being yourself?"

"Be myself?" I repeated, crunching on a salty, greasy chip. "It took him three weeks of regular tutoring to ask me out. And look at me now." I waved my hand in front of my red, puffy face. "No guy is going to want to date me once he sees this."

He took some chips from the bag. "I think you'd be surprised."

"No, trust me. Being myself wasn't getting me anywhere." I grabbed one of the Cokes from the table and cracked it open before taking a sip. "Anyway, I said the fourth one was my favorite, so he suggested we watch it yesterday, but we had to watch the three before it first."

"That's too bad. Anyone with any taste knows the original is the best."

"Seriously? You couldn't tell me that the other day? Maybe if I'd said that we could've watched the first one and stopped there. Now I have to sit through the rest of the movies next weekend."

Cooper grimaced. "Yikes."

"What about you? Anything new or exciting in your life?"

"Oh yeah." He took a sip from his drink. "Life sure is thrilling when you're stuck in a big empty house with no car and nowhere to go."

"Like you don't have friends to hang out with."

He looked at me. "Most of my friends are busy with soccer, and when they're not, they're at some dumb high school party."

"Hey, I go to some of those dumb high school parties. They aren't that bad. What about your parents? How are they doing?"

He shrugged. "Fine, I guess. They're both going to be home later this week for the first time since Thanksgiving. Mom's flight gets in Tuesday night from the Bahamas, and Dad's getting a few days off starting Wednesday morning, so I'm preparing for the fallout. Neither of them is leaving again until Friday."

"It may not be that bad. They've been apart so long, they could actually be happy to see each other."

"I highly doubt it."

An idea came to me. One that I would probably regret the moment it was out. "I could come over one night, if you want. Maybe with me here they'd try to be civil with each other." Not that I particularly wanted to spend time around his mom and dad, but the thought of him alone in a house with two bickering parents made my chest hurt. And if he really meant what he'd said earlier...

"It's more likely they won't be in the same room together." He gave me a crooked smile as he tilted his dirty-blond head to the side. "But yeah, you should come over."

"Really?"

"Sure." He shrugged. "I mean, you're hardly the first girl desperate to spend time with me—"

I chucked a couch pillow at his face, and he chuckled. "Okay, okay. I take it back." He returned the pillow to its spot between us. "For real, though, you should come over. It'd be nice to have you here to help warm the frigid atmosphere. That is, if you think you can handle it."

"I'll be sure to wear a warm jacket just in case."

He grinned, the sight of it warming me from head to toe. "Perfect. You up for another classic?"

"Not if it's as depressing as the last one you forced on me."

"Don't worry, we'll go with something lighter this time. How do you feel about John Hughes?"

"You mean like the eighties? Do those really count as classics?"

"Well, maybe not to our parents. But yes, there are definitely a few of his that have become iconic."

"Fine. Who am I to argue with the master? But no crying this time, promise?"

He shook his head and laughed. "Fine, take all the fun out of it."

Chapter 10

Liam and I sat at my usual lunch table the next day, me admiring the way his bicep looked whenever he ran his hand through his light hair, and him glaring down at the equation in front of him like it was created by a prince of Hell specifically to torture him.

"I don't get why I need to know this stuff."

I drew in a deep, slow breath. I'd probably tutored over fifty different people in the last several years, and they all said the same things. *When will I ever need this in the real world?* And *why can't I plug it into my phone like a normal person?* Every time, I told whoever it was to suck it up, quit whining, and get on with it already.

Only none of the other forty-nine people had been my almost boyfriend. I wasn't a dating expert, but I was pretty sure telling the guy I was currently seeing to grow up and be a man wasn't a great idea. Not if I wanted him to ask me out again.

"Hey," I said, putting my hand on his notebook and sliding it away. "Why don't we take a break, get your mind off it for a second? Then when you come back to it, maybe it will make more sense."

He grinned, clearly liking the idea of putting off his homework. "Okay, why don't we talk about what you're doing tonight? That rapper I was telling you about the other day is performing in Greenville, and I thought maybe we could go."

"I'm babysitting tonight and tomorrow," I said, only a little disappointed. As much as I wanted to spend time with Liam, even I had my limits. Especially when it involved listening to an Eminem wannabe spew out SAT words seemingly at random for several hours.

He frowned. "He's only going to be in town for tonight."

"Oh, that's too bad." I'd never been so happy to have to watch my little brothers and sister in my life.

He perked up again. "How about we do something Wednesday?"

I shook my head. "Wednesday I'm hanging out with Cooper."

Liam's brow creased. "Cooper? As in Cooper Bradshaw?" I nodded. "Is it a date or something?"

My hand wasn't fast enough to stop the laugh that exploded from me. "No way, it's not like that. Cooper and I are friends." Barely even that.

His eyes narrowed. "You two are spending a lot of time together lately."

"Not really. I'm giving him rides to school and back home." I lowered my voice. "He's having a tough time with his parents right now. They're both home this week, and I'm trying to help take his mind off it some. That's all."

"Fine. But you have to promise to come to the game Friday night. It's the first one of the season, and I'd really like it if my girlfriend was there cheering me on."

"Did—did you just call me your girlfriend?"

He grinned. "If that's okay with you."

"Yeah." I cleared my throat. "I mean sure. That's cool."

"Nice. So, you'll be there Friday?" He took my hand in his, tracing the lines on my palm.

"I wouldn't miss it."

"Good." Liam studied something over my shoulder. I moved to follow his gaze, but before I could, he cupped my face and kissed me. His lips were soft against mine, and any thought I had vanished in an instant. I kissed him back, not caring who was watching and I was in the middle of the school cafeteria involved in a highly frowned-upon public display of affection. On the contrary, I was relieved that after three dates, Liam had finally made the move and kissed me.

And not only that, but he'd also called me his girlfriend less than a minute before. Any doubt I had of Liam really liking me was gone.

The bell rang, and Liam pulled away, leaving me in a dreamy, post-kiss haze. When my eyes finally focused, he watched me with a crooked grin. "See you later." He placed another quick kiss on my lips before shooting up from his seat and out the nearest door.

I sat dazed for a moment, almost unsure of what to do next or which class I was supposed to be heading to. When I was finally able to gather my wits, I scanned the cafeteria for any faculty who might've seen the show.

But as I searched my mind eased. Then I checked behind me, remembering the look on Liam's face as he stared at something over my shoulder right before he kissed me. But whatever it was had to be gone now. All that was left was a bunch of empty tables on the far side of the cafeteria.

***

Instead of cutting straight across the cul-de-sac to my house when Dr. Caldwell got home Wednesday afternoon as I usually did, I turned left and headed down the sidewalk and up the stone path to Cooper's.

The sun was getting ready to set over the trees behind me, casting a warm glow on the glass in the front door.

Inside, I tossed my backpack to the side, the loud thump it made amplified in the large, empty foyer, and I closed the door behind me. Noises came from the kitchen down at the end of the hall, and I imagined Cooper in there fixing up some sort of pre-movie snack or whatever takeout he'd had delivered for the night. My stomach grumbled, and I hoped whatever it was involved some sort of greasy, salty goodness.

"What movie are we watching?" I called out, taking slow steps down the hallway. I'd been here two other times in the last couple weeks, but I had yet to take the time to really look around.

Photos of the Bradshaw family lined the main hallway. A few of Coop's parents were scattered here and there, along with several of Caitlyn from when she was growing up, her hair lighter than Cooper's and always pin straight. She wore an infectious smile in each photo, not only because her picture was being taken, but because that was the kind of girl she was. She could always find something to smile about.

Several shots of Coop hung scattered randomly throughout the mix. I recognized most of them from when we were kids and even found one of the two of us together. We were ten or so. The day Mrs. Bradshaw took us to the zoo that summer. My hair was dark and short, barely hitting my shoulders, and I had on a pair of overall shorts, a bright pink T-shirt, and sneakers. Cooper stood several inches taller than me, his messy, dirty blond hair hanging down in his face in sweaty streaks. When I looked closer, I could make out the freckles plastered over his nose and cheeks.

We posed for the camera, our arms around each other while I held the stuffed panda he'd convinced his mom to buy me. We grinned like we were the happiest children on the planet, my eyes on the camera, Cooper's eyes on me.

"Coop?" I gave the picture one last look before following the noises down the hall. "This better not be some trick so you can get me to cry again," I warned. I turned the corner into the kitchen.

And froze.

"Oh, sorry, Mr. Bradshaw. I thought you were Coop."

He looked at me from behind the kitchen island, a glass of amber-colored liquid in his hand. He swirled it around before taking a sip. "I guess you don't bother to knock before barging into someone else's house."

Crap. My brain must have been on autopilot. I used to walk in whenever I wanted when I was a kid. "Sorry, old habit, I guess." I searched the kitchen and living area, looking anywhere but at the squared-shouldered man in front of me. "Where's Cooper?"

"Around somewhere." The drink in his glass sloshed over the side as he waved it around in his meaty hand, and I allowed myself to get a good look at him.

He wore a thin, black sweater and dress slacks. His blond hair visibly thinner since I'd last seen him and his cheeks and neck redder than my brother Xander's that time his friends dared him to eat a ghost pepper his sophomore year. Something told me this wasn't Mr. Bradshaw's first drink of the day.

He gave me a thorough once-over before letting out a sigh. "I have to say, Bentley. I'm a little surprised you of all people are hanging around my son."

"I don't know what you mean."

"I thought you had better sense than the other girls he sleeps with."

"Oh." I stepped back as the words hit me with an almost physical force. My cheeks burned. This was not the Mr. Bradshaw I'd grown up knowing, the one who—when he wasn't bickering with his wife—used to laugh and take his son and me to baseball games. That man would never have said anything so crass as this man did.

"It's not like that. I have a b-boyfriend." After only three days, the word still felt awkward on my tongue.

Mr. Bradshaw shrugged. "The stories I've heard, I don't imagine that makes much of a difference to him." He took another long sip from his drink, then came around the kitchen island, past me, and down the hall, never saying a word as he took the curved staircase up to the second floor.

Even Coop's dad knew about his son's reputation. How could he possibly have heard about all the college parties Coop went to, all the girls he'd been with? It had to be an awfully long list, the knowledge of which had never bothered me before.

But now I'd been accused of being on that list. Was that what people thought whenever they saw me and Coop together? It wasn't like we were together all that much. Aside from the rides to and from school, we barely saw each other. We'd barely gotten to the point where we acknowledged each other in the halls. And yet the mere sight of me in his house had Coop's dad thinking I was sleeping with him.

No wonder Liam had sounded disgruntled with me for hanging out with Cooper. But, I mean, this was *Cooper Bradshaw* we were talking about. Everyone knew he went for college girls, and I was an average high school student. How could anyone ever think there was anything between us?

I was still frozen and gaping when he came down the same stairs a minute or two later. The corners of his mouth turned up. "Hey, Bent. I didn't know you were here already."

I shook myself, hoping to erase the last several minutes like the lines on an Etch A Sketch. "Yeah, sorry. I kind of forgot to knock."

"No worries. So…" Cooper pulled a bag of pretzels from the pantry. "If you really haven't seen any John Hughes movies, you've got to start with *Ferris Bueller*. It really doesn't get any better than that."

"Isn't that the one where they skip school?"

Cooper hung his head. "First you call the main characters of *Top Gun* Maverick and *Goat*, now you call this 'the one where they skip school.' You disappoint me."

"Then what would you call it?"

"The quintessential teen movie, the anthem of all high-school-aged youths. Bueller is an idol to all who know him. In the first few lines alone, he shares more wisdom than men twice his age."

I laughed. "Why don't you start the movie, and I'll decide for myself?"

"Fine," he said, making his way over to the shelves of DVDs and Blu-rays. I took the same spot on the couch I had last time. "But you'll see I'm right."

He put the movie in.

***

An hour and forty-five minutes later, the screen went black. Cooper set the remote down and turned to face me. "So, what did you think?"

"It was okay."

"Okay?" He shifted in his seat. "That's all you have to say? It was *okay*?"

"Don't get me wrong. I thought the story was amusing and exciting."

"So what's the problem?"

"It wasn't realistic."

He looked like I'd slapped him. "Of course it wasn't realistic. It's a movie."

"And you said you liked movies that were real," I shot back. "If you and I decided to skip school, it wouldn't be near as multifarious as that."

"But this was better than real. This movie is a goal to aspire to. Bueller takes life by the balls—so to speak—and he lives it. He took what was going to be a boring, regular day of going through the motions and made meaningful memories out of it."

"And tomorrow he'll be right back at school going through the motions again like everyone else."

"Exactly."

"But how meaningful can it all have been if life goes back to normal the next day like none of it ever happened? He'll go to school, sit through his boring classes with the rest of them. He didn't really accomplish anything. He got bored and found a way to avoid his responsibilities for a day."

"It's not about avoiding responsibilities. It's about giving yourself a chance to put everything else aside and do what you want, be who you want," Coop said, scooting closer. His eyes shone, his words tumbling out as he spoke. "It may have been only for a day, but at least when he looks back on it a few years down the line, he'll have no regrets."

"Is that what you're doing every weekend at those college parties? Being the person you really want to be?" I didn't know what made me say it. Perhaps the run-in with Mr. Bradshaw had affected me even more than I thought. But it was too late to take it back. "And all the random girls you've been with. You're honestly telling me you have no regrets in regards to them?"

I waited for Coop to yell at me and tell me it was none of my business. Or worse, show a cocky sense of pride at the mention of all his female conquests.

His mouth opened, but no words came out. Then he looked down at his hands. "I have only two real regrets in my life, Bentley," he said, his voice lower than I'd ever heard it, "neither of which I plan on discussing with you."

We sat in a tense, awkward silence.

"Hello? Anybody home?" a cheery, female voice called from down the hall.

Coop perked up, his forehead wrinkling. "Caitlyn?" he called back. "We're back here." He jumped to his feet, the recent turn in our conversation forgotten, and a smile came to his face as his older sister appeared in the archway. A tall man with brown hair and glasses followed behind her.

"Hey, stranger." She threw her arms up and ran over to her brother, wrapping them around his muscular frame.

Cooper hugged her back. "What are you doing here?"

"Mom didn't tell you? Owen and I came to have dinner with you guys."

"She must've forgotten to mention it." He turned to me with a wry smile. "Bentley and I just finished a movie."

I stood as Caitlyn looked my way, her mouth falling open. "Oh my god," she squealed, and in seconds, I was trapped by her arms. In the years since she went to college, I'd managed to get a good two inches on her, making it hard to believe she was eight years older than me. She still looked like a teenager. "Look at you. I didn't know you two were still hanging out."

"Bentley is an old family friend," Cooper told the man who'd come in with his sister. "This is Owen, the boyfriend I told you about."

We waved at each other, neither of us having much to say.

"Actually," Caitlyn said, holding up her left hand to show us the sparkly diamond sitting on her finger, "Owen is my fiancé."

Coop's eyebrows shot to the roof and a massive grin spread across his face. "What? When did this happen?"

"A week ago. Mom and Dad still don't know. That's why we're here. I wanted to tell you all over dinner since they were both going to be in town."

He kissed his sister's cheek. "Congratulations. And you—" He walked over to Owen and gave him a pat on the back. "—I've always wanted a cool older brother. I guess you'll have to do."

Owen laughed, and the two started roughhousing the way my brothers did. It was obvious when they came in that Owen was on the shy side, but the way he and Cooper wrestled with each other one could hardly tell.

Caitlyn looked back at me, taking my hands in hers. Her long blonde hair was pulled up with a few carefully placed wisps framing her face. "You've got to stay for dinner. Mom's getting carryout from my favorite restaurant, and I'd love for you to celebrate with us."

"Not happening, Caitlyn," Cooper told her. "You can't ask Bent to sit through dinner with our parents."

She shrugged. "Why not? She's already been over here at least a couple hours and she hasn't run home crying yet."

"That's because we've been safe in here while Mom and Dad are hiding from each other at two different ends of the house. She hasn't seen them all evening. You're asking her to sit at a table with them…together. That's cruel and unusual punishment."

"You, shut up." She poked Cooper in the chest. "This is my engagement dinner. When you're the one getting married, you can invite whoever you want." She turned back to me expectantly.

I grimaced. "I don't know. This is a big family thing, and I don't want to intrude."

"Please. You're practically family. And if you're here, maybe Mom and Dad will be on their best behavior and try to get through the night without screaming at each other."

It was the same logic I'd used on Coop, only now I knew what a load of bull it was. I'd been here all of two seconds before Mr. Bradshaw started accusing me of sleeping with his son. The last thing I wanted was to be stuck in a room with both of their parents at the same time.

"Come on. You're the closest thing to a little sister I've got. Do this for me," Caitlyn said quietly, her expression soft and pleading.

I didn't have the heart to say no. I looked to Cooper for guidance, but he gave me a sympathetic smile like he already knew what my answer was going to be.

"Fine, if you're sure you want me here." I took in Caitlyn's red dress and Owen's slacks and dress shirt for the first time, then glanced down at my frumpy sweatshirt and jeans. "But I have to go home and change."

Caitlyn's smile stretched from one ear to the other, the same way it did in all those pictures out in the hallway. "Of course. Take all the time you need."

Chapter 11

I brushed my hands over my dress, staring at my reflection in one of the dark windows on the Bradshaws' porch. I'd tried to change as quickly as possible, ultimately taking five minutes to go through my closet and settle on one of the dresses I loved but rarely got the chance to wear: a simple black number with a boat neck collar and elbow-length sleeves. It clung at the chest and waist then flowed at the hips and down to my knees.

It was modest when it came to skin exposure but still hugged my curves in the right way. It felt classy yet sexy. Not that I was going for sexy in particular tonight. But anything that boosted my self-confidence was preferable after the way Coop and Caitlyn had described whatever this was I was walking into.

I was all but terrified.

After checking every inch of the dress for wrinkles or hang-ups, I ran my hands through my hair. I'd managed to take it down from its ponytail and quickly touched it up in a few places with the curling iron, making it look practically good as new. I hadn't bothered with anything more than the natural makeup look I already wore, not when I'd taken too long to get ready. Besides, it was dinner at Coop's house. Who would I need to impress there?

Once I was sure everything was in place, I rang the doorbell. A dark figure approached on the other side of the frosted glass window. Then the door opened, and Cooper stood before me.

The air froze in my lungs. His hair was damp and his face clean-shaven. He'd put on dark jeans and a cobalt blue dress shirt, which looked striking against his tan skin. I'd never known him to dress up for anything, and tonight he looked...

I couldn't think of a single word that did him justice.

"Hey," I said, as if I hadn't seen him fifteen minutes ago.

"Hey." His voice was deep and froggy as his eyes slid down over my dress. He attempted to clear his throat. "You look beautiful."

My heart stopped beating. I couldn't remember the last time anyone other than my parents had called me that. Something about the way he said it left no doubt in my mind he meant it.

When my heart started again, it came back ten times faster than before. It was the kind of reaction I would imagine most girls had to Cooper Bradshaw, but I certainly never expected him to have that kind of effect on me.

I forced a smile, feeling my cheeks heat. "Thanks. You clean up well yourself," I teased, hoping the light banter would ease the stressed tightness residing in my stomach.

Coop didn't laugh, and I noticed he look me over once again. I hadn't bothered to wear a coat for the hundred-foot walk over, so I hugged my arms to my chest, partly from the chilly night air and also as a defense from his inexplicably intense gaze. "Can I come in?"

"Right, sorry." He jumped back from the door and pulled it open wide. "Everyone's getting into the dining room, so you're right on time."

"Great." My hands fidgeted as we walked down the hall together, and I cringed at the resounding clack of my heels on the wood floor. As promised, Caitlyn, Owen, and Cooper's parents were all waiting in the dining room.

"*Bentley*," Mrs. Bradshaw gushed from one end of the table. Her hair, the same dark shade of blond as Cooper's, sat in a carefully constructed twist high on her head. She adjusted the light gray cardigan covering her blue dress. "I didn't realize you would be joining us this evening. Cooper really should have said something."

"It was pretty last minute," I admitted.

"I invited her, Mom. It's been so long since I last saw her, and I wanted the chance to catch up with her," Caitlyn said, winking at me. She and Owen sat in the two chairs on the far side of the table. I waved, and Owen smiled back politely.

"Well, sit, sweetie." Mrs. Bradshaw waved at the two chairs directly in front of me and Cooper. "Mitchem and I are always glad to have you over. Aren't we, dear?" The man at the opposite end of the table lifted his glass in silent greeting, but I couldn't bring myself to meet his gaze.

Cooper stepped forward and pulled out the chair closest to his mom for me.

Caitlyn was shaking her head from across the table. "I am in love with that dress, Bentley. Cooper, doesn't she look stunning?"

"What do you want to drink?" he asked, barely meeting my gaze. His shoulders were impossibly tense, nothing like the way he'd relaxed into the sofa beside me only half an hour ago. All because his parents sat in the same room. I couldn't imagine my mom and dad ever making me that uncomfortable, even on their worst days.

"Water's fine, thank you."

Cooper disappeared out the door, and the five of us at the table sat silently for what felt like ages. I glanced around at the various platters of food, which, according to Caitlyn, were prepared somewhere in town and was delivered all the way out here. When she'd said Mrs. Bradshaw was ordering carryout, I'd assumed Chinese or something. But this spread looked like something out of a five-star restaurant.

Coop returned with a glass of water and set it in front of my place at the table before taking his own seat.

"Well, now that we're all sitting, let's dig in." Mrs. Bradshaw gave me a high-wattage smile, and everyone else at the table slowly started filling their plates. There was a heaviness in the room, almost like a large blanket settled over the entire table and its guests.

"So, Bentley," Caitlyn spoke up after a few minutes of awkward, silent eating. "How's everyone in your family doing?"

"Everyone's good. Mom is working almost night and day on another health book, and she's hoping to have it done and published sometime in the next year. Dad's still coaching at the high school and teaching underclassmen PE."

"Do you have any siblings?" Owen asked.

"Five, actually." I almost laughed when he gave me the typical wide-eyed reaction. "My sister, Addie, is three. And my little brothers, Caden and Noah, are fourteen and twelve."

Caitlyn took a sip of red wine. "And Xander and Theo? They've got to be in their twenties now," she said, the wonder clear in her voice. Of course, she would find it hard to believe, seeing as she used to babysit us when my older brothers were only ten and thirteen.

"Theo is. Xander turned nineteen in August."

"Are they attending college anywhere?" Mrs. Bradshaw asked. She'd yet to actually eat anything and was pushing food around with her fork.

"Yes, ma'am. They're both at Coastal Carolina right now. Theo is a senior and Xander's a sophomore."

"And what about you? What are your plans after graduation?" she asked.

"Definitely college, though I'm not sure which one yet. Probably something in-state."

Caitlyn gave me an encouraging smile. "What are you interested in studying?"

Geez, why was everyone so interested in me tonight? Surely one of them had a question for someone else at the table or a new story to tell. But Caitlyn and Mrs. Bradshaw kept their eyes on me, waiting for my response. Owen smiled, and I imagined he was glad not to have all the attention on himself.

"Teaching," I finally told them.

Caitlyn nodded her approval. "Any particular age or subject?"

"I really enjoy math and science. I'm not sure what ages I'd want to teach, though. I'm taking an early childhood education class this year, but I have more experience tutoring middle and high schoolers."

Mr. Bradshaw scoffed at the far end of the table, and all eyes turned to him. "So, you're saying you don't plan on making any money."

"Dad, don't," Coop warned, the first time he'd spoken since he sat down.

"Everyone knows you don't go into education for the money. And knowing what I do about her parents, she's not prepared to rough it on a lower-middle-class income."

"I think it's lovely," Mrs. Bradshaw interjected with a kind smile directed at me. "Do what makes you happy, the rest will sort itself out. I think working in any field you love is commendable."

"Oh, I absolutely agree," her husband burst out. "At least you know what you want to do and aren't shitting your time away like my son here." He emptied the drink in his hand. "And you're willing to work and earn your cut in life instead of taking the easy way out and mooching off whatever rich man you can get your hands on, so you've already surpassed two people at this table."

"I don't mooch anything," Mrs. Bradshaw practically yelled. "I never needed your money. My parents left me an inheritance and a trust fund."

"We both know you burned through that measly sum before the kids were even born."

"Can we please not do this tonight?" Caitlyn pleaded. "Not in front of Bentley and Owen."

"What the hell do I care if they hear? You think they're going to come into *my* house and dictate what I can say to my own family?" He slammed his glass on the table. "Face it, Sandra. Me and my money are the only things keeping a roof above your head and food at your table. Not that you ever say thank you."

"Oh yes. Thank you for constantly belittling me in front of our children. Thank you for embarrassing me when our neighbor and guest are here. And *thank you* for reminding me yet again why I can't stand the sight of you anymore."

"Fine, if you're that sick of me, why don't we tell the kids and get it over with? That way we can both stop trying to pretend either of us gives a fuck about this marriage anymore."

Coop's gaze ping-ponged between his parents. "What's that supposed to mean?"

Mr. Bradshaw stared at his wife. She glared back murderously. "Your mother and I are getting a divorce. There, Sandra. Happy now? I'm the bad guy once again."

"Wait, what?" Caitlyn cried out. Owen took her hand gently in his. His gaze met mine, and I felt this strange sense of camaraderie at being the other non-family member forced to witness this. "You two can't be serious. You pick the night I'm trying to announce my *engagement* to tell us you're splitting up?"

"Oh, honey, you're getting married?" her mother cried at the same time Mr. Bradshaw muttered a loud, "Good luck with that."

The three of them yelled at each other about life-ruining mistakes and poor judgment.

"I think I should leave," I whispered to Coop, not knowing what else to say. He'd been sitting in stunned silence while raised voices flew around him. When he looked at me, it was as if he only just remembered I was there. His dazed expression turned hard as he stood and followed me out into the hallway. No one else seemed to notice.

Voices carried down the hall all the way to the front door. Coop closed it softly behind him, cutting off the sound of his mother screaming obscenities at her husband.

I shivered, and my breath clouded the air in front of us.

"I'm sorry you had to see that." Coop's hands slid into his pockets as he looked to the lamp-lit cul-de-sac.

"Don't be. None of this was your fault. And it's not like I don't ever see my parents fight."

Coop shook his head, not saying anything. We both knew my parents had never once had a fight like the one we witnessed. He turned back to the door.

"Wait, Coop." I reached out and set my hand on his arm. "I know this sounds awful and stupid, and I wish I could know what else to say right now to make this all better for you. But if you ever need anything, or want to talk, I'm here for you. Okay?"

He looked at me, his eyes wet and shining, and the prettiest shade of green I'd ever seen thanks to that damn shirt that was honestly the perfect color for him.

I wanted to hug him, to hold him close to me and pour every ounce of strength I had into him like when we were kids. But I knew him, like I knew the only thing he wanted right now was to be alone while he processed everything. So I let my hand fall from his arm.

He sighed, letting out the breath he'd apparently been holding, and turned back to the door. "I'll see you tomorrow."

"See you tom—" But the door closed before I could finish.

Chapter 12

"Okay, this is getting ridiculous." It was Friday night, and I was supposed to be getting ready to go see Liam's first soccer game of the season. Instead, I was glaring at the phone, willing it to spring to life like an obsessed girlfriend.

Only it wasn't my boyfriend I was so anxious to hear from. It was the next-door neighbor who didn't have the decency to give even the most basic indication of life on the other end.

I'd texted Cooper at least a hundred times since Wednesday night, but the only answers I'd gotten were at seven the last two mornings telling me he didn't need a ride to school.

After that horrifying dinner, it was no surprise when both of his parents' cars were gone come Thursday morning. Which meant Coop was in that big, empty house all by himself. He could've choked on one of his stupid potato chips and died and none of us would be the wiser.

"Screw this." I tugged on my light blue Oakcrest High hoodie and grabbed my wallet, keys, and phone from the bed before barreling out my bedroom door and down the stairs.

"Have fun at the game," Mom called from the kitchen where she and Addie were eating an afternoon snack of apple slices and peanut butter. Dad and the boys had left for the field half an hour ago.

I didn't slow as I crossed the lawn between our porch and Cooper's and shoved his front door open.

"All right, Bradshaw," I bellowed. "Get your ass up off the couch so we can go." I raced down the hall and around the corner. Coop sat on the sofa, watching some black-and-white movie. A man in a pinstriped blazer and a black fedora took up the screen, standing on stacks and stacks of newspapers.

Coop angled his neck to look at me over the back of the couch and then turned his focus back to the screen. "You really shouldn't come into people's houses like that. You never know what you could be walking in on."

"Maybe if people around here had enough common sense to lock the front door it wouldn't be a problem." I rounded the sofa and stopped between him and the TV. Cooper slouched back into the cushions in a pair of gray boxers and no shirt to cover his bare chest.

His *obscenely muscley* bare chest.

"What are you doing here, Bent?"

I blinked slowly, trying to remember myself. "You've skipped school two days in a row. Now I'm here to drag you kicking and screaming back into reality." I grabbed the remote from the coffee table and turned off the TV. "You have got to stop sulking and get out of this house, so you and I are going to go to the soccer game tonight."

"You really think going to the first Oakcrest High soccer game I'm not playing in in the last three years is going to make me feel better?"

"It's better than sitting around watching a bunch of movies all day."

"Movies help me process my deep-seated, complex emotional state," he said dryly.

"Come on." I stepped forward, offering him my hand. "What would Bueller do?"

For a brief moment, he wore a hint of a smile. "Fine." He stuck his hand out, and I pulled him—with some effort—up from the sofa.

He stood inches from me, his hair shining and heavy while his jaw and chin were hidden beneath what had to be several days' worth of scruff. "When was the last time you showered and shaved?"

He rubbed his chin. "Wednesday night?"

"Okay, shower first and then we go to the game." I pulled him by the arm, but he didn't budge, so I resorted to circling him, placing my hands on his bare back, and shoving him ahead of me into the hall.

Coop glanced back over his shoulder. "You know," he said, grinning as we turned to climb the stairs. "I don't think any girl has ever wanted to get me into the shower quite *this* badly before."

Unbidden images of Cooper in the shower danced in my head, and I almost tripped up the step. "Maybe your usual girls don't have the keen sense of smell I have." If there was any justice in the world, he didn't notice the way my voice shook.

He chuckled, and the hard muscles of his back tensed under my splayed fingers. "Good god," I muttered.

"What was that?"

"Nothing." We reached the top of the stairs, and I forced him down the hall and through the doorway I knew led to his room. I pushed him into his attached bathroom, started the shower water, and grabbed him a towel—pretty much everything short of stripping him naked and throwing him under the spray of water myself. A wave of heat rushed over me from head to toe.

"Hurry up and shower so we can go."

He turned to face me, and I couldn't keep myself from taking in each defined muscle of his exposed chest.

He grinned. "You're looking a little flushed there, Bent. You sure you don't want to hop in for a second with me so you can cool off?"

More unwanted images of him in the shower, only this time I was there too.

He chuckled, the sound dragging me back to the real world where I stood overheating and a little bit dizzy. I think I'd forgotten how to breathe for a minute. "Bite me," I barked, marching past him and slamming the door closed between us.

Muffled laughter followed me all the way to the stairs.

***

Coop rubbed his gloved hands together as we walked to the ticket gate. "It's cold."

"Weatherman says this is the last cold spell. It's supposed to start heating up after the weekend."

"I could be home sitting on a warm couch right now if it wasn't for you."

"If it wasn't for me, you would have already succumbed to death by potato chip."

He eyed me but said nothing.

Mrs. Stanton, the office assistant in charge of selling tickets, smiled at me as we approached. Then she saw Cooper, and her brow furrowed. "Oh, Cooper. I'm surprised you're not out on the field tonight."

"I'm taking the season off to focus on my grades," he lied with apparent ease, and I had to fight not to blurt out the truth. Knowing what I did about his hope for Liam's scholarship chances, I hated how little credit the false story about his grades gave him.

She smiled. "Good for you. Two tickets?"

Coop nodded and gave her the money before I could offer to pay for my own. She handed him the tickets, and he gave one to me.

"I could've paid for mine." I glanced around at the other students and faculty nearby. "People might think we're on a date or something." Okay, that might have been a stretch, especially given Cooper's widespread reputation. But still, my relationship status with Liam was still new, and it seemed wrong to let another guy pay for my ticket. Even if it was Cooper.

"I had a ten and didn't feel like waiting for change. It's not a big deal. And who cares what other people think?"

"Easy for you to say," I muttered.

We worked our way through the bleachers to find seats, and my dad waved from his spot with my brothers down on the sidelines. Players were starting to take the field, half in Oakcrest's blue and white, the other half in black and gold. I searched the blue jerseys for Liam. I waited for him to look up into the stands to see me wave, but he was too focused on the field to notice.

Coop and I said hello to a few who passed by. Most of them were surprised to find Cooper wasn't playing this year. Many walked away with their heads hanging a little lower. It seemed a lot of the soccer fans weren't quite as sure of our win without Coop.

Finally, the ball went into play. We watched in silence as it passed from player to player, but Coop didn't stay quiet for long, and soon he was cheering with the rest of the crowd. It got colder as the sun set, and by the end of the first half, Cooper and I were huddled close together on the bleacher trying to keep ourselves warm.

"S-see, this isn't s-so bad," I said through chattering teeth. The teams had left the field for the locker rooms at halftime, Oakcrest leading by two goals.

"It's not so bad." Blond stubble he hadn't had time to shave surrounded his small smile. "Thank you for this."

"You're welcome." I rubbed my gloved hands together, unable to hold his gaze.

Cooper stood. "I'm going to get some stuff from the concession stand. You want to come?"

I practically jumped out of my seat at the chance for warm food and hot chocolate.

The stand was close by at the top of the bleachers, which meant we were able to get to it before the line got too long. Cooper asked for two hot dogs, some boiled peanuts, and two hot chocolates, then pulled out his wallet and handed over the money again before I could object.

"Coop, you don't have to keep doing that. I'm the one who dragged you here. The least I can do is pay."

He shrugged, handing me my hot dog and drink. "The way I see it, I owe you for dinner the other night, seeing as you barely got through the green beans before the yelling started." I frowned. "Fine, if you really want to pay me back, I've been craving brownies lately."

"Deal." I led the way down the steps to our seats, and looked back to see Coop still standing at the top of the concrete bleachers, talking to an older man in a thick black coat.

Coop gave him a polite smile, and the man nodded as he spoke. Then Coop pointed out at the empty field. The man grabbed a pen and a small notepad from his coat pocket, quickly scribbling as Coop spoke. Then notepad guy said something and patted Coop on the back.

"Who was that?" I asked through a mouthful of hotdog when he sat down beside me.

"Scout from Coastal. Wanted to know why I wasn't playing tonight."

"What did you say?"

He shrugged. "Same thing I told Mrs. Stanton. That I needed to focus on my grades. Then I told him to keep an eye on Liam if he wasn't already."

I nudged his side. "You're really a great friend."

"Not as good a friend as you think." Instead of elaborating, he tore open his foil-wrapped hot dog and took a bite, then eyed me. "How's everything going between you two?"

"It's fine," I murmured. Because what else could I say? We'd been on four dates in the last two weeks, and I'd officially been his girlfriend for five days now. But between soccer and my big sister babysitting duties, we still had yet to spend much time alone together.

"So…he's treating you all right?"

I laughed, both at Cooper's concern for my well-being and at the absurd thought Liam would do anything else. "Of course, he is."

"'Cause if he doesn't, all you have to do is say the word…"

"Geez, I feel like I'm talking to my dad all of a sudden. Liam is the perfect gentleman when it comes to women, unlike y—" I stopped short when Cooper's glare whipped up. "I'm sorry. I didn't mean that."

He looked out at the field. "Yes, you did. But that's okay. Why should anyone in this town think otherwise?"

"If it helps, I think there's a lot more to you than that, but you don't let other people see it."

"People see what they want to see. I've got good grades and I'm a great soccer player, but my dad only sees me as a promiscuous, womanizing teen with zero drive or ambition to do anything important with my life."

"Why do you think that is?"

"I don't know. Probably because looking down on me means he doesn't have to look too closely at himself."

"But how does your dad even know about all the girls in Columbia?"

"Same way everybody else does." He scanned the full bleachers around us. "People in this town like to talk. And the guys at his country club *really* like to talk. Not that Dad's ever in town to visit the club, but people still call him when they hear my name being whispered around. It's like nobody has anything better to do."

"If you don't like what people are saying about you, then why do it? Why actively seek out weekly flings with college girls when you know the news will spread?"

One of his eyebrows lifted.

"Aside from the obvious reasons," I quickly added.

"That's an incredibly loaded question." He didn't say anything else, and I knew I wasn't going to get anything more than the usual *it's complicated* line he gave when he didn't want to talk about something. "Oh look, your boyfriend is taking the field again."

The team emerged from the locker room and hustled across the field and over to the sideline, my dad following them with intense focus. Liam made his way over with the other players, then stopped and looked up at the stands for the first time all night.

I waved as his eyes landed on me, and he grinned. But the smile fell when he took in Cooper, who was too focused on his boiled peanuts to notice Liam glaring daggers at him.

He didn't so much as look at me before turning away, his entire body noticeably more tense as he took the field.

Chapter 13

Cooper and I waited for Liam by the locker room door. My stomach clenched whenever the door opened, and a weird mix of relief and disappointment flooded my gut each time I saw it wasn't him.

The second half of the game had dragged by with only one goal made by each team. Realizing how little I knew about the technicalities of the game—being the coach's daughter didn't automatically make me an expert—Cooper patiently talked me through everything happening on the field. It was a nice change considering I usually sat at the games with Aubrey, who knew even less about the sport than I did. At least with Cooper I had a good idea of what was really going on.

I'd only half-listened, though, while the other half of my brain focused on Liam as I willed him to look up at me, to smile and reassure me that everything was okay.

He wasn't happy about something. His anger was evident in his playing, and he'd had two fouls called on him. Cooper didn't say anything about them, only shaking his head, and I'd wondered if he also suspected he was the reason Liam acted this way.

Whatever his issue with Cooper was, I hoped Liam would get over it. But he hadn't looked at me once through the entire second half. So I stood outside the locker room waiting to congratulate him on his win like a girlfriend was supposed to. But I was fairly certain of the mood he'd be in when he came out, and part of me wished this girlfriend could get away with calling him later once he'd calmed down.

The locker room door swung open again. Liam's hair stuck out in wet clumps from under a thick black beanie, and he had on a fresh pair of warm clothes. Maybe the victory and post-game shower had helped lift his mood some. But then he froze when he saw me, debunking that theory.

"Great game out there."

He glanced past my shoulder where Cooper talked animatedly with Will Benson while his girlfriend, Heather, stood under his arm and rummaged through her purse. "What's he doing here?"

"Aubrey had a date with Beth tonight so I invited Coop to come see the game. A last-minute sort of thing."

Cooper walked over to us. "Hey, man, nice job out there." He made no indication he was aware of the awkwardness flowing between the three of us, though how he could not feel it was beyond me. "You played a good game, though I think you could have eased up on seventeen a little." He was referring to the guy Liam forcefully shoved to the ground right in the middle of a play.

Liam's eyes narrowed. "Haven't seen you at school the last couple days. I thought you were at home sick or something."

I glanced at Coop. He hadn't told Liam what happened Wednesday night. Why wouldn't he tell his best friend of all people? Did it have anything to do with why Liam looked like he wanted nothing more than to punch Cooper in the face right now?

Cooper shrugged. "I'm feeling better. Bentley thought it would be a good idea for me to get some fresh air."

Liam stared at him a few seconds longer, then forced a smile. He put an arm over my shoulder. "That's my girl, always thinking of others." Then he pulled me to him and slammed his lips to mine.

It was a powerful kiss, like he'd put every ounce of his earlier anger into it, and it took me a moment to work past my shock and kiss him back. I'd expected it to end quickly, especially with so many people around.

But then his hand trailed up to my neck, pulling me even deeper into the kiss as his tongue brushed my bottom lip. I gasped, and the moment my lips parted, he slipped his tongue in to mingle with mine. It was too much, and in front of too many people, and while the kiss made my heart race, it also filled my veins with ice.

I pulled away, my gaze falling to the ground as a torrent of heat rose to my cheeks. And not the good kind.

Technically speaking, it was a good kiss. A great one even. One that was meant to carry passion and fire. But what little passion there was had felt more for the public eye than for me. Like Liam had staked his claim in front of everyone watching, including Cooper.

I'd suspected it before, especially after the glares and the brutal anger he'd played with on the field, but now there was no question. Liam was jealous of Cooper.

By the time I finally lifted my eyes, Liam was grinning. "So," he said, his mood significantly brighter now. He pulled me tighter into his side. "Thomas is throwing a victory party at his house tonight. What do you say we swing by and have some fun, celebrate my great game?"

"Oh..." My mind spun. Too much had happened in that last— was it really only a few moments—for me to think straight. "Um, sure. But I have to take Coop home first."

"No way. Coop should come too. How long has it been since you wrecked the Maserati? Six, seven weeks?" He stared at Cooper, and he seemed to hold some sort of challenge in his eyes. "You've got to be dying for a good party by now."

"He doesn't go to high school parties," I told Liam. Then I turned to Coop. "It's not a big deal. I don't mind dropping you off first."

Cooper's lips curved in a smile that rivaled Liam's, but I recognized the tension in the corners of his mouth. "That's okay. Maybe I should check this one out, see what I've been missing all these years." His eyes were hard as he stared back at Liam. *Challenge accepted.*

I swallowed. "Um, okay. Great." I tried to sound optimistic, but I had this nagging feeling the night was only going to get worse.

***

Thomas Lancaster lived approximately five minutes from the high school, which meant including the slow progression to get out of the overcrowded parking lot, the three of us had to sit in awkward silence for fifteen minutes. But as most awkward silences go, it felt like ten times that.

Since Liam's mom was working all night, he'd had to get a ride to the game with one of the other players. Once he told Keith he was riding with me, he'd snaked his arm around my waist and started leading me to the parking lot, Cooper following behind us.

As we neared the car, I typed out a quick text to my mom about heading to a victory party with Liam and Cooper. Liam took the front seat and held my hand the whole way while the radio played low in the background.

Thomas was a senior I'd tutored on several occasions for many of his classes and one of the more popular guys in school who threw parties at least once a month. By the time we pulled up, his entire street was already crowded with cars.

"Quite the turnout." Liam rubbed his hands together like a child about to enter a candy store. I wouldn't have thought Liam would be so enthusiastic about a high school party, especially when he'd been dragged to so many college parties with Cooper over the last two years.

I got out, and Liam took my hand in his, steering me toward the music-blaring house. The lights were on, and from the outside, I could see at least a hundred people inside dancing and laughing, nearly all of them with red plastic cups in hand.

Thomas's house wasn't quite as big as mine or Cooper's, but it had plenty of room for the partygoers inside, and the many more I was sure were on their way. The open floor plan meant I could see almost everyone in the living room, kitchen, and hallway. A group of girls chatted and danced up on the second-floor overlook while Travis Bishop and Adam Walsh leaned over the banister and looked like they were attempting to drop pennies down the shirts of the girls below. *Classy.*

The house was warm, and I pulled off my hoodie and tossed it into a dark study on the right that tonight served as a temporary coat room. Liam did the same with his.

"You want to dance?" His voice was barely audible over the music. I nodded, then turned to tell Coop we'd be back, but he wasn't there. A quick look around and I saw he was in the kitchen talking to some of his friends on the soccer team.

Liam led me to the center of the living room where several couples were already moving to the music. We danced, smiling and laughing at each other's moves, and I could feel some of the night's tension slowly dissipate. Maybe this whole thing wouldn't be so bad after all.

He took my hand and twirled me a few times, pulling me in close and moving our hips together.

Several songs later, Liam and I were both smiling, our faces flushed from the heat of the growing crowd around us. He pointed a thumb back to the kitchen behind him. "Let's get a drink."

We worked our way through the sea of bodies to where considerably fewer people stood talking and topping off their drinks from a massive keg. Thomas and some of the other players hung around, but Cooper had moved on elsewhere.

"Well if it ain't my best tutor and my favorite left winger," Thomas called out when he saw us. He pulled Liam into a hug and patted him on the back, and I got the distinct impression he'd had a few drinks already. He grabbed a full red cup and handed it to Liam. "Have a drink with me, my man."

He took it graciously and nearly downed the whole thing in one go. The boys around us cheered.

"I thought you didn't drink," I said in his ear.

"This is a special occasion. I'm celebrating." He handed his cup to Lincoln Randall, who filled it again. "You want one?"

I shook my head. "No thanks." I was going to have to be the sober one tonight. Not that I minded. I usually didn't drink at these parties anyways. "I'll take a water."

Lincoln nodded, grabbing a bottled water from the package on the counter. At least someone had thought to bring something other than alcohol.

The guys recapped the game while I took slow sips of my water and Liam went through two more cups. With each drink they got louder and rowdier until my head started to pound listening to them.

"Hey, Thomas, where's your bathroom?"

He sobered up long enough point to the doorway on his left. "Down at the end of the hall, on the right."

"Thanks." Water bottle in hand, I followed his directions out the kitchen door and down the hall. At the end, instead of turning right and into the unoccupied bathroom, I went straight out the back door to the deck.

The backyard was dark, the only illumination coming from underneath the crystal-clear water of the in-ground pool. It was blessedly quiet though, and I could already feel the ache in my head easing. The good thing about it being so cold outside was no one went out to the backyard.

The bad thing about it being so cold was that it was *really freaking cold.*

I wrapped my arms around myself tightly, regretting I hadn't grabbed my hoodie from the study first. My purple sweater was thick but not near warm enough. I was about to run back inside when I spotted movement on the deck steps.

"Cooper?"

He whipped around, his winter coat on and his elbows resting on his knees. He smiled. "What are you doing out here?"

"It's loud in there. Got a headache." I took a few steps forward. "What about you? I would have thought you'd be inside getting drunk with the rest of them."

"Don't drink."

My soft snort filled the cold night air. "Good one. So why are you really out here?"

Coop looked out over the shimmering water of Thomas's pool. "Wanted to hide out for a bit."

"Well, that's unfortunate because the back deck happens to be *my* favorite hideout at parties."

He scooted over and patted the spot next to him. "Share it?"

"Sure." I crossed the rest of the deck, set my water bottle down as I sat, then refolded my arms. "Why are you hiding?"

"There's only so much of these things I can take."

"Yeah, me too." I bumped his shoulder with mine. "You probably think this party's pretty lame, huh?"

He chuckled. "Actually, they're all pretty much the same. College parties tend to have less underage drinking and more of the other legally questionable activities."

"There's something to look forward to, I guess." I pulled my arms in tighter. "So then why don't you come to any of the high school parties if they're like the ones you and Liam go to in Columbia?"

He scratched the scruff on his chin. "Trust me, I get my fill on the weekends. Besides, most of the parties our classmates throw are on the weekends too. The ones that aren't, I miss because I have more important things to do."

"Like practicing your female seduction techniques in front of the mirror?"

Coop rolled his eyes, but he was smiling. "Like homework, studying, maintaining my athletic physique." For a sport he wasn't even playing, I nearly pointed out. "It's not like those things are handed to me, you know. You don't get my GPA and *mad* athletic skills without some serious time and effort," he said, throwing a subtle wink on the end.

"You don't say. Who would've thought the secret to Cooper Bradshaw's enviable grades and talent was that he actually worked for them? I guess the question on everyone's mind is how you manage to balance your athletics, schoolwork, and social life while still maintaining your carefree, youthful glow."

"What can I say? I'm good at keeping my priorities straight. School first, then soccer. As long as those are taken care of during the week, I'm free to go to Columbia for the weekend."

"What about Liam? Where do his needs fall on your list of priorities?"

"All right, technically I guess Liam comes first. Then the rest of it," he said with unabashed honesty. Cooper truly was an amazing friend, the evidence in his actions, the ones most people knew nothing about. He'd sacrificed his own wants and happiness for Liam's. No one who knew that could doubt how much Cooper cared about his friend.

After hearing the stories Liam told of their weekends together, where Liam had looked out for Cooper's safety time and again, there was no doubting how much Liam cared for Coop in return.

So then why were they acting so weird around each other?

"Can I ask you something?"

Coop snorted. "Would it stop you if I said no?" I said nothing. "Yes, you can ask me something."

"What's going on between you and Liam? Ever since the first day he came back to school, it's like you two barely know each other. Which is impossible since you spend almost every weekend together."

His smile slipped, and it seemed he had to think about his answer. "Three years is a long time, and people change. Liam and I are two different people now. It's not as noticeable when we're together a few days at a time. But now that he's back and I see him every day, those differences are starting to catch up to us."

He shook his head and looked down at his fidgeting hands. "Sometimes I think if Liam and I met each other as we are now, without all the history we have, I don't think we'd give each other a second thought."

"Wow. I had no idea." *People see what they want to see.* What else had I come across in life that was so drastically different from the way I saw it? The thought sent a shiver down my spine and into my belly until my whole body shook.

"Jesus. You're freezing out here." He shrugged off his coat and set it over my shoulders.

His lingering heat instantly warmed me, and I managed to keep my teeth from chattering when I spoke. "Thanks, but won't you be cold?"

"I'm a man, Bent. Besides, my beard will keep me warm," he joked, rubbing his hands over the dirty-blond scruff. Despite being only a few days old, it was surprisingly full.

Which made one more thing to add to the list of ways Cooper had been unfairly blessed. He had the talent and the brains. Not to mention the near perfect set of abs I'd seen only hours ago combined with the way the muscles in his back felt like thick, hard cords under my hands.

My body grew even warmer, and I hardly noticed the freezing night air anymore.

He definitely had the body and the looks. And now he had a beard that most high school boys would kill for. I laughed to myself at the injustice.

"What, you don't like it?"

On the contrary, I liked it a lot. Probably more than I should. Not that he needed to know that. "I'm wondering if it's exhausting living the perfect life."

"You of all people know my life isn't perfect." Cooper smiled, but it looked wan. Tired. Dark circles rested under his eyes, and I guessed he'd barely slept the last couple days.

"Still processing the divorce thing?"

"Yeah, I guess," he said quietly. "I know it's been two days, but I still can't believe they're actually doing it."

"I would've thought you'd be happy. When we were kids, you used to tell me all the time how badly you wanted them to split up."

Once, he'd told me he spent every night praying his mom and dad would finally get a divorce. I hadn't understood it at first. Most kids thought their parents splitting was the end of the world. I certainly would have. But then one day we'd been sitting in Cooper's room, listening to the angry words his parents shouted through the walls, and I realized the kids who took the divorce so hard were the ones who never witnessed how screwed up their parents' marriage was.

"I know I should be happy, and I think I am deep down. But now that it's real, I have no idea what's going to happen. Like my dad said, my mom's inheritance is probably used up. She doesn't have a job, and she lives off his income. I don't know what's going to happen to her or where she'll go. Add that to the stress of our senior year coming up and then college, and it's all too much right now." He shook his head and rubbed his gloved hands together. "I don't like not knowing what's going to happen."

"Look." I put my arm through his and rested my head on his shoulder. It was meant to comfort him, but in a way, I was comforting myself too. "I won't pretend to know what's going to happen. But I know that things will work out the way they're supposed to. There's nothing you can do to change it. So maybe instead of putting everyone else's needs in front of yours, you could try focusing on your own for once."

"That's a lot easier said than done." Coop squeezed my hands and leaned his head on mine. "But thanks for the pep talk. I'll try to keep it in mind."

"No problem, Goat."

He snorted. "How many times do I have to tell you it's *Goose.*"

"Oh, I know, but I like how annoyed you get when I call you that."

His shoulders bounced, and his head rolled slightly on top of mine. For the tiniest nanosecond, I thought I felt his lips brush over my hair, but just as swiftly, the feeling was gone.

"Try to remember your parents' problems have nothing to do with you. Because you're great." I squeezed his hands, he squeezed mine back, and it felt like we were those thirteen-year-old kids again, sitting on his bed and talking while we waited out the storm.

A throat cleared behind us, and Coop and I jumped. I spun around in my spot on the steps. Liam stood at the back door, glaring.

Chapter 14

Liam's glare morphed into an innocent smile. "I thought you were going to the bathroom." His gaze traveled between me and Cooper.

I pulled my arm from where it was still tucked around Coop's and stood. "I was. But then I saw Coop alone out here and we got to talk—"

"Could you give us a minute, Cooper?"

Coop stood, shoving his hands in his pants pockets, and glanced at me. "I'll see you guys inside." He walked past Liam and into the house, shutting the door quietly behind him.

"Everything okay?" I asked.

Liam's jaw clenched and his nostrils flared, his eyes glassy from several cups of alcohol. "Let's forget for a second you two were snuggled up alone in the dark." I opened my mouth to contest, but he rushed on. "You're supposed to be at this party with me, your boyfriend. Not out here with him."

I knew this would be about Cooper, but I'd hoped otherwise. "What has gotten into you? First you were acting weird at the field, now you're mad because Coop and I were talking?"

"Do you like him? Is that it?"

"I already told you, it's not like that between me and him."

"So, you're not cheating on me?"

"The fact that you're even asking me proves you're even more drunk than I thought. Let me take you home. You can sober up, and then tomorrow we'll talk about this all you want—"

"No, I want to talk about this now. I want to finally know what's going on between you two."

"How many times do I have to say, we're just friends?"

He took a step forward. "You brought him to the game tonight."

"So what? I'm not allowed to hang out with my friend? It's not like we were making out or secretly dating behind your back."

"You've clearly thought about it though, or you wouldn't feel the need to defend yourself."

"I'm defending myself because you're accusing me of cheating. I wouldn't do that to you, and neither would Cooper. He sure as hell wouldn't do it with me of all people."

"Oh come on," he scoffed. "Are you really that naïve?"

"What do you mean?"

"He's—" Liam stopped and sucked in a long breath, slowly regaining some of his calm. "You've heard about his reputation. He'd do it with any girl that moves. He's not that picky."

I didn't respond for several long moments, refusing to show how much the insult stung. He was worried about me cheating with Cooper, not because I was so desirable, but because Coop's standards were that low.

"He needed someone to talk to. You were busy drinking and goofing around with Thomas and the rest of the team. I didn't think stepping out for a second would be such a big deal."

"You're saying you'd rather talk to Cooper than spend time with me."

"He just found out his parents are splitting up. He's going through a rough time right now, and I'm trying to be a good friend and help cheer him up."

"That's not your responsibility. You two weren't even friends before I came back. You're not the one who's supposed to make him feel better or worse or anything at all."

"You're right. It's not my responsibility. It's yours. You're his best friend. You're the one who's supposed to be there for him, supporting him. But since you aren't really talking to him, it falls to me."

"Why should I talk to him? He was out here trying to steal my girlfriend."

"Can you hear how ridiculous you sound?" I ran my fingers through my hair, then lowered my voice. "I don't want to do this right now. Not out here in front of everyone, and not when you've been drinking. Can we please leave and talk about this later?" Hopefully in the morning he'd be able to see all of this for what it was: two friends talking while he'd acted like an irrationally jealous ass.

Liam was quiet. When his glare finally softened, he shoved his hands in his pockets and looked down at his feet. "You're right, this isn't the time or place. Go get your sweater, and I'll tell Cooper we're ready to go. I'll meet you at the car."

"Okay." I didn't bother to question the turnaround or his sudden willingness to speak to Cooper after what happened. Instead I walked past Liam to get to the door. "Thank you."

It didn't take long to find my bright blue hoodie in the sea of coats and jackets. I shrugged off Coop's oversize coat and pulled the hoodie on over my head. With his coat draped over my arm, I headed for the car, muttering quick good-byes to the few people out on the porch who noticed my exit.

I yanked the car door open and fell inside, wasting no time before I cranked the engine and blasted the heat. I closed my eyes and sucked in a deep breath of rapidly warming air.

Liam and I had been officially dating all of five days, and we'd already had our first fight. And boy it'd been a doozy.

But at least it was over. For now. Come tomorrow when he was sober, we'd be able to make up and pretend it never happened, chalking it all up to a bad case of underage drinking. In the morning he'd realize how stupid he was being about the whole Cooper thing, and we'd move on.

The passenger door opened, and my gaze went up as I pasted on a smile solely for Liam. Only it wasn't Liam sitting next to me.

"Where is he?" I asked Cooper. I searched the road toward the house, but there was no sign of Liam or anyone else approaching.

"He said you were leaving and I could either get a ride with you or someone else, but he wasn't ready to go yet."

"Oh." So, the fight wasn't over. It was stupid of me to think it would be. Liam was still angry. So angry he'd lied to me, basically telling me to go home so he wouldn't have to see me again tonight. "Did he say anything else?"

Cooper's eyes narrowed as he stared out the front window. "Not anything you need to hear." Great. "You okay?" I shook my head and fought the tears springing up in my eyes. "If you want to go back in—"

"No. Let's go home." I threw the car into drive and pulled away from the curb.

We said nothing as we crossed town. He didn't bring up Liam's ridiculous accusations, though I knew from the waves of tension emanating off him he knew exactly what Liam and I argued about. He didn't bother turning on the radio, and without music to drown out the silence, I had nothing to distract me from the accusations playing on repeat in my head.

Liam had been so sure there was something going on behind his back. Something between me and Cooper.

In Liam's defense, a few hours ago, you were picturing Cooper in the shower after one brief glimpse of him shirtless.

What did that prove though? That I found him attractive? Fine, but so did anyone else with eyes. That hardly made me special.

What mattered was I was with Liam, and I was happy with him. Not only did his concerns show a major lack of trust in me, but he really didn't trust Coop. If he only knew what Coop was doing for him.

Besides, I didn't want to be in a relationship with Cooper. At least, not like that. I was fine being his friend, hanging out with him. Sure, he made me laugh, and at some point, I'd even started to look forward to the time I spent with him, but that was all a friend was. Someone to goof around with.

Liam was the one I could see myself with in the long run. He was kind and sweet, and most importantly, he was the kind of guy who looked for a real relationship, and not a bunch of weekly hook-ups. Cooper had a long list of his own great qualities, but it didn't change that he wanted girls for nothing more than meaningless sex. I could never be with someone like that.

Why was that so hard for Liam to understand? Clearly, he didn't know me.

We pulled into my driveway, and I cut the engine. It was a little after eleven and the lights in the lower level of the house were on, which meant my parents were still up.

The moment I walked through the door my mom would be in my face asking how my night with Liam went. I didn't want to have to explain what happened. I wasn't ready to face the reality of it all yet.

Maybe I'd sit out here in the car for an hour or two. They'd have to go to sleep eventually.

"You up for a movie tonight?" Coop asked as if reading my mind. I mean he was sitting here with me while I'd been staring at my house for the last three minutes without making any moves to get out of the car.

I looked over at my wingman and considered his offer. Given the fight Liam and I had, spending more time with Cooper was a bad idea. Terrible. But compared with the impending line of questioning I'd face when I walked through my front door and the inevitable loneliness and worry I'd feel sitting in my room wondering what Liam was doing, what this meant for us, this particular bad idea sounded like exactly what I needed.

"Sure."

We got out, and Cooper led the way to his front door. I glanced back at my house where my parents waited, then pulled out my phone and typed out a quick message to my mom.

We left the party early, but we're going to watch a movie at Coop's place. I'll be home in a little while.

No need to tell her *we* didn't include Liam.

Cooper turned on the foyer light before heading back to the kitchen and living room. "You want anything?"

"No thanks. I'm good." My phone buzzed in my hand.

Don't stay up too late. Can't wait to hear about your night.

My eyes pricked with the beginnings of tears, and I knew I'd made the right decision. I shoved my phone in my pocket.

Coop sorted through various containers of leftover takeout in the fridge. In all seriousness, how did he manage to stay in such great shape eating all that junk? It had to be some sort of medical mystery.

Or a serious case of *insane teenage metabolism*, as my mom called it.

"What movie are we watching?"

"Don't worry." He'd settled for a box of pizza and some pretzels, laying them on the wooden coffee table. "I've got just the thing."

I took my usual spot on Cooper's sofa—something I thought I'd never have again—while he grabbed a case from his collection and started setting up everything.

For the next hour and forty-five minutes, we sat next to each other, laughing and getting lost in the story of Peter and Ellie in *It Happened One Night*.

Chapter 15

"We're going to be late," Cooper yelled up the stairs.

I stood in front of my bathroom mirror, carefully finishing the thin layer of eyeliner on my left eyelid. "No, we're not." I clicked my phone to life and checked the clock.

Damn. He was right.

I forewent the lip gloss and mascara for the sake of not getting my first tardy slip. While Liam might not mind being late, I certainly had no plans to be. I knew the same went for Cooper.

I ran to my closet, grabbed a random jacket, and threw it on over my short-sleeved shirt. It had grown markedly warmer outside in the last month, but the early morning chill still lingered.

I raced down the steps two at a time and around the corner into the kitchen. *"Oof."*

I slammed into Cooper, his grip on my arms the only thing keeping me upright. He let me go, then shoved my travel mug and a breakfast bar into my hands.

"The car—"

"I started it five minutes ago." He grabbed his phone from the counter as well as the coffee mug that was basically his now. "All the lights are off, and our bags are in the car."

"You're the best," I said, smiling.

"Yes, I am. Remember that when you get home tonight and see half of that cheesecake you made is missing. Now let's go."

He spun me around and pushed me to the door.

"Why are you in such a hurry?" Not that I wasn't used to Cooper pushing me around in the mornings. This had become our routine in the last few weeks. What with my hair and makeup taking a good fifteen minutes longer than before Liam.

It was a good system, and since both my parents were usually gone before Cooper came over, there were no complaints on my end.

It also helped I had two younger brothers to blame the missing food on when Coop got hungry waiting for me each morning.

"I have to talk to Will Benson before class. We have a project in Spanish coming up, and I couldn't get ahold of him all weekend."

"Oh." I took a quick sip of my coffee, dark roast with several scoops of sugar, exactly the way I liked it. "That's probably because Heather broke up with him Friday night at Leah Hannover's party."

"She did? Poor guy." Will and Heather had been together since middle school, and everyone had expected them to be *the* couple to survive through high school, college, and beyond. Now as seniors with their graduation approaching, the news of their breakup had spread like wildfire. "But you weren't at Leah's party. How do you know?"

"It's called Instagram, Coop. You would've known too if you had it." I knew for a fact he didn't, thanks to a little digging I'd done a few weeks back. The morning after my big fight with Liam.

He'd called me, like I expected, apologizing and ranting about how it must have been the beer—understandable since he never really drank at the parties he went to—and of course he trusted me and it was all so stupid. He'd begged me to forgive him so we could forget about the whole thing, and I'd readily agreed.

After we'd confirmed our date for that afternoon and hung up, I'd taken to the Internet. We'd survived our first fight, and I was ready to officially announce our relationship on all my accounts, which I was probably way more excited about than I'd ever admit to Aubrey or Cooper. But when I went to tag Liam in a photo of us on Instagram, I realized he didn't even have it. Or TikTok.

I'd checked for Cooper's accounts next, thinking maybe Liam was there somewhere but his accounts were private. But no pages came up in my search for Cooper either.

What did come up were a lot of posts from some of the University of South Carolina students giving shout-outs to their favorite party animal. While there was no official handle to tag Cooper Bradshaw to their posts, it didn't stop them from name dropping all over theirs and their friends' pages.

Before long I'd looked through several of those girls' posts, curious about what exactly Coop got up to at the infamous parties. There were several—including some asking where Cooper had been in the last couple months—but never any pictures or details that could give me more insight.

Ironically, Coop's name was all over the Internet, but he was nowhere to be seen.

"Instagram is inane," Coop said after a long sip from his mug. "Along with Facebook and all those other apps that are ruining the way society communicates."

"Geez, tell me how you really feel."

"We're replacing quality time and the spoken word with pictures and idiotic shorthand. What happened to real communication, face-to-face?" He lifted his hand in the small space between us. "Like this?"

"I can't believe I've never noticed it before, but you sound like a grumpy old man." Most people would probably be annoyed by his purist rants about movies and social media, but I found it entertaining. Who would have thought, aside from his phone, the amazing Cooper Bradshaw was a borderline Luddite?

"I might have to start calling you Grandpa Goat now." Especially if it irritated him as much as Goat did.

"Laugh all you want, but don't come crawling to me the day your Internet goes out and you don't know how to do anything."

Instead of arguing, I changed the subject. "How did it go after your dad came home Friday night?"

Coop took a bite out of his breakfast bar, somehow still hungry after supposedly devouring half a cheesecake. "For once it wasn't so bad. We kind of had a good time."

I glanced at him from the corner of my eye.

"I mean, we didn't go to the park for a game of catch or anything. But we did order takeout and watch a few basketball games on TV. And this time he even managed to stick around a few days instead of taking off the next morning like he usually does."

"Wow."

He shook his head. "I know. It's weird. He was relaxed and somehow stayed sober the whole time. Like he was a completely different person. I can't remember the last time he acted like this."

"That's great."

"Yeah. The divorce isn't finalized yet, but they already seem happier getting the process started."

"Good." Because the happier they were, the less stress it put on Cooper, which made me happy.

"Dad was in such a good mood, he even mentioned getting me another car soon."

"Oh." The balloon of relief in my chest deflated.

Coop looked at me with a crooked grin. "Hey, that was supposed to be good news, Bent. I would've thought you'd be tired of carting my ass across town every day."

"I don't know. I've gotten used to having someone start my car and make my coffee." Not to mention having someone to talk to and joke with, whose presence put me in a good mood for the rest of the day.

"All right, then when I get my new car, we can take turns driving. That way we save gas and all that other environmentally friendly stuff."

"That sounds…responsible. I approve of this new plan of yours." I frowned. "But I still have to drive the twins home after school."

"You're not the only one who can chauffeur two private-school terrors around, you know."

"You'd be okay with that? Picking them up after school." Despite things between Cooper and the twins having gotten remarkably better in the last few weeks, I'd still expected he'd be glad to be rid of them.

"Sure. I mean, yeah, it means no hot two-seater sports cars in my near future. But I think that's a sacrifice I can make."

I grinned at him. "You know what I think?" One eyebrow hitched as he waited. "I think you secretly like them." Why else would he be helping train Sebastian for his soccer games after school? It was obvious while he and Samantha still bickered back and forth, they both loved it.

The other day while the boys were kicking the ball around outside, Samantha had let it slip she thought Cooper was "not so bad…I guess." I suspected the twins were starting to like Cooper even more than me. But I wouldn't complain. Not when Samantha had been boning up on her vocabulary in anticipation for their verbal quarrels and Seb looked happier playing soccer than I'd ever seen him.

"I'm right, aren't I? Those *private-school terrors* have finally grown on you."

"Hmm." His mouth twisted as he considered it, then transformed into a playful grin as his eyes met mine. "I won't tell if you won't."

***

My phone shook in my pocket as I shoved the Algebra II book in my messenger bag. My locker door clanged shut, and I pulled the phone from my pocket.

Need you to take care of Addie and the boys tonight. Have to work.

Of course she did.

"What's got you looking so down?" Aubrey asked. She put in her combination and yanked the door open, exchanging her Spanish and history books for English and chemistry.

I shoved the phone back in my pocket. "Mom needs me to babysit tonight. Like I have for the past four nights. And every night last week."

"Geez. Why are you in such high demand?"

"She's reached a serious stride in her writing, which means she's staying holed up in the basement office. With Dad's coaching and the fact that the boys can't be trusted to watch themselves, let alone a temperamental three-year-old, I am Mom's only option."

"Why don't they get a babysitter?"

"Who needs to pay for a babysitter when they've got a live-in, free sitter right here?" I muttered.

"You could try standing up for yourself. Tell her you can't tonight."

"But then she would freak out, accuse me of not wanting her book and her career to do well." Aubrey gave me a look. "That's how she gets when she's in her zone. She wouldn't mean it, and she'd feel really bad and apologize tomorrow. But it's not worth it in the end. I'd rather babysit like she asked me to."

"Are you supposed to babysit tomorrow too?"

"I don't know yet. It depends on how much she gets done tonight." I threw my hand over my mouth, attempting to stifle a massive yawn.

"Whoa, open that mouth any wider and you could land a plane in there. Everything all right? You've been exhausted the last two weeks."

"I was up late at Coop's."

"You said you were watching the kids last night."

"I was. After Addie was asleep and the boys' homework was done, I went over to Coop's to watch a movie and didn't get to bed until late."

"Ooh, late nights with the not-so-innocent boy next door? Tell me everything."

"It's not like that and you know it. After a long afternoon of cooking, cleaning, and bossing Addie and the boys around, hanging out at Coop's is a good way for me to relieve stress. So I grab my backpack and enough of whatever I made for dinner for both of us and go next door to work on homework and unwind."

"You bring him food? That's so cute. And, hey. You don't have to convince me." Her grin turned downright wicked. "I bet Cooper Bradshaw knows all kinds of ways to help relieve stress."

I punched her arm.

"Ouch. Geez. I was kidding." She rubbed the spot gingerly. "Could you blame me for thinking it, though? You do realize any girl in this school would kill to be up late every night with him. Even if you are only doing homework and watching movies."

"Well, none of those girls are already happily dating Liam, are they?"

She shrugged. "You've got me there. How does that wonderful boyfriend of yours feel about you spending your late nights with another guy?"

I bit my lip, paying extra attention to a black scuff on my locker door.

"Bentley?"

I sighed, turning to face her. "He doesn't know."

"So you've been lying to your boyfriend? You can't be okay with that."

"Not lying so much as…omitting. And I mean, obviously, I'd prefer not to have to hide what I do each night from Liam. But he's made it clear he doesn't like me spending so much time with Cooper, and the chances of him being okay with it any time soon are next to nothing."

"I think I can help with that." Aubrey grinned as something over my shoulder caught her eye. "Hey, Liam, come here for a sec."

I spun around as he reached us. He put his arm around me and kissed my cheek before he turned to Aubrey. "What's up?"

"Beth and I are catching a movie tomorrow night. You guys want to double date?"

Liam's eyes widened and his lips tensed a fraction of a second before the tight smile twisted into a frown. "I wish I could, but I've got a big test I have to study for. I think it's going to take me all night." He turned to me. "But you should totally go. Don't miss out because I'm busy."

"Bentley doesn't want to feel like a third wheel," Aubrey said before I could so much as breathe. "But that's okay, we can bring a friend. Let's see, who should we invite?" She tapped her chin innocently while scanning the hall. "Oh, I know. What about Cooper? You guys are friends, right?"

Liam stiffened at my side.

"Aubrey, I don't think—"

"Hey, Bradshaw," she yelled before I could finish. A dirty-blond head shot up from down the hall. I hadn't noticed him there with his soccer friends. The way Liam's jaw clenched, I guessed he hadn't either.

Coop said something to the guys before jogging down the hall to us with his textbook in hand. "Yes, Miller. What can I do you for?"

"Beth and I were going to see a movie with these two tomorrow night, but Liam said he can't make it. You up for it?"

"Uh…" He looked unsure at first, but it took one quick look from Aubrey before he seemed to understand her whole master plan. He studied Liam, whose hand gripped my shoulder tighter than my little brothers' around their PlayStation controllers.

Coop grinned. "Sounds like fun."

"Great. Let's say we all meet at the theater at six?"

Coop's smile grew. "It's a date." He glanced from me to Liam. "See you guys later."

Liam's eyes narrowed as Cooper strutted off down the hall.

"You don't mind, do you?" I asked quietly. "I could always cancel."

He turned his attention back to me, forcing a small smile. "It's fine. You should have fun tomorrow." He leaned in, his lips grazing my ear. "Maybe you could swing by my place sometime this afternoon before you have to watch Addie tonight. We could get a head start on all the studying I have to do tomorrow."

Something stirred low in my stomach. The way his heated eyes locked with mine, there was no doubt his idea for the afternoon had little to do with studying. "Sounds like a plan."

He leaned in and placed a quick peck on my cheek. "I have to get to class. I'll see you later." He took my hand and squeezed it before heading down the long, crowded hall.

"How did you do that?" I asked Aubrey once he was out of earshot. She'd somehow managed to set me up for some quality time with my boyfriend at his house as well as a fun hangout session with two of my closest friends, all without breaking a sweat.

"Easy. Liam gets super weirded out whenever I mention Beth, so I knew he'd say no."

I winced. I'd noticed that the last few times Beth came up in conversation, though I'd hoped Aubrey hadn't managed to pick up on it. "I'm sorry. I have no idea why he's like that."

"It's not that hard to guess. He's hardly the first person to be weirded out by two girls dating each other."

"Liam isn't one of them. He'd never treat anybody differently over something like that. Besides, he was totally fine with the two of you the couple times we were together." It wasn't until after the third or fourth double date that he'd started avoiding hanging out with Beth. Which was a shame, since it felt like they'd really hit it off right before then. They'd spent over an hour talking about their hobbies, families. Then all of a sudden it was like he wanted nothing to do with Aubrey's girlfriend.

"It is what it is," Aubrey said. "Anyway, since I knew he'd say no, I figured it was a good way to get him to agree to you hanging out without him there. Then it was a matter of inviting Cooper before Liam could stop me. This way you get to hang out with him with your boyfriend's okay."

It was kind of brilliant. If only it didn't take a well-laid plan like Aubrey's to hang out with Cooper guilt-free.

"Thanks. You're the best, really. I'm sorry you had to go all diabolical for this. I'm pretty sure a normal person wouldn't have to go through all these crazy hoops to hang out with her best friend."

"Whoa." Aubrey's hand shot to her back pocket. She whipped out her phone and started tapping like a mad woman.

"What's wrong?"

"You referred to Cooper Bradshaw as your best friend. I'm checking the news to see if there's anything about hell freezing over."

"Funny."

"If someone told you two months ago you and Cooper would be besties again, you would have laughed in their face."

"It kind of slipped out." But even so, it didn't feel wrong. Actually, if felt oddly satisfying in a way. Like fixing a peg in a hole that was exactly the right shape or fitting two puzzle pieces together perfectly.

Cooper was my best friend, had been for most of our lives. I'd forgotten that for a little while.

"No worries. There can be two of us. You're lucky I'm not the jealous type, unlike your boyfriend." Aubrey pulled out her last book for class and shut her locker door. "You know, you guys don't have to come to the movies with us if you'd rather do your own thing."

"Of course we're going to the movies with you. I haven't seen Beth in weeks. Besides, I think Coop will appreciate getting out of the house."

"You say that like he's a complete shut-in. Doesn't he have other friends to hang out with?"

"He has friends. But all they ever want to do is go to parties, and he says he gets enough of those during his weekends in Columbia. The rest of the week he likes to hang out at home studying and watching movies. He's kind of a homebody."

"Cooper Bradshaw, the guy who drives two hours to a college town every weekend to drink and get laid, is a homebody?"

"I know, it doesn't make sense to me either." But Cooper hardly ever made sense to me these days.

"Maybe it's less about staying home and more about who he's staying home with." She shot me a side-eyed glance.

"Me? Please. That makes even less sense than him being a homebody. Besides, I've tried to invite him out with me and Liam, figuring there's no way Liam could disapprove of us hanging out when he's right there with us. But Coop's never interested."

"Who can really blame him when all you and Liam do is make out the whole time?"

"That's not all we do."

"Oh no? So last week at Whitney Lance's party, you two weren't huddled in a corner sucking face for two hours straight?"

"How do you know about that? You weren't even there."

"I have my sources. And I wouldn't want to be the third wheel with you and Liam either."

I shook my head. "It's not that. Things between Liam and Coop are worse than ever since Thomas's party a few weeks ago."

"You mean the one where Liam got drunk and accused you and Bradshaw of hooking up behind his back?"

"That's the one. They're completely silent in the car in the mornings, and now they're barely friendly at school even when I'm not around. It's like I'm walking on eggshells around them for fear of making things worse. Hence the secret movie nights."

"Poor Bentley." Aubrey put her arm over my shoulder, ushering me down the hall and on my way to class. "Two gorgeous guys vying for your time and attention. How do you get by?"

"Bite me." I shoved her arm off with minimal force. "Liam needs time. As soon as he gets used to me and Coop being friends and realizes there's nothing going on between us, and the two of them finally get over their issues, maybe the three of us can all go back to being friends again."

Aubrey smirked. "Yeah, you keep telling yourself that."

Chapter 16

"I'm really glad you came over."

"Me too."

The sheets on Liam's bed wrinkled beneath us as he rolled me over onto my back. His hands traveled down my sides and under my shirt while kissed me again and again. They were hard, almost forceful kisses.

"Hey, let's slow down, okay?" I pulled at his hands under my shirt, and he reluctantly gave in, moving them to my hair. But his kisses became more hurried, trailing down my neck and over the skin on my collarbone. I ran my fingers through his shaggy hair.

"Bentley." His warm breath puffed against my neck. My skin tingled wherever he touched me, my insides practically screamed in need as his body covered mine.

"I said slow down, Liam." My voice was shaky but louder this time.

Then his hands were at the button of my jeans, and the warning bells in my head screeched at maximum volume. "No, stop." I grabbed his hands, pushing them away. "I said stop."

I shoved him off me, and Liam fell back at the other end of his mattress. He ran his hands over his face and through his hair as he groaned.

I sat up, allowing time for me to catch my breath and for Liam to get his bearings. Aside from our heavy breathing, the bedroom was silent. If anyone else had been home, I'd swear they could hear us panting from the other side of the house.

Liam's bedroom had enough space for a twin-size bed, dresser, and a cozy little desk in the corner that was currently piled over with papers and books on auto repair and other non-school-related subjects. Posters of either world-famous soccer players or fast cars with scantily clad women posing on or beside them covered the wood-paneled walls. Everywhere except over his bed, where several rows of shelves held up his expansive assemblage of rap music and a movie collection that paled in comparison to Cooper's.

"You okay?" I asked after a minute.

"Yeah." He let his hands fall from his face. "Sorry. You know how hard it is for me to stop when I get going."

"I know, and I'm sorry, but I'm not ready for...*that*."

He laughed humorlessly. "If by *that* you mean sex, then yeah, I remember. Though if you plan on being ready any time soon, you may want to work on saying the actual word first."

My cheeks flushed hotter than they already felt. I couldn't meet his eyes, instead staring down at the pale-blue bedsheets we'd tangled beneath us. "Hey." He scooted closer and rested his hand on my cheek. "It's cute you're nervous. But I've already told you, sex is just sex. It doesn't have to be that big of a deal."

"And I've told you, I want it to be a big deal."

He laughed with genuine humor this time. "I know. I guess I keep hoping you'll change your mind."

"I'm serious, Liam. I've never done this before, and I want my first time to be meaningful. Not the result of overworked hormones while trying to hurry before your mom gets home."

"Okay, okay. You're right. Our first time will be special. You deserve that much." He leaned forward, cupping my face and bringing his lips to mine once again, parting them and caressing my tongue with his.

I pushed him away, this time gently. "Can we talk for a little while? I have to be home in less than an hour, and I feel like you and I have barely had a real conversation in the last three weeks."

Aubrey's accusation that all we ever did was make out had been bothering me all day. I hadn't wanted to admit it, but the more I thought about it, the more I worried she might be right.

Liam's lips curled into a mischievous grin. "But it's so much more fun to kiss you." He leaned forward, leaving me no choice but to back away from his advance.

"Fine." He sighed, finally giving up and falling back on the bed again. "What do you want to talk about?"

"How was soccer practice? Dad sounds really optimistic about the game this weekend."

"It was fine. The guys like to give me a hard time, saying Coach takes it easy on me since I'm dating his daughter." He grinned, eyebrows waggling. "But I'm pretty sure that'd change if he knew what we've been up to behind closed doors."

I chucked a pillow at his head. "I talked to Aubrey. She and Beth might be able to make it to the game to help me cheer you on. Maybe after the game the four of us can grab a bite to eat, do something?"

"Ah. I don't know. I'm usually pretty tired after a game. Maybe next time, though."

I sat back against the wall at the head of his bed. "I don't get it. You liked Beth the first few times we hung out with her, then out of nowhere you started avoiding her like the plague. Is it because she's gay?"

"No. I told you, it's more complicated than that. I don't care she's gay, I...don't think we get along."

"You sound like a homophobe," I said under my breath.

"I'm not. I've got nothing against Beth or Aubrey." He sat up again, his eyes hard on mine. "Though I don't appreciate her setting you up on double dates with guys who aren't me."

"She offered for you to come first. It's not her fault you turned her down."

"Yeah, well, she could've invited anyone else. It didn't have to be him."

"You're starting to sound jealous again," I warned with a playful smile, praying he'd return it with matching ease. He didn't. "Hey." I scooched closer to him, bringing my knees flush with his, and wrapping my arms around his neck before placing a quick, chaste kiss on his lips. "You're okay about tomorrow night, aren't you? I told you, you've got nothing to worry about. It's not like that with me and Cooper. We're friends. Why would I want to be anything more with him when I've got you?"

He finally smiled. "I know. You're right. I'm being stupid. I mean, you said it that night at Thomas's. It's not like you're even Cooper's type. He goes for hot college girls with experience." Liam crawled off the bed and headed for the kitchen. "What would he want with a high school junior who can't even talk about sex without blushing?"

"Right, exactly," I said, forcing a smile he couldn't see. "What would he ever want with a girl like me?"

***

I tried not to think about it.

As I drove through town on my way back home, I tried not to think about how true Aubrey's words were. That aside from our tutoring at lunch, all Liam and I ever seemed to do anymore was wordless make-out sessions. We'd barely spoken to each other in the last few weeks, and despite my lack of extensive relationship experience, I knew it wasn't normal.

I tried not to think about how sexually frustrated Liam was getting. It wasn't like he tried to hide it. And based on his carefree attitude when it came to sex, I assumed he had a lot more experience than I did. A realization that probably should've bothered me. But it didn't, which worried me more about our relationship than anything else

I tried not to think about Liam's jealousy or that he'd probably only said what he did as a result of the jealousy. Because why else would he?

He goes for hot college girls with experience. What would he want with a high school junior who can't even talk about sex without blushing?

More than anything else, I tried not to think about how much the truth of those words bothered me. Because there was no reason for them to. Cooper was my friend, my best friend. I didn't want him the way Liam worried I might, and I didn't want him to want me either, not that way. Which was good because if I did, it would only be a matter of time before he ended up disappointing me. Maybe if things were different…

No. There was no point in thinking like that. It was exactly as Liam said: Coop didn't want that from me. I knew what Liam wanted me to do, and I had to admit, things would be a lot easier if Cooper and I went back to being neighbors who barely spoke to each other.

But I couldn't go through that, not again. Not after how hard losing his friendship the first time had been. I'd done everything I could to reach him after Liam left, but in the end I'd lost my best friend in the entire world.

Coop and I were finally in a good place again, like when we were kids and would spend every day chasing each other around our yards. Or when we'd play in our favorite spot in the clearing by the tiny creek hidden a quarter of a mile deep in the woods behind our houses. We never told anyone about that spot, not even Liam after he moved in next to Coop in sixth grade, because it had been our special place.

I hadn't thought of that spot in years. Remembering it now filled my chest with that familiar warmth I always felt as a kid when I was with *my* Cooper. The same warmth I felt whenever I was with him the last several weeks. It was so consuming I wasn't sure whether to be happy to feel it again or amazed I'd somehow managed to survive so many years without it.

I did know I wasn't going to lose that feeling again and I'd do whatever it took to keep it. If that meant walking on eggshells around my boyfriend and using Aubrey's diabolical plans to hang out with him without sneaking around, then so be it. Liam was going to have to accept Cooper Bradshaw wasn't going anywhere.

Of course, saying all of this in my head was one thing. Telling Liam to his face was a whole different story.

When I got home, Mom stood behind the kitchen island with Addie on one hip and a cellphone held to her ear.

"Benny," Addie called.

Mom looked up and smiled when she saw me. "Okay, Esther, I understand." Addie squirmed until Mom finally set her down. Then she came running around the island and into my waiting arms.

"Listen, Bentley just got home, so I'm going to head down to the office and start on those suggestions you made and then send you the changes as soon as I can. Yeah, all right. I'll talk to you tomorrow. And thanks. Bye." She hung up and set her phone back in her pocket. "Hey, sweetie. I was starting to get worried."

"Hey, sorry I'm a few minutes late. I went to Liam's for a little bit, and we lost track of time."

"That's okay, honey." She rounded the island and gave me a quick hug. "I went to the store and got some stuff for you to make Mexican tonight. Your dad should be home in a couple hours, so if you could get everyone fed and make sure the boys get all their homework done—"

"They haven't done it yet?" It was almost seven at night. What did she let them do all day?

"I Know, I Know. I Meant For Them To, But I've Been On The Phone With My Editor For Hours. I Sent Her The First Several Chapters, And She Tore Them Apart, Which Is Why I Have To Get Back To The Office."

Her phone chirped from her back pocket. She whipped it out, frowning. "Even more notes from Esther." She started moving for the door.

"Hey, Mom?"

She stopped, her gaze glued to her phone. "Yeah."

"Aubrey and Beth invited me and Coop to see a movie with them tomorrow night, so I won't be able to watch the kids." Addie jumped at my side, pulling at my shirt and leaving me no choice but to scoop her up. "That okay?"

She struggled to pull her gaze from her phone screen. "Uh...yeah, sweetie. No problem. Now I really have to get to work. This is going to take me all night."

"Don't work too hard," I called after her, but she was far too gone to hear me. I looked at Addie. "Now we have to do dinner and get the boys to start homework. Maybe we should tag team. How about I start the food while you tell the boys to get to work?"

"No way." Addie squirmed until I let her down, then she ran straight for the den while singing the theme song from *Daniel Tiger*.

It looked like I was handling dinner, the boys, cleanup, and getting Addie to bed all by myself, all while still trying to find time to do my own homework. Again.

I took a deep, exhausted breath. I conjured all my negative thoughts, doubts, worries, all the stress over Liam and Cooper and what the heck I was going to do about them, and I pushed them away, down into a deep, dark hole, for another day.

Chapter 17

"I'm sorry Aubrey dragged you into this," I told Coop as we pulled into the parking lot of Oakcrest's small movie theater. It was a popular enough spot to hang out during the week, though most of the high school student body was currently, or at least soon would be, wasted and rowdy at a party tonight.

"I know you wanted to watch a movie at your place, but I haven't had a night out with Aubrey and Beth in a while."

"Don't sweat it. I don't mind hanging out with Miller and her girlfriend."

"Really?" I pulled into an empty space. "It's not weird for you?"

"Why would it be weird?"

"No reason." I opened my door and climbed out, locking it behind me. "Anyway, thanks for doing this. Between Liam and my mom, it's been hard to find a free night to spend time with Aubrey, and I feel like I haven't seen Beth in ages. I know the movies here aren't really your type."

Coop stood in front of me, his gaze on mine. "It's fine. I can handle a bad movie every now and then. Especially when there's a small chance I get to catch Aubrey and her girlfriend making out in the middle of it."

My mouth fell open. "You're such a perv. No wonder you agreed to this."

He laughed, a sound that was quickly becoming one of my favorites. "I'm not a perv. It's called being a guy."

"Nice," I muttered. I pulled my phone out to check for any messages, then went ahead and silenced the ringtone before I forgot.

"I'm only kidding...mostly. Besides, if all I really wanted was to see two girls make out, I could've gone to Jay's party tonight instead. Seriously, though, even if this movie turns out to be total crap, which is pretty much a guarantee, I like spending time with you. No matter what we're doing, I'm happy."

My gaze flew to his. "Me too," I admitted, fighting a grin and failing. "So can we go in now? I told Aubrey we'd meet them in the lobby five minutes ago."

"Yeah, yeah." Coop led the way to the theater's main doors. He studied each of the movie posters on display outside as we walked up. "So which one of these are we seeing anyway?"

I hesitated before telling him the title, and he groaned.

"Oh relax. I'm sure it won't be that bad," I said, reaching up to give him an encouraging pat on the shoulder. "Who knows? Maybe you'll actually enjoy it."

***

Coop and I were still laughing as we all headed out to the lobby.

"I am never watching a movie with you two again," Aubrey grumbled from beside Beth.

The four of us walked together, Aubrey and Beth holding hands on my left and Cooper towering over the three of us by several inches on my right. I tried not to stare at my friend and her girlfriend.

Aubrey had on bright red skinny jeans, black boots, and a skintight black Rolling Stones T-shirt. Beth wore a completely different look: her long, black hair falling in dozens of tight braids over the straps of the white spring dress that stood out beautifully against her dark skin.

They were adorable together, both looking amazing and clearly dressed for a date. For a split second I wondered what people thought when they saw me and Coop with them, if maybe it looked like a double date. I glanced over at Coop in his cargo shorts and button-down shirt, then remembered my own messy hair and the same jeans and blue top I'd been wearing all day.

What a joke. It didn't take a genius to see Coop was way out of my league.

"I don't think you two ever stopped making fun of it," Aubrey went on.

Cooper shrugged. "I'm sorry, but seriously? The whole thing was so ridiculous. The only thing that kept them alive while drifting around in outer space was *their love*? That's so lame."

"Not to mention the cheesy dialogue," I added. Coop nodded his agreement.

"I'll give you that," Beth said. "But you have to at least admit that the romantic chemistry was there."

"True," I allowed. "But romantic triangles are seriously overused these days. Way too predictable."

Aubrey snorted. "It's a romance. Predictable is in the definition."

"Except in this case, where the wrong guy got the girl in the end," Coop said.

Aubrey, Beth, and I all stopped in the middle of the lobby and stared at him. He slowed and turned around to the three of us. "What?"

Beth's forehead crinkled. "You're kidding, right?"

"You expected her to choose the other guy?" Aubrey asked.

"Yeah, why not? He was a great guy who obviously cared about her. Why couldn't they end up together?"

"He was the friend guy," Beth said.

"So?" He looked down at her, his creased brow now matching hers. "Why should that matter?"

"Girls in movies don't pick the friend guy. Not when the main guy is obviously hotter," Aubrey said. "Unless that one turns out to be a major asshole."

He looked at her like she was trying to explain quantum mechanics to him, which ironically, he probably would have had an easier time understanding. "So because his competition isn't an ugly jerk, he has to stay friend-zoned forever? How's that fair?"

"Because she doesn't like him like that," I said. "Look, it's just like Andie and Duckie."

Cooper rolled his eyes. "Not this again."

"What?" Beth asked as she turned to me.

"It's the Duckie Scenario."

"Wait, there was a duck in the movie?" Aubrey looked uncertainly at Beth.

"Duckie is a character from *Pretty in Pink*," Coop clarified.

Beth's face lit up with recognition. "Oh, I think my mom has that movie."

"Look," I said to Coop. "Duckie was a great friend and funny, and yes, he cared about her more than anyone else in the world. But it didn't matter because he never stood a chance. The friend-guy can be the best guy in existence, but the girl isn't going to pick him if she isn't attracted to him."

He looked dumbfounded, pointing down the hall we'd come from. "You're really telling me you didn't find him attractive? I'm not into guys, and even I can tell you he was hot."

"Of course, he is. I'm not saying he's not attractive. But he's…he's like Lucille Ball."

Coop gasped, and several people in the lobby turned toward us. "What do you have against Lucy?"

"Nothing, she's great. But if you were asked to choose between her and Marilyn Monroe, we both know who you would choose."

He seemed to think about it. "Maybe," he said, looking back at me. "Though full disclosure, I'm more of a Hepburn kind of guy."

"That's not really the point," I muttered before looking around. Aubrey and Beth had already moved on from our conversation. At some point they'd found their way out the lobby doors and now were talking excitedly on the sidewalk.

I glanced sideways at Coop. "Katherine or Audrey?"

He gave me that smile that never failed to put one on my own face. "Always Audrey."

"I hope you two aren't ready to call it a night yet," Aubrey said once Coop and I caught up to them. "Because the ice cream shop next door is calling my name."

I looked at Coop. "I'm game if you are."

"Fine, but only if it's my treat. As a sort of *thank you* for letting me hang out with you lovely ladies tonight, and to make up for talking through the whole movie."

Aubrey considered his offer. "Normally I would object to letting someone else treat my woman to ice cream. But considering your house is three times the size of mine, I think I'll make an exception."

She took Beth's arm in hers and the two walked ahead of me and Coop, leading the way to the ice cream shop while whispering and giggling to each other.

"There's only one problem with your Duckie theory," Coop said beside me as we followed.

"And that is?"

"You say that the more attractive guy gets the girl. But if that were the case, then Sabrina would have picked David over Linus."

I shook my head, thinking back to the movie he'd chosen for us to watch earlier this week, along with his complete and utter shock that I'd never even heard of *Sabrina* before. "I said that the girl picks the guy she's attracted to, not the one who is more attractive. While William Holden was obviously the hotter of the two, Audrey's character was also attracted to Humphrey Bogart. It was the way he treated her and he wasn't a serial womanizer that won Sabrina's heart."

Beth and Aubrey stopped in front of the ice cream shop and eyed the selection of small, bright green tables outside.

"So you're saying if Andie had been attracted to Duckie even in the slightest, she would have picked him?"

I shrugged. "Probably. If he stopped being such a jerk about Blane."

Aubrey spun around to face Coop. "So how about you and I go in and get the ice cream while Bentley and Beth get a table for us?"

"Sounds like a plan." Coop looked at me. "Rocky road?"

"Aw, you remembered."

He winked before he and Aubrey disappeared inside. Seeing as there were only four tables available outside, it took only a second for me and Beth to pick one.

"How long have you known Cooper?" she asked once we sat down.

"Um, since we were eight. My family moved in next to his when my dad got the coaching job at Oakcrest. Coop's dad wasn't around much, so my dad would invite him to play soccer with him and my older brothers in our backyard most nights. It wasn't long before he and I became best friends."

"I didn't know you had older brothers."

I nodded. "Xander and Theo. They go to school at Coastal Carolina, though I'm pretty sure they play soccer and party more than they actually attend class."

"I would love to go to a school near the beach," she said with a wistful smile. "But then I'm not sure I'd ever go to class either." She let out a soft laugh that made me smile.

Beth was easily one of the sweetest, nicest people I'd ever met. Which made it all the harder to believe Liam when he said they didn't get along. There had to be something more to it, but no matter how desperate I was to ask Beth what Liam's problem with her was, I couldn't risk hurting her feelings. Especially when she'd given zero indication she disliked him or even realized he'd been avoiding her the last few weeks.

"Is that where you want to go when you graduate? To Coastal Carolina with your brothers?"

"Not really. I've spent years being identified as their little sister or the coach's daughter. The last thing I want to do is go to a school where I'm known only for my family."

Beth grimaced, twisting a braid through her manicured fingers. "What schools do you have in mind, then?"

"I've been looking at the University of South Carolina the last few weeks. Mostly because it's close to home and has one of the best early childhood education programs in the state. I'm actually thinking about going down there one day over spring break to take a look at the campus."

"My cousin goes to school there," Beth said, perking up even more. "I'm sure she'd be happy to meet you and show you around."

"Really?" I'd thought about asking Liam to go with me since he knew the campus so well already, but he was so busy with soccer and school, and it didn't really seem like something he would be into.

Cooper, on the other hand, seemed to have all the time in the world to hang out with me. I knew we'd have fun together. But for some reason—other than my boyfriend would hate it—I got this weird feeling in the pit of my stomach whenever I thought about asking him.

Beth nodded. "I can give her your number, have her get in touch."

"Yeah, that would be amazing."

"Amazing, you say?" Cooper's deep voice called. "I assume you're talking about me."

He held up a cute little cup of rocky road ice cream. I took the sweet treat as he lowered himself into the chair at my left. Aubrey had taken her seat next to Beth, a small ice cream cone in each hand.

"Thank you." Beth planted a kiss on Aubrey's cheek and took the ice cream her girlfriend offered.

I looked at Coop. "Yes, thank you." I tried a small spoonful of the ice cream and almost moaned in pleasure. Living with a health nut for a mom, we didn't come by ice cream often at my house.

"You're welcome. Now please, feel free to continue discussing how *amazing* I am."

"I was telling Bentley my cousin goes to school in Columbia and could show her around campus," Beth said.

Aubrey's eyes widened. "I completely forgot Maya went to school there. Maybe you know her, Bradshaw."

Coop stilled, his smile faltering. "Not likely. It's a big campus."

"You sure? She's in one of those sororities I hear you like so much." Aubrey's eyebrows lifted twice. "Maya Freeman, you know her?"

His face scrunched, suddenly entirely focused on his chocolate chip cookie dough ice cream. "Nope. Not ringing any bells."

"Do you have friends there or something?" Beth asked.

"Not really."

Her eyes narrowed. "But you know people?"

Aubrey laughed. "Oh, you could say that. Seeing as he's slept with about half of them, Bradshaw here is kind of an expert when it comes to the female collegiate population in Columbia."

"I wouldn't go that far," he muttered.

"Wait." Beth's eyes nearly doubled in size. "You're not telling me…you're Cooper Bradshaw? As in *that* Cooper Bradshaw?"

Coop grimaced as something hard settled in my stomach.

"You've heard of him?" I asked, not feeling near as amused as Beth sounded.

She nodded. "Maya talks about you all the time. You're like a celebrity at that school."

Coop said nothing beside me. He'd stopped eating his ice cream and was swirling it around with his spoon. Mine was all but forgotten in my hand.

"I had no idea you were in high school, though. Maya was sure you were in college somewhere. So what, you drive down for the weekend to party and pick some lucky girl to spend the night with?" She didn't sound appalled. On the contrary, she sounded quite impressed.

A seed of unease began to sprout in my gut as a series of images of Coop with a different girl every weekend involuntarily took up residence in my mind. It grew as I imagined him kissing, touching, and doing much more with those girls until I felt downright queasy.

"It's more complicated than that," he said casually while I sat there battling nausea.

"She tells me stories about you at those parties all the time, and it sounds like you two really got to know each other…if you know what I mean." She laughed. "You really don't remember her?"

"He said he doesn't," I barked. "Look, if we're being honest, there's been so many girls, it's probably impossible to keep track of them all. Sorry, but your cousin is one in an extensive list of girls whose names he doesn't remember. Let's drop it, okay?"

I took a deep breath, hazarding a quick look at the three people around me. Cooper stared down at the table. Poor Beth looked absolutely horrified, and the nausea in my stomach shifted into a heavy feeling of guilt.

Then I looked at Aubrey, staring at me from across the table with wide eyes. She glanced at Cooper, and a second later her eyes softened with a mixture of understanding and something much worse. Pity.

Why would she pity me? Feel sorry for Beth or Maya, or maybe even Cooper. But not me.

None of this even had anything to do with me.

I shook my head. "I'm sorry. I think I'm tired, and the ice cream is giving me a headache," I said, pointing to the mostly melted and barely touched bowl on the table in front of me. I looked at Coop. "Is it okay if we call it a night? I should get home soon anyway."

Coop nodded. "Sure." He stood from his chair, addressing Beth and Aubrey, both of whom seemed to be watching me warily from across the table. "Ladies, it was fun hanging out with you tonight. It was great to meet you, Beth, and I hope I see you around again soon."

"You too, Cooper. Drive safe, Bentley. I'll see you around." She sounded sincere despite the awkward tension after my unexpected outburst.

"It really was good to see you, Beth," I said, hoping she could hear how much I meant it. "I'll see you tomorrow, Aubrey."

She still had that unnerving look on her face, the one that said she knew something that I didn't. She gave me a small, sad smile. "See you."

I grabbed my uneaten ice cream bowl from the table and dumped it in a trash bin before turning quickly to the parking lot, Cooper close on my heels.

"You want to tell me what's wrong?" he asked once we were out of earshot of the other two. He was practically jogging to keep up with me.

"Nothing, I'm fine."

"You could've fooled me." We reached the car, and I went to pull the driver's side door open, but Cooper stopped me. "Hey, I don't have to be a mind reader to know you're upset."

I couldn't bring myself to look up, gazing at my hands, the car, the parking lot—anywhere but him. When he spoke again, his voice quieter, almost hesitant. "If this is about Beth's cousin—"

"It's not."

"I swear, it's not as bad as you think it is."

"You don't owe me an explanation. You don't owe me anything. You're my friend, and what you choose to do with your time has nothing to do with me," I said, still unable to meet his gaze.

"Bent..."

I leaned against the car, crossing my arms. "If you choose to sleep around, well, that's none of my business. You do whatever you want, and I have no right or reason to complain." I didn't know where it was all coming from, or the anger steadily rising in my voice, the same anger that had me snapping at Beth only a minute ago.

He shook his head. "It's not that simple."

"It never is," I said, laughing humorlessly.

"Why do you even care?"

"I don't," I said too quickly. "I shouldn't. Other than I know you're better than this. You're *so much* better than this. But you do it anyway. You have sex with girls like Maya, and then you don't even remember them afterward. And the worst part," I went on, unable to stop myself, "is that you don't seem to care. You don't care what anyone says or thinks about you. Your parents, your friends, even complete strangers."

"Don't do that. Don't pretend you know how I feel about it," he said, his voice rising to match mine. "There's no point in worrying about what other people think or say, so I don't. I don't care what anyone else thinks about me. Except you."

My breath caught at the strain in his voice, the vulnerability I didn't think I'd imagined there, but he didn't give me the chance to speak.

"You think I liked hearing Beth talk about it? Being constantly reminded of my reputation, especially in front of you? You really think I like being the guy the whole town gossips about?"

"Then why do you let them? Why give them a reason to?"

"You don't understand."

"So explain it to me. Please." The last word was soft, and I could feel that dull ache in the back of my throat and the prick of oncoming tears.

He turned to the side with his hands shoved into his pockets, no longer looking at me. Instead, his gaze was on something far away, eyes darker than I'd ever seen them. He was done, completely closed off. "I can't," was all he said.

I let out the breath I'd been holding. "Fine, whatever. Let's go home." He stood to the side while I opened the car door, climbed in, and started the car. He didn't move. I rolled down the window. "Coop."

He took a step back. "I think I'm going to check out that party."

"What?"

"Jay's house is a few blocks away," he said. "I'll walk there and get a ride home from someone else."

"You don't have to do this. Let me take you home."

"It's fine, Bent. Go home. I'll see you in the morning."

He turned to walk away. "Coop," I tried to call after him, only to be ignored. The ache in my throat grew tenfold, and it felt like I was choking. "Cooper."

I watched him go and felt a wave of déjà vu, remembering vividly the only other time he'd walked away from me like this. Liam's mom was backing the U-Haul out of the driveway. My lips still tingled from where Liam had surprised me with my first kiss. I'd watched the van, tears streaming down my face, until it turned the corner onto the next street and was gone. Only then had I looked over to my best friend, who I knew would be as equally devastated as I was.

But he wasn't there anymore. I searched the driveway, the green grass, only then finding his retreating back as he darted across the lawn and up the steps of his front porch. "Coop," I'd yelled over and over. But he never turned, never answered. Through blurry eyes, I'd watched him until he disappeared through his front door.

The same way my gaze followed him now, glued to him until he was no longer in sight.

Then the tears finally started to fall.

Chapter 18

When I finally pulled into my driveway, it was almost ten. Technically, I could've been home twenty minutes ago, but I rode around the streets of Oakcrest, waiting for my eyes to lose some of their redness and swelling. For as long as I could remember, Cooper and I had never fought like that. Not even that day Liam moved away and Cooper stopped talking to me. Then there had been no arguments, no words at all, really, only quiet distance.

How had our fun night out gone so horribly wrong? I tried to think back to when exactly it had all started to go downhill, but that wasn't a difficult leap.

You're Cooper Bradshaw? As in that *Cooper Bradshaw?*

I put the car in park and pulled my phone out of my pocket. I tried to convince myself to put it away and go inside, but my curiosity got the best of me. I hit the button, flipping on the screen. There were a few notifications, but I ignored them for the moment as my mind stayed fixated on something else. Before I knew it, I had Instagram up and was typing in a name.

It took less than a second for a list of profiles to pop up, and then another moment to find the right one. I opened it up and came face-to-face with Maya Freeman. Her hair was sleek and straight, her skin dark, but a few shades lighter than Beth's. The profile picture showed her grinning and posing with her arms around two girls I assumed were sorority sisters in flowy sundresses and strappy sandals, one on each side.

To say she was pretty was an understatement, and it was easy to understand why and how she would have caught Cooper's eye. She looked outgoing, mature, and sexy. Three things I wasn't sure I'd ever felt myself.

I scrolled through her pictures, looking for any sign of Cooper Bradshaw. And like my previous searches, I found nothing. No pictures of the two of them together—thank god—or any other photos of Cooper at one of these infamous parties. The tightness in my chest eased ever so slightly.

I found one of her many selfies. She was a complete stranger, a girl I'd never seen before in my life. And yet, as I sat in my car staring at her, I resented her.

It sounded like you two really *got to know each other.*

It made my stomach churn. This was the first time I'd heard about Coop's sexual encounters. Going to high school with a bunch of gossiping teenagers, it was practically all anyone talked about half the time. Until tonight, it had never really bothered me.

So why had hearing Beth talk about his past with her cousin made me so angry and sick to my stomach? Why did picturing him with all these other girls make me want to hit something?

Jealousy.

I closed my eyes as the word hit me in the chest like a brick. That couldn't be it. But as I replayed the mental images of Cooper with various girls and the feelings that went along with them, it became impossible to deny.

Oh god, I really was jealous.

Which was the last thing I should've been feeling. Jealousy didn't manifest for no reason. It was always accompanied by something else, something much more complicated. Something a girl should not be feeling for her best friend, especially when she already had a boyfriend.

I cut off my thoughts there, burying them down along with the phone I shoved back into my pocket. I had to process the cause of these new feelings, but that didn't mean I had to do it alone. I needed advice, and the one person who was almost always willing to give it.

I forced myself out of the car and up to the house, not stopping until I was inside, then walked into the kitchen after locking the front door. I went straight to the medicine cabinet, grabbed some ibuprofen, and swallowed them dry, hoping they would be enough to lessen the headache before I went in search of my mom.

The sound of rushed feet thumping down the stairs filled the otherwise quiet house. "Where have you *been?*"

I spun around to find my mother, blonde hair and clothes disheveled, her eyes wide and on me.

"What's wrong?"

"I Have Been Calling And Texting You For Hours. I Needed You To Watch The Kids Tonight. I Was Supposed To Send Esther My Revised Chapters, And I Needed You Here. I Asked Your Father To Come Home Early From His Meeting And Take The Boys Out Somewhere To Get A Little Quiet, And Now Addie's Upstairs With A Fever And I've Gotten Zero Work Done. Where Were You?"

"You told me I could go to the movies with my friends."

Her eyes got even bigger. "What? When did I say that?"

"Last night. I asked you while we were standing right here."

She shook her head, strands of hair falling from her messy ponytail. She placed her hands on her hips. "Why would I have said that when I knew I needed you here? Why didn't you call me back? I must have left you five messages."

I winced, remembering the notifications I'd ignored when stalking Maya's Instagram account. I'd seen Mom's name, but I didn't count how many there were. "I had my phone on silent for the movie, and then I forgot to turn it back on while we got ice cream. Then Coop and I got in this fight—"

"So while I've been here trying to work and take care of a sick toddler, you've been off goofing around and ignoring my pleas for help."

I took a step back. Was she seriously yelling at me right now?

"I'm sorry," I said a little icily. "But, you know, I did ask you. And you did say yes. It's not my fault you weren't paying attention when I talked to you."

Her eyes narrowed to slits. "You know that my work keeps me busy, Bentley. Is it too much to ask that you help me out just a little bit?"

A laugh escaped my lips before I could stop it. The anger I'd felt at the ice cream shop and in the parking lot was creeping back. "You're joking, right?"

"Excuse me?"

"I've been home almost every night for the last two months getting the boys' homework done, making dinner, getting Addie bathed and to bed. That's not even including the time it takes to get my own homework done. And you expect me to do *more*?"

Her hands fell to her sides, her anger faltering for a beat. "That's not—"

"I'm sorry for trying to hang out with my friends and have a life outside of school and this house." The words tumbled out on a tidal wave. "But maybe instead of assuming I have nothing better to do, you could try pretending you care as much about spending time with your family as you do about your stupid book."

Her eyes grew even wider, the slight twitch in her brow a sign of her anger. "Now hang on just a minute, young lady. You do not get to speak to me like that."

"Really? Because I'm starting to think someone finally should. All you do is write in that basement and expect everyone else to fend for themselves. Only they can't, so it's all left to me. You expect me to cook and clean and make sure everything gets done around here. That's fine every once in a while, but I'm seventeen years old, Mom. I'm supposed to go out with my boyfriend and my friends, and be a kid. Not a full-time mom."

She stared at me silently for the longest time as I stood by the kitchen island, breathing heavily while adrenaline pumped through my veins. Gone was the rage that'd turned her face red, quickly replaced by the wet shine of unshed tears in her eyes. Now instead of angry, she was hurt. And I'd caused it.

"Bentley…" she said softly, then stopped there when she seemed to have no other words.

I closed my eyes, bringing my fingers to the bridge of my nose. "I can't do this right now," I said quietly. I didn't want to see the pain in her eyes, not when I had so many other thoughts and feelings to sort through. I had enough guilt to deal with already—fighting with Cooper, lashing out at Beth, jealousy over a guy who wasn't my boyfriend—I didn't want to add yelling at my mom to the mix. At least not yet. "I'm going up to bed."

Without another word from either of us, I darted past her, out of the kitchen, and up the stairs to my bedroom.

***

I didn't check the messages on my phone until half an hour later when I sat down on the bed. My brown and pink hair was dripping wet after a long shower, soaking the T-shirt I'd put on with my cotton pajama shorts.

The screen came to life with a list of missed calls, texts, and voicemails that were mostly from my mom, except for a picture from Liam. Nothing from Coop.

I read my mom's texts first.

Where are you? When will you be home? Call me ASAP.

Followed by the panicked voicemails she'd left after two hours of me not answering those texts. She sounded irritated as she complained about the work she was supposed to be doing, but there was also worry in her voice, bringing the guilt I hadn't wanted to feel after yelling at my mom to the surface.

Once I'd finished listening to her messages, I moved on to Liam's. He'd sent me a photo of him doing a keg stand with two of his teammates helping to hold him up.

A crowd of mostly juniors and seniors had gathered around him, cheering him on. No comments or caption saying *Miss you* or *Wish you were here*, only a picture of him getting drunk on the night he claimed he'd be too busy studying to go to the movies with me. I rolled my eyes and closed the image.

It was almost eleven, which meant Jay's party still had another hour or two to go depending on how much beer was left. I should call Liam, let him know that I was home and make sure that he had worked out some sort of ride since he'd been drinking. But after feeling so responsible for everyone else in my house the past few weeks, I didn't want to have to be responsible for Liam too.

Besides, he wasn't really the one I was dying to call.

I walked to the window beside my bed, looking over to the dark, vacant house next door. So far I'd seen zero cars pull up to Coop's house, which meant he was still probably at Jay's. In the shower, I'd gone through our fight over and over until all the anger had washed off and swirled down the drain with everything else from the day. By the time I'd cut off the water, I had no fight left in me.

I was too tired to be angry anymore. And after the horrible night I'd had, the only thing I could think about was how badly I wanted to hear his voice and know everything was all right with us. To hear him tell me everything would be okay.

Before I could lose my nerve, I dialed his number. I had no idea what I was going to say, and I had no time to think of anything. He answered almost instantly. There was a long silence before he spoke, and I could hear the faint sound of music in the background. "Hey."

His deep voice sounded resigned in my ear, filled the same exhaustion I felt.

"Hey," I said back, hugging one arm into my stomach while the other held the phone. "Are you still mad at me?"

There was a pause, then a sigh. "Not mad. To tell you the truth, Bent, I'm not sure I could ever be mad at you even if I wanted to."

"Good," I said softly, letting out the breath I'd been holding. I sniffled and wiped at the moisture collecting in my eyes. "Because if you ever walk away from me like that again, Cooper Bradshaw, I'm going to kick your ass."

I could almost hear the grin in his voice when he said, "I'll definitely keep that in mind."

That was it. The hard part was over, and it was us again. Two friends who didn't need apologies because the words were understood.

I took another deep breath and let it out before sitting back down on the bed. "So, how's the party going? Are you still there?"

"I am. It's pretty lame, which isn't really all that surprising since pretty much everyone is drunk and acting stupid. Myself excluded, of course. I've been sitting out here on the front porch making sure these idiots don't try to drive home."

"Ah, so you haven't gotten wasted and started dancing half naked on the kitchen counters yet?"

This time his laugh rang out clear over the line. "No, though I think I did see your boyfriend attempting the Cha-Cha Slide on the coffee table about half an hour ago."

"I bet. You know, for someone who says he never really drinks, he sure does seem to get wasted a lot." Come to think of it, I couldn't think of a single party Liam and I had gone to that hadn't ended with me driving him home while he struggled to even sit up straight.

Cooper fell quiet. "Well, you know what they say about actions speaking louder than words."

"Yeah. Maybe you're right."

"I usually am."

Silence dragged, and my fingers toyed with the fraying hem of my pajama shorts as I tried to work up the courage to speak. There were so many things I wanted to say to him. Like how sorry I was for letting myself get so bent out of shape over Maya and those other girls. The fact that I was jealous of all these girls I didn't know while feeling nothing more than mild annoyance when my boyfriend did keg-stands and played beer pong with Ashley Morales and all her obnoxiously flirtatious friends. Or how my mom and I had this huge blowout at the exact moment I went seeking her advice about what all these things meant.

I wanted to tell him how scared I was, the heaviness weighing down on me, a feeling like something was changing between us. Something that maybe only I could sense, feelings that would put our recently revived friendship at risk. Especially knowing how impossible it was he would feel them too.

I wanted to say all of that. Only I didn't dare, for fear of his response.

"So you're really telling me if given the choice between Marilyn Monroe and Audrey Hepburn, you wouldn't pick Marilyn?" I asked instead, my voice light. "Isn't that against some sort of guy code or something?"

"Maybe I'm not like other guys. I mean, don't get me wrong, Marilyn's a knockout. It's not like I don't find her attractive. I guess I prefer a woman with more substance and class."

"Like Audrey."

"Exactly. Compared to Audrey, Marilyn is a total Duckie."

I smiled, nestling back into my pillows while we spent the next two hours pretending our fight in the parking lot never happened.

Chapter 19

Cary Grant or Clark Gable?

I thought for a moment, pulling up images of both men in my mind.

Clark Gable

Then I quickly typed out a second message.

Debbie Reynolds or Ingrid Bergman?

He replied almost instantly.

Reynolds. Come on, Bent. At least make this a little hard.

I rolled my eyes as I stared down at the phone, waiting for the text I knew was coming as they'd been coming on and off since Cooper and I got off the phone at one in the morning last night.

The phone buzzed in my hand.

Jimmy Stewart or James Dean?

"Hello, Earth to Bentley."

My head snapped up. Aubrey glared at me from across the table, her hand raised and waving what looked like an oddly colored chicken strip between us. "What?"

She stared incredulously. "Oh nothing. I've been talking to you for the last ten minutes about whether you think this is real chicken or some sort of poisoned meat substitute the lunch lady gave me."

"Why would the lunch lady give you poisoned chicken?" I asked at the same time typing a quick response back to Coop.

James Dean.

"To get back at me for suggesting she use an extra hair net for that lady beard she's growing on her chin." My gaze flew up to hers, praying she was joking.

"I didn't say it to her face. But she did manage to overhear Pete Whitmore repeating it to his girlfriend. There's no way she can know for sure I said it, but judging by the death glares she gives me with my French fries every day, I think she suspects."

I studied the chicken strips on her plate again. "Definitely poison."

"I knew it." Aubrey pushed her plate away, grabbing her wallet as she stood. "I'm getting something from the vending machine. Want anything?"

I shook my head, staring at my phone as I chose my next words carefully.

Greta Garbo or Lauren Bacall?

Buzz.

Greta Garbo.

I turned my focus to the turkey sandwich sitting on my plate, took a bite of it, then set it down with all the other food I'd barely touched.

Buzz.

Chris Pratt or Chris Hemsworth?

I looked up slowly from my phone screen and across the lunchroom, my gaze instantly meeting his. He had a smug look on his face, knowing how difficult it was for me to choose between any of the Chrises ever since our debate over all the hype people were making about the latest superhero movies. This one, at least for me, was especially difficult.

Neither.

I glanced up in time to see his eyebrow raise as he watched the screen. He typed back.

Forfeit?

I sighed, then bit my lip in concentration as I typed a response.

Fine…Pratt.

I hit Send, then typed again.

Happy?

Very. Though I don't imagine he will be if he ever finds out.

"Well, there were no more Cokes in the machine, but I did manage to convince one of the stoner kids out there to trade me his unopened drink for a piece of gum and an expired McDonald's coupon I found on the ground. Score." Aubrey sat back in her seat across from me, a giant bottle of Coke she'd already seriously depleted in one hand and several different bags of chips in the other.

"Nice," I muttered.

Doris Day or Claudette Colbert?

Buzz.

No brainer. Colbert.

"Are you even listening to me?"

"Of course. You traded Coke for gum and an old coupon," I said without looking up.

"Oh good, I'd hate to think you were too busy texting someone fifty feet across the room to pay attention to me," she said, taking a long sip from her drink. "What's so important he's got you glued to your phone like this?"

Han Solo or Indiana Jones?

I looked up at Aubrey, who was watching me intently. "We're playing a game."

Her eyes narrowed. "A game."

I nodded. "We started it last night. Basically, we give each other two names, two choices, and we have to pick which one of the two is the Duckie."

"Duckie? Oh right, from the movie you were talking about last night."

"Exactly. So if I gave you, say, Scarlett Johansson and Jennifer Aniston, the Duckie is the one you'd have to friend-zone. And whoever can't pick a Duckie loses." I glanced down, quickly typing back.

They're the same person.

"I see. And you two have been texting this game back and forth since last night?"

"Pretty much, aside from the drive to school and during classes," I said.

I'm waiting.

I sighed, rolling my eyes. Aubrey tore open a bag of chips and pulled one out. "Everything is okay between you two, then?"

"Yeah. Why wouldn't it be?"

She popped a SunChip in her mouth, followed by a satisfying *crunch.* "Things were a little tense when you guys left, is all."

"We're fine. We worked it out."

"Good." She grabbed another chip. "Any idea how long you'll be grounded for yelling at your mom last night? You know, so I can start deciding the best way to celebrate your freedom someday."

"I wouldn't go making any plans yet. After what I said to her, I'm expecting a month, at least." That was not a conversation I looked forward to when I got home tonight.

Han Solo. Too scruffy looking.

I grinned as I hit Send, knowing he'd like it.

Across the cafeteria, Cooper ignored his friends from the soccer team laughing and joking around him as he checked his phone. An unbearably adorable smile spread across his face. It was so infectious, my own grew bigger in turn.

"You two are cute together."

My face fell. "I'm not sure what you mean."

"You know." She shrugged. "You two were all flirty and stuff last night, joking about the movie and all."

"That wasn't flirting, that was us talking."

She shrugged again. "Whatever you say."

My phone buzzed in my hand, but I ignored it. "What?"

"I'm wondering if maybe there's a little more than friendship going on there."

I sat back in my chair and crossed my arms. "You sound like Liam." I sounded defensive even to my own ears. I'd managed to ignore the confusion of feelings I'd had around Coop all day. I didn't want to have the subject forced on me in the middle of my lunch break.

"Well, maybe he's got a point. I mean, did it ever cross your mind maybe Coop likes you?"

"He doesn't."

"You sure?" Aubrey glanced over her shoulder at his table, where I currently refused to look while having this conversation. "Because I've been getting vibes he's majorly into you."

"The only thing Cooper Bradshaw is ever into is sex, remember? You said last night he's slept with half the girls at South Carolina. What would he possibly want with me?" It was the same thing Liam had said two days ago. And after looking at Maya's profile, I was even more convinced he was right.

"Do you see him hanging out with any other girls? Because I don't. I'm telling you, he would get all up in that if he could."

I shook my head. "Even if he was attracted to me like that, we still know he'd never want anything more than sex. He's not the kind of guy who's interested in a relationship."

"But you would be interested in a relationship with him?"

My heart fluttered at the idea of Coop and me holding hands, kissing, and dating. There was a thrill to it, anticipation, along with a strange feeling like I needed it, missed it even though I'd never had it. "That…that's not what I said. And besides, I have a boyfriend."

"Liam."

"Yes, Liam." The name alone was like a weight on my chest. I grabbed my sandwich, avoiding her stare as I took a giant bite.

"See, the only problem I have with that is that, when I said Coop's name, your face lit up. But whenever I mention Liam…" She didn't say anything else, and let the thought hang there.

I finished chewing my mouthful and swallowed. "Coop is my friend."

"I've been your friend for three years, and you've never looked at me that way. Not that I'm complaining."

"It's not like that," I said, my voice getting lower. "I've had a crush on Liam since I was fourteen. He's all I've ever wanted."

"Sometimes the things we think we want, once we get them, we realize there are other things out there. Better things. Things we want even more." She sighed. "Look, I'm not trying to tell you your business. I'm merely saying maybe there's more to this thing with Bradshaw than you want to believe."

I had no response and was saved from coming up with one as the bell ending lunch filled the cafeteria.

"I'll see you later," she said slowly. She stood and came around the table, patting my arm with that same pitying look she'd given me last night. "Think about what I said." She didn't wait for a reply before she turned for the cafeteria doors with the rest of the students rushing to their next class.

I made a much slower show of gathering my stuff together. I checked Coop's table, both grateful and disappointed to see him gone. I felt like I needed him beside me, making me feel better, though he was the last person I needed to be near right now.

Reality was starting to set in, and it was not coming gently.

I paid almost no attention to the cacophony in the hall as I found my locker, my mind occupied with the thoughts and feelings I'd been denying all day. *Maybe there's more to this thing with Bradshaw than you want to believe.*

I hadn't known what to say to Aubrey, mostly because part of me had begun to worry she might be right. She'd come to the same realization I'd been on the verge of discovering last night. The possibility I may have somehow—so slowly I had no idea it was even happening—started falling for Cooper Bradshaw. How else could I explain the mix of excitement and longing in my stomach at the thought of holding his hand, or the jealousy I felt hearing about the other girls Coop had slept with? Especially when thinking about Liam's past sexual encounters had me feeling almost nothing.

What did it mean about my relationship with Liam? The feelings I'd once associated with him were almost completely gone. Sure, there was still that rush I felt when I remembered the way he kissed me so many years ago. But when I thought about the more recent kisses, even the heavy make-out session in his bedroom the other night, those feelings were dulled, muted as if watching a movie through an old television set. The picture was blurred with static, less real, less exciting.

I switched out books for my next class, then I allowed myself to close my eyes and imagine those scenarios again, the kisses, making out on the bed. Only this time, I let myself imagine it was Cooper.

My breath caught, the thought of his mouth on mine and his hands on my skin making my heart beat faster and my body grow hot all over. The feel of his warm breath on my neck, his lips curling upward as they caressed my jaw. The sound of his deep voice whispering in my ear.

"Bentley."

I jumped, my eyes flying open to find Liam standing next to me. The sight of him, along with the knowledge of what I'd been thinking about so unfaithfully, made my cheeks burn. He looked almost as uneasy as I felt, like a dog waiting to be scolded for messing in the house when I was the one who'd been fantasizing about kissing another guy.

Oh god. I was going to hell. "Hey."

He frowned. "I knew you'd be mad."

"Mad?"

"For ditching you at lunch. I know we usually study on Friday, but Thomas had some ideas for the game tonight that he wanted to go over. I'm sorry."

"Oh." The weight on my chest grew even heavier. I'd been so caught up texting with Cooper I hadn't realized Liam was missing from what was supposed to be my lunch with him. "That's okay."

"So you forgive me?"

I nodded, turning to face him. "How was the party last night?"

He grimaced. "It was all right. Got a pretty nasty headache, though."

"Coop said there was a lot of drinking," I said, not surprised. Especially after the keg-stand photo.

"Cooper was there?" His brow furrowed, but after another moment he nodded. "Oh yeah. You know, I think I caught a glimpse of him right before he went off into one of the back rooms with some girl."

"He what?" I almost dropped the book in my hand. "I mean, he didn't mention anything about a girl."

"No? Well, you know how Coop is. Can't keep him away from them for long. I'm amazed he lasted as long as he did."

I nodded, my body going numb inside. "Yeah."

Was that really all it took? One fight with me, and he went running back to the one-night comforts of strangers. It shouldn't've been surprising, knowing his reputation. And yet it surprised me.

I was an idiot. I'd allowed myself to fantasize, however briefly, about what a relationship with Cooper Bradshaw would be like. But the truth was, there would never be a relationship with Cooper because it wasn't his style. Even if he did like me as Aubrey claimed, how long would it be before he got bored with me and went back to his one-night stands in Columbia?

It was one thing I could count on Liam for, one reason dating him made so much more sense. I was safer with Liam. My heart was safer. With Cooper there were too many variables, and the certainty if he was interested in more than sex with me, in the end someone would end up hurt.

And that person would most definitely be me.

"You want to do something after the game tonight?" I asked, pushing thoughts of Cooper far away. "We could get something to eat, go somewhere fun."

He gave me a small smile. "I would, but I already made plans to hang out with the guys after the game."

"Okay. What about this weekend?"

"Maybe. I'm not really sure what I've got going on." He leaned down and kissed my lips gently. "I have to get to class, but I'll see you later."

He started to turn away, but impulsively, I grabbed him and pulled him back to me. My lips crashed against his as I kissed him deeply, desperately, willing myself to feel some of that same excitement I'd felt when I imagined it was Cooper I was kissing.

Liam was quick to indulge once he got over the initial shock. His tongue slid into my mouth and made its presence known. A few whoops and catcalls rang out around us, but I ignored them. When we finally parted, Liam grinned.

"This weekend, you said? I think we can figure something out."

He turned away while I stood by my locker with throbbing lips and a distinct hollowness spreading through me.

Liam was the right choice. I was sure of that much. I'd hoped that kiss would unleash all the same feelings his first kiss had three years ago, further reassuring me in my decision.

But despite my best efforts, the kiss had not measured up to the secret one in my imagination.

Not even close.

Chapter 20

I sat through the rest of my classes in a daze. Most girls would be hopped up on adrenaline after kissing their boyfriend so publicly in the middle of the school hallway, and maybe a week or two ago I would've been. But all I could think of was how hurt and angry I was with Cooper.

I didn't want to be upset he was with another girl the night before, probably only minutes before I'd called him. But it *did* bother me. Much more than it should. And there was nothing I could do about it.

After the last bell rang, Cooper waited at my car like always, and it didn't take him long to see I wasn't in the mood for our usual banter. I still hadn't looked at the last message he sent me during lunch, and I half expected him to ask me why I'd never responded to his latest round of The Duckie. But he said nothing.

Both of us were quiet as we reached Oakcrest Academy, but when I moved the car to the front of the line, it filled with the familiar sounds of Sebastian and Coop discussing the various superhero movies coming out in the next several months while Samantha argued all of them looked stupid and predictable—a point Coop didn't disagree with.

When I finally pulled into my driveway, I practically jumped out. The twins darted for their house across the cul-de-sac as they usually did, but Coop stood on the other side of the car, watching me.

"I'll see you later." I gave him no time to respond before I grabbed my bag and followed the twins across the road, ready to dive into homework and think about anything other than Cooper Bradshaw.

***

Being a game night, it wasn't long before Dr. Caldwell got home, and I was finally able to cross the cul-de-sac to my own home. I surveyed Coop's house as I walked past, taking in the barely visible lights shining out through the downstairs window and the absence of cars in his driveway. He was home and he was alone, and along with the not-so-subtle pang of guilt, I felt relieved.

I climbed the steps of my front porch, sat on the top step, and finally pulled out my phone. The text I'd ignored all day still waited for me when I opened my messages. I expected to find whatever two names Cooper had come up with next for the game, but there were no names. Only pictures.

Two pictures, to be exact.

At first, I almost didn't recognize what I was seeing. Both pictures were bright, with overhead lights and sunshine streaming in through the familiar cafeteria windows. In the center of each photo was me, sitting at mine and Aubrey's usual lunch table, and I had on the same green blouse I wore now.

In the first shot my head was down, an undeniable grin lighting up my face as I studied the phone in my hands. It wasn't like any snap I'd ever seen of myself before. I wasn't sure when the last time I smiled like that was.

The second picture was a stark contrast to the first. Where I'd been smiling only moments before, now my expression was stone cold. My eyes were focused on Aubrey on the other side of the table, the phone in my hand forgotten. There was no way for him to know we were talking about him, but it was clear whatever Aubrey was saying, I wasn't happy about it.

You okay?

My heart thawed at his show of concern, even if it was from several hours ago and before I'd gotten jealous and given him the cold shoulder the entire drive home.

I sighed.

Coop was a good friend, even if he was an unapologetic man-whore. Being nothing more than that, I had no right to let what he did at the party come between us.

I'm fine. Have a lot on my mind.

His reply was almost instantaneous, like he'd been waiting for it.

You sure?

A couple of seconds went by before another message came in.

You want to talk about it?

I smiled.

Yes, I promise. And not really. I'll see you later.

The next message didn't come near as quick. I wondered if he was going to respond at all when my phone finally beeped.

Sure.

My screen went dark before I shoved the phone in my pocket. I felt lighter as I stood, one of the many weights I'd been carrying through the day lightening. As I stepped into the house, another weight grew increasingly heavy. My parents sat at the kitchen table, waiting for me.

Clearly, the time to discuss my punishment had come. And while I knew I should apologize—I'd never snapped at my mother, and since I'd lost it I was totally embarrassed—but I also knew I was right. Whether she saw it that way was another story.

"What's going on?"

Dad patted the chair next to him as he curled his other hand around my mother's on the table. "Take a seat, Bentley. We need to have a talk." Mom was having trouble making eye contact. I dropped my bag by the door and slowly crossed the kitchen to the chair my dad had indicated. He took a deep breath. "Your mom told me about what happened last night," he said quietly. He glanced over at her, and I saw her give him the tiniest nod. "And while there's no excuse for talking to her the way you did, we agree your anger is not unfounded."

This was my dad: calm and cool in the face of confrontation. I'd never seen anyone with as much self-control. It was part of what made him such a great coach.

My mom, on the other hand, was a tearful mess. "I'm so sorry, sweetie," she cried after finally looking at me.

"No, Mom—"

"I had no idea the kind of pressure you were under, the expectations we've piled on you. It's not fair to you."

The back of my throat ached, the tears I'd been fighting all afternoon building. "Don't cry, Mom. I'm sorry for blowing up at you. I don't mind helping out. Really, it's okay."

She shook her head. "It's not okay. You're right. I've asked way too much of you lately, along with everything you're already dealing with. There's no excuse for it. I'm so, so sorry."

Dad placed his hand on Mom's arm and squeezed. "Your mom has talked to Esther and they've agreed to let her take the next couple weeks off to rest and give you a break from some of the responsibilities we've been putting on your shoulders lately."

"You don't have to do that."

"I want to," she said. She took a deep breath. "We both deserve a break. You've been working so hard taking care of Addie and the boys, watching the twins and tutoring, and all while keeping up with your own schoolwork. Sometimes we forget how much you already have on your plate, and we are so proud of you for keeping it all together the way you do. So, so proud."

"As a reward for your hard work," Dad added, "and a thank you for all you've done to help us, your mom and I have made plans to take the boys and Addie to the coast to visit Theo and Xander the weekend after next. That way, if you like, you can have the house to yourself for a couple days for some R and R."

"That's...that would be great." An entire weekend of sleeping in and having the whole house to myself? It sounded perfect. I couldn't think of the last time I'd had a weekend completely sibling free. "Thank you," I said quickly before they could take it back.

Dad held up a finger. "We do have a few conditions. We're putting a lot of faith in you, and we expect that faith to be honored. That means no parties, no drinking, and no boys inside the house while we're gone."

"Understood."

"I expect you to be safe and get home at a decent hour each night. I can have a talk with Liam if he has a problem with any of this."

"He won't," I assured him. When neither of them said anything else, I stood and hugged them. "Thank you. This means a lot."

Mom smiled, hugging me back. "You've earned it. Now why don't you go upstairs and get ready so we can all head to the field together for the game."

I nodded. "I'm really sorry about what I said last night."

"I know, sweetie. Now run upstairs before your dad decides to make you wash the team's dirty towels tonight as punishment." She was only teasing, but I wouldn't put it past my dad to do it. I grabbed my bag and rushed up the stairs to my room.

A whole weekend to myself to do whatever I wanted. I was almost too excited to believe it. Granted, I had to make it through the next two weeks, but still the promise of it was there. I grabbed my phone from my pocket and sat on the bed as I pulled up my messages, ready to share the good news with someone. Then I froze.

The first person I'd wanted to tell was Coop. The thought of the two of us spending the weekend watching movie after movie, eating takeout, and comparing the merits of the old-time classics to those of the beloved teen rom-coms of the eighties. It would be so easy.

Too easy. Too easy for me to fall farther down that slippery slope that was Cooper Bradshaw.

I put the phone down by my side. I needed to put some space between us. Cooper was my friend, and I hoped he always would be. The only way that could happen was if I put whatever feelings I had for him aside. The risk of losing my best friend over them wasn't worth it.

There was no future in my feelings for him, and the sooner I realized it, the better off I would be. If spending all this time with Coop was enough for those platonic feelings to evolve into something more, surely taking a step back would help to lessen them.

***

Despite his promises to figure something out for the weekend, Liam and I barely spent more than two hours together. After a major win Friday night, he'd spent the evening out with the guys celebrating with lots of partying and alcohol involved. At least, that's what I'd gathered from the ten-minute voicemail I had on my phone early Saturday morning.

He called me again around eleven—this time infinitely less inebriated—and invited me over to his aunt's house after his mom left for work around noon. I'd gone with the hopes of going out for lunch or maybe to see a movie, but he'd insisted on staying in and picking up where we'd left off with that kiss in the middle of the hallway Friday afternoon. But no matter how hard I tried, I wasn't in the mood.

After enduring my lack of enthusiasm, he hadn't been in the mood for much else.

Even our three lunches together during the week had been long and awkward, so much so Liam didn't bother to show up at our table for lunch the week after. Something Aubrey noticed without much comment.

The honeymoon was over. Even Aubrey and Coop could tell, though neither of them had said anything about it. It wasn't until the Friday afternoon before my big weekend in the house alone I realized how close the end was for us.

"Bentley?"

I stood at my locker after the final bell as Liam came over, his eyes grim and the corners of his mouth tipping downward.

"Hey, everything okay?" I asked him. "Aren't you supposed to be getting ready for practice?"

He nodded. "I'm headed that way." His weight shifted from foot to foot, his hands in his pockets.

"So my parents are leaving with the kids for Myrtle Beach after the game tomorrow morning. I know Dad said no friends in the house while he's gone, but I thought maybe you and I could go out and do something."

He said nothing for a while, and part of me wondered if he'd even heard me. "I'm not sure…" he finally replied. "Do you think I could come by your place after practice today? My mom should be back with the car. I can drive over as soon as I get home and get a shower."

I hesitated. This didn't seem like Liam at all. I thought he'd jump at the chance when I reminded him I was home alone for the weekend. "Sure, that's fine. Is everything okay?"

"Yeah, I…we really need to talk."

My stomach dropped, and I knew this was it. The end. Thanks to Coop, I'd seen enough movies now to know when your significant other said the words *we need to talk*, it meant you were done.

"Oh, okay. Sure. I'll see you then," I said, the words coming out flat. He turned and walked down the hall before disappearing around the corner. Not knowing what else to do, I made my way out to the student parking lot. It was sunny out, the heat of the sun's rays beating down on me the instant I stepped outside. But I hardly felt them, my mind too caught up in trying to process what had happened.

Cooper stood by the trunk of my car, leaning against it while he waited. "Finally. I'm getting fried out here." He stood tall when I reached him, the grin on his face falling away as I got closer. "You okay, Bent?"

"Fine," I muttered, unlocking the door and yanking it open. "Let's go home."

He watched me a moment longer before finally getting in without a word. The silence stretched as we drove through town to the twins' school, the car then filling with the sounds of Samantha and Coop arguing playfully while Sebastian tried to talk strategy with Coop over his soccer game later that night.

Coop kept throwing glances my way, but he said nothing, instead focusing his attention on the two redheaded preteens in the backseat.

Meanwhile, I focused on the road as I tried to make sense of my jumbled thoughts.

Chapter 21

An hour later, both twins had finished their schoolwork in record time. As they always did, Samantha ran upstairs to talk on the phone with her friends while Sebastian went outside to the backyard to start his required hour of practice with the soccer ball.

Not quite ready to think about the impending talk with Liam, I decided to scour the cabinets for ingredients to make cookies. Luckily, Dr. and Mr. Caldwell always kept their pantry stocked, and I had perfectly good dough ready for the oven in no time.

I put in the first batch of chewy chocolate cookies and set the timer when the back door burst open. In flew Sebastian, an enormous grin on his face as he ran across the kitchen and living room to the stairs.

"Whoa. Where's the fire?" I called as he started up the steps two at a time.

"He's coming to my game," he shouted. "I have to tell Mom."

"Who's coming?" But Seb was already in his room and out of earshot. I turned to the window, looking out at the backyard. My hunch at who might be out there put that kind of smile on Sebastian's face was correct.

Cooper stood by one of the two soccer goals Mr. Caldwell had insisted on keeping in the massive backyard. Coop kicked at the ball, flipping it up in the air with his foot, his knee, his head, over and over, never letting it touch the ground. He was so focused, his concentration zeroed in on that ball each time it rose and fell. And yet, behind the furrowed, sweaty brow and the intense set of his eyes, I could see the joy he felt whenever he manipulated a ball like this. As I'd seen it every other time he coached Sebastian in the backyard.

I stepped outside as Coop bounced the ball around a few more times before letting it fall to the ground. He looked up at me with a wide smile.

"What was that about?" I pointed over my shoulder to where Sebastian had burst through the house.

"That?" He nudged the ball with his foot and shrugged. "He was bummed his dad can't make it to his game tonight, so I told him I'd go as long as it was okay with his mom."

"No wonder he was so excited." I crossed the deck and down the stairs. "You're really something."

He glanced at me, then looked back down at the ball. "It's nothing," he said, shaking it off. Only I didn't want him to shake it off. I wanted him to see and recognize this amazing side of himself the way I did.

I grabbed his arm and his attention. He looked down where my hand met his warm skin and then up at my face, the ball between his feet stilling. "I'm serious. You're a good person. What else do you call it when a guy agrees to go to a kid's soccer game when he could be doing anything else?"

There was a beat of hesitation before he said, "Not anything."

An image of Coop with Maya Freeman popped up into my brain. Of course. The one thing he really wanted to do still remained out of reach. At least until his dad got him a new car.

My hand fell from his arm, and I took a step back. *Distance.* I'd done so well the last two weeks, cutting back on our movie nights, limiting the messages we sent back and forth, but it hadn't lessened how badly I wanted him near me. The "space" hadn't changed that he was the first person I wanted to talk to about my day or whatever crazy drama he was missing on social media.

Whenever the loneliness without him felt too sharp, one word echoed in my mind like a mantra. *Distance. Distance. Distance.* To his credit, Cooper didn't try to fight or question me on my sudden step back. He gave me the space he seemed to understand I needed.

Of course, his understanding made it hurt all the more.

"What's wrong?" he asked, stepping closer.

"Nothing." I pasted on a smile. "What makes you think something's wrong?"

I froze as he lifted his hand to my cheek. He rubbed his thumb over the skin growing warm from his contact and proximity before he pulled away. "You have flour on your face."

"Oh." I wiped at my cheek, hoping to remove the flush in my cheek along with the stray white powder.

"You've been baking, which means something is bothering you. Tell me."

I was prepared to stand strong and tell him it was nothing. This wasn't his problem, and the more space I put between him and my relationship with Liam, the better. But then the tenderness in his eyes shredded my resolve.

"I think Liam is going to break up with me."

His brow furrowed. "What?"

"His precise words were 'we need to talk.' It's not exactly rocket science."

After a long pause, he said, "I'm sorry." He shoved his hands in his pockets and nudged the soccer ball with his sneaker. "You must be devastated."

He was right. That's what I should've felt. I should've been heartbroken, a big wailing mess. Wasn't that what girls did when they were on the verge of losing the person they cared most about? And yet, I wasn't.

I'd been struggling to sort through my emotions ever since Liam came up to me in the hallway at school. I should've been upset, but instead I felt this strange sort of calm. Peace.

"I'm...surprisingly okay." His head tilted. "I mean, I'm bummed, I guess. But I think I knew this was coming, you know? We've been distant lately. We barely talk, and all he wants to do is..." I didn't want to say the words, but I was sure he got the gist. "And even that's been getting less and less. So it's not really like it's out of the blue or anything."

"I had no idea."

I looked down at my fidgeting hand. "I guess you were right. He's not the right guy for me."

"Well, if it makes you feel better, he's a bigger idiot than I thought. But don't worry." This time Coop placed his hand on my shoulder and squeezed it. "The right guy is out there."

"Yeah, maybe," I said.

"He is. And I'll prove it."

My mouth fell open, my heart galloping as I instantly thought of several ways he could do that. My eyes fell to his lips. *Distance. Distance. Distance,* the rational side of my brain reminded me.

Shut up. Shut up. Shut up. "How?" I whispered.

He smiled, letting go of my shoulder as he stepped back and grabbed the ball at his feet. "We'll let Fate decide."

I shook off the fog looking at his lips had created, staring uncertainly at the ball in his hands. "Fate plays soccer?"

"No, but I do." He positioned himself in the middle of the makeshift soccer field and placed the ball on the ground. He pointed to the spot of grass halfway between him and the nearest goal, an indication I should stand there. "I get the ball past you and score it means I'm right."

Was he kidding? "You realize this whole thing is rigged, right? How the heck am I supposed to stop you?"

"Hey, I don't make the rules. You don't like it, take it up with Fate." I made a show of rolling my eyes. "You ready?"

"Fine, whatever."

I got into position in front of the goal, bending my knees and shifting my weight from side to side as my dad had taught me years ago, feeling utterly ridiculous.

Coop nudged the ball with his foot, gently at first, then with more skill and effort.

Once he'd warmed up and had the ball moving, he shifted, readying to get past me on my right side. I was a step ahead of him, cutting him off and pushing him farther back from the goal.

"Not bad." He looked genuinely surprised I'd blocked him, but I had a feeling he was taking it easy on me. He moved the ball between his feet again, this time lunging to my left side much quicker than last time. Still I was there, a proud smile on my face.

I wasn't sure how I kept up with him. Maybe I'd absorbed more of those childhood lessons with my dad and brothers than I'd thought. Coop moved again and again, each time coming face-to-face with me. His focus sharpened as he feinted left, then spun around, taking the ball to the right.

I darted forward, sweeping my foot through and taking control of the ball. I had it in my possession for all of three seconds before he grabbed me. Out of nowhere, Coop swooped down and caught my waist, lifting me into the air and over his shoulder.

"Coop." I yelled into his back, half squealing and half laughing. My hair fell around my face and I gripped his T-shirt, acutely aware of the taut and tense muscles working underneath my fingers. His firm hands secured my thighs as he carried me to the goal. His foot thumped hard against the ball and the net rustled as it went in.

"Goal," he yelled, his arms flying in the air, leaving me teetering on his shoulder. I shrieked, and his hands came down to steady me.

"That's cheating," I felt the need to point out.

He shrugged, the movement jostling my entire body. "How was I supposed to know you were actually a decent defender?" I slammed my eyes closed as he spun around once before he set me down.

I swayed at the sudden shift and grabbed his shoulders reflexively. We both panted, his face dangerously close to mine. He grinned down at me, his green eyes bright.

His grip tightened on my waist while his left hand cupped my cheek, his thumb caressing the same spot where he'd wiped away the flour.

"I told you the right guy is out there," he said quietly. "You just have to see him."

I see him, I wanted to say. *I see you.*

"What the fuck are you doing?"

Cooper and I broke apart at the sound of Liam's booming voice, exactly as we had at Thomas's party over a month ago. My stomach plummeted knowing what this must look like, and I felt guilty. Liam hadn't dumped me yet, which meant technically, I was still dating someone else while Coop and I were…whatever we were doing.

"What are you doing here?" I asked breathlessly, smoothing down my wrinkled shirt.

"I told you I was coming by after practice to talk to you. I went to your house, but your brothers said you were over here." His glare shifted to Cooper. "I would've come sooner if I'd known my best friend was trying to steal my girl."

I took several steps toward him. "He's not. It's not like that. We were kicking the ball around. Right, Coop?"

I looked back at him, begging for his aid. But he stayed resolutely quiet, meeting Liam's glare with full force.

"Really?" Liam said. "Because it sure looked like he was making moves on my girlfriend."

"Coop wouldn't do that to you."

"No? Let's ask him." He stared at Coop with a weird sort of grin I'd never seen before. Cruel and terrifying all at once. "You the kind of guy who would screw over his best friend?"

Silence stretched as they stared at each other, both looking livid, and once again I got the feeling there was more going on here than I was aware of.

Finally, Coop sighed as he ran his hand through his dirty blond hair. "Whatever, man. We're good here." The words were flat, lifeless. "She's all yours." Without another word, Cooper turned away from us and disappeared around the side of the house.

"One of these days I'm going to kick his ass."

I shook my head. "Stop. The twins are inside. The last thing I need them to see is the two of you fighting. Now you said you wanted to talk, right?"

He glanced at me, then back to where Coop had been. I braced myself, sure of what would come next. "Your parents are out of town this weekend?"

"I—" I froze, wondering if I'd misheard him. "Yeah…yes, they are. Right after the game in the morning."

He smiled, stepping closer and wrapping his arms around me. "Good. Because I've got a special night planned. What do you say to a reservation for dinner at this great place in Greenville?"

It was so far from what I'd been expecting I didn't know what to say. "Oh, um, sure. That sounds good."

"Good. I'll pick you up at six." He grabbed the back of my neck and pulled my lips to his. He kissed me gently before letting go. "I'll see you tomorrow."

I nodded, not trusting myself to speak.

Liam turned and followed went to his car, which I presumed was parked in my driveway.

What the hell just happened? One minute I was preparing for what I thought was the inevitable breakup, the next I'd agreed to a romantic dinner.

Not knowing what else to do, I made my way back into the twins' house. I opened the door as the insistent beep of the oven timer told me my first batch of cookies was done.

I grabbed a mitt and opened the oven door, too distracted to care the cookies were hard and blackened on the pan.

Chapter 22

"Tell me that was not the best meal you've ever had," Liam said from the driver's seat.

"Mmm," I moaned next to him, remembering the way the pork loin practically fell apart in my mouth, so moist and flavorful. I was going to have to find a similar recipe to try at home because that was too good to have only once.

I laid my head against the headrest and placed my hand over my full stomach.

Liam glanced my way. "I hope you're not too full."

"Are we going somewhere for dessert?" I asked, subtly pulling the phone from my black clutch and checking the screen for the billionth time today. Nothing. Cooper hadn't answered any of my calls or texts since the episode with Liam the day before. I was starting to worry.

"Something like that." Liam winked at me, placing his right hand on my knee. I didn't know what he meant, but I had to admit I was more than a little curious.

Dinner had been a surprising success after our awkward encounter in the twins' backyard. I wasn't sure what kind of mood he'd be in when he picked me up, especially considering the major loss the soccer team had suffered that morning. Dad was especially disappointed, and I was glad he'd be spending the weekend in Myrtle Beach instead of moping at home.

I'd spent almost two hours getting ready, doing my hair, makeup, nails, the works. The only part I struggled with was deciding what to wear, not sure what was appropriate for a fancy dinner, but also not wanting to overdo it. Aubrey came to my rescue, sitting at the end of my bed while I tried on literally every dress in my closet. After going back and forth, we finally agreed on a strapless azure blue cocktail dress, which hit a couple inches above my knees.

When Liam arrived a few minutes after six, he'd grinned from ear to ear as he got out and opened the passenger-side door for me. "You look amazing," he said, taking me in from head to toe. "I hope you're ready for the best night of your life."

His mood had stayed in the clouds all evening, even after paying what to me seemed like a ridiculous bill for pork tenderloin and shrimp parmesan. He was so excited for whatever was coming next I couldn't help but feel it too.

"Here we are," he said about ten minutes after we left the restaurant. He pulled into the shared parking lot of a laundromat, a drab-looking motel, and a Chinese restaurant called the Hidden Dragon. "Surprise." Liam pulled his mom's car into a spot, turned it off, and quickly climbed out.

I sat there, not sure what exactly I was supposed to be surprised about. He came around to my side and opened the door. I climbed out with my black clutch, and he took my hand. "Are we getting fortune cookies?" I asked, still hung up on the promise of dessert.

"Nope." He pulled me in close, his hands wrapping around my waist. He lips grazed my ear. "I'm getting us a room."

"Wait, what?"

"Don't worry. I thought with my mom home tonight and your house being off limits, this is a way for us to get a little privacy. I know things have been weird between us the last couple weeks. I thought this would be a good time for us to talk and be together."

"I don't know." This night had the potential to end incredibly badly if I said no, but the twist in my gut told me this was not where I wanted to be.

He grabbed my hand again and pulled me gently to the motel. "Come on. Trust me."

I didn't want to go in there, but I also didn't want to make Liam mad. Not after all the effort he'd already gone through tonight. More than anything, I didn't want to ruin the amazing date we'd had so far.

"Okay. But to talk."

He tugged on my hand again, this time pulling me along with him. I gripped my clutch tightly in the other as he steered us to the office where a woman with a stained white T-shirt and the voice of a lifelong smoker took Liam's cash in exchange for a key.

The room was small, the dark green carpet worn out in a circle around the bed and leading to the tiny, stained bathroom. The off-white walls had standard cheap motel room paintings.

Liam locked the door behind us, then took my hand and led me over to the bed. He placed his phone and his keys on the nightstand and sat down, patting the questionable-looking bedspread. Not knowing what else to do, and feeling the usual pain that came with standing in three-inch heels, I sat next to him.

"See, nothing to worry about." He smiled at me, then brought his hand up to draw slow circles on my exposed back. He ran his fingers through my hair, twirling one pink curl on his finger. "Have I told you how incredible you look tonight?"

"Liam, I don't think we should—" My breath caught, stopping my words short when he brought his lips to my shoulder. It was soft, gentle, and felt so good. But not good enough to ease the ice prickling in my chest. All I could think about was how Mom and Dad told me I could have this weekend alone to relax, and this was definitely not what they'd had in mind.

"I thought you said we were going to talk." My voice shook as his kisses moved from my shoulder to my neck and up to below my ear.

"We are talking," he mumbled. Then he moved to my jaw, placing a few quick kisses there before finally bringing his lips to mine. The kiss was slow and sweet, and my lips responded. We stayed like that for a while, the two of us taking the time to explore each other's kiss for the first time in almost two weeks, and my body started to relax. This part wasn't so bad, pleasant even. If we could stay like this...

Liam cupped my cheek, then he slowly pushed me back so I lay flat on the bed beneath him. "Liam," I warned. I tried to push myself up, but he was too heavy.

"Shh. Relax." His mouth left mine and started trailing kisses down to my chest.

I pushed harder this time, but unlike the times I shoved him away in his bedroom, he didn't budge. "No. I didn't agree to this."

He pulled his lips from my collarbone and looked up at me, the fire of need unmistakable in his eyes. "I know you're scared, but I promise there's nothing to worry about. Once you get the first time out of the way, you'll feel so much better." He gripped my knee, slowly dragging his hand under my dress and up my thigh.

My mouth fell open with a gasp, but he mistook my shock for pleasure and shifted his hand to the inside of my leg, then higher, then he pushed his lips hard against mine.

"Liam, no—" I cried between his lips, and my voice shook with fear. I squirmed under his touch. "Don't. I want to go home."

"I'll go slow. It will only hurt for a second," he coaxed. His hand traveled higher. I couldn't breathe.

"No." I cried again. He pulled his face from mine for a moment to catch his breath. Not knowing what else to do, I threw my hand flat across his face, the echoing smack filling the room.

"Son of a bitch," he yelled, jumping off the bed and bringing his hand to his face. It was bright red, and only from where my hand had collided with his cheek. "Jesus Christ, Bentley. What the hell is your problem?"

I panted, adrenaline coursing through me while each of my nerve endings tingled like live wires. I curled in on myself, wrapping my arms around my middle as I sat up on the bed and scooted away from him.

"My problem? Didn't you hear me say no five times? And don't give me any of that shit about how I make it too hard for you to stop. I told you I'm not ready."

His hand fell from his cheek. "Not ready to have sex, or not ready to have sex with me?"

"What does *that* mean?"

"You weren't this shy when you were hanging all over Cooper," he yelled, glaring down at me.

"What are you talking about? How did he even come into this?"

"Yesterday, when I caught you two in the backyard. Or how about the time I found you cozied up on Thomas's back porch? You two could've been sleeping together this whole time for all I know."

I shook my head. "You sound crazy, you know that?"

"Admit it," he said, pointing an accusing finger at me. "You'd rather be with Cooper, wouldn't you?"

"Honestly, yes. But that's probably because he's not the one trying to force me to do something I don't want to do."

He scoffed. "Please, you don't show up in a dress like that after a guy says he's got a special night planned if you're not ready to put out."

I glanced down at my dress—the dress I spent over an hour picking out—and pulled my hands in tighter, trying to cover myself under his leer.

"You know what you are? You're a tease." He crossed over to the nightstand where his phone and car keys sat, yanking them up and leaving only the room key. "I'm done with this. I should've ended it yesterday like I planned."

"Liam…" So he *had* come over to end things. Why had he changed his mind?

He reached the door in three long strides, unlocked it, and yanked it open. "The room's paid for. Why don't you stay here until you figure out what you want?"

The door slammed behind him.

I sat still and silent on the bed, waiting for him to cool down before he did the decent thing and came back to get me and drive me home. But several minutes had passed.

He wasn't coming back.

The tears started running down my face, a dam breaking open with no sign of stopping. I could hardly believe what had happened, let alone I was stranded in a moldy motel room almost an hour from home. I had to get out of here.

I stopped my tears long enough to grab my clutch where it sat on the other end of the bed and pulled out my phone. I dialed the first person I thought of, then wiped the tears from my face as it rang in my ear. After several rings, it went to his voicemail.

"Dammit," I shouted, almost losing my nerve and breaking down into another round of wet, hopeless sobs. Instead, I tapped his name again and put the phone to my ear.

This time he picked up after three rings. "Look, Bent, I'm not really in the mood right now—"

"Coop, please." My voice broke on the last word. "I—I need you… I need you to do me a favor."

"What's wrong?" His tone became tender. "You sound like you're crying."

"I need you to go into my house and get my car keys from the table by the door. Then I need you to come get me at a motel a little outside of Greenville."

"Why the hell are you at a motel?"

"I'll explain later. Please come get me. I'll send you the address."

I hung up before he could ask any more questions.

***

Nearly forty-five minutes later, I watched through the window as my white Camry pulled into a spot in the dark parking lot. I grabbed my clutch, leaving the key on the nightstand where Liam had set it. My heels clicked as I crossed the parking lot, and I was acutely aware of the swelling around my eyes, a sure sign I'd been crying for almost an hour.

Coop's glare was glued to the windshield when I opened the passenger-side door and fell into the seat he usually occupied. I waited for him to put the car in drive, but he didn't move, his hands clenching the steering wheel so hard his knuckles were white. After an excruciating silence, when I tore the high-heeled sandals from my aching feet, he finally spoke.

"Care to tell me why you're all dressed up and stranded at a motel in the middle of the night?"

Not really, I wanted to say, but he wouldn't accept that. "Liam and I were on a date. He wanted to surprise me and brought me here. When I told him I wasn't ready, he kept pushing."

His hands gripped the wheel tighter. "Did he..." He cleared his throat, his focus remained on the windshield. "Did he force you?"

"No. But he got mad, and he stormed out and left me here."

His chest rose and fell at a slow, deliberate pace, then he reached down with his right hand to put the car in drive. His foot fell heavy on the gas, and I was thrown back into my seat as the car spun around and shot out onto the road, narrowly avoiding oncoming traffic.

"Coop," I screamed. "What are you doing? Slow down."

The engine roared as the car went faster and faster. "I'm going to kill him," he said through his clenched jaw. "If he thinks he can hurt you like that..."

"He didn't, Coop." The words came out in a rush. "I'm fine, really."

"And then he just leaves you there. Anything could have happened to you."

"Stop, Coop. Listen to me. I said I'm fine." I placed my hand gently on his arm, begging him to listen. "Please, please calm down and take me home. I really want to go home." My voice grew heavy with exhaustion. After everything that had happened with Liam, I had no more fight left.

Cooper must've heard it. His foot eased off the gas some. I moved my hand from his arm and grabbed one of his hands where it clutched the steering wheel. He let me pull it gently from the wheel and curl it around my own. "Please, Coop."

He hesitated, then let out a heavy sigh and allowed the car to ease to a reasonable speed. "Fine."

"Thank you." I loosened my hold on his hand, but instead of letting it go, he spread his fingers and intertwined them with mine, holding on even tighter.

We drove silently for several minutes before Coop asked, "So you're not hurt?"

I shook my head. "I'm fine except for my hand." I lifted my right hand and wiggled my red and tender fingers.

"What did he do to your hand?"

"Ran into it with his face," I said, hearing the pride in my voice. I thought I saw the tiniest hint of a smile on Coop's lips, but it was gone.

"You two didn't have sex?"

"God no. You really think I'm going to let someone take my virginity in a Motel 6?"

His left hand on the wheel loosened even more. "You and that Louis guy never…"

"We dated for three weeks at summer camp. I barely knew him. But I'm glad you think so highly of me."

"That's not what I meant," he said quickly. He glanced at me before looking back to the road. "But I'm glad you didn't."

"You are?"

"You deserve better than a guy you knew for three weeks or an asshole who can't hear the word no. Liam didn't deserve it. No guy does unless you're willing to give it. Your first time should be special, with someone you really care about and who cares about you."

"Was yours?"

He went quiet, and I realized what I'd said. "Sorry," I muttered as my cheeks heated. "I didn't—that's none of my business."

"It's fine," he said, but there was a finality to it, letting me know he wasn't going to answer my question. Neither of us said anything more, sitting through the rest of the drive home in complete silence while his hand held mine.

It was after ten when Coop finally pulled into my driveway and turned off the car. Reluctantly, I let go of his hand and grabbed my clutch and my heels. The light, chilly breeze ruffled the skirt of my dress and my long brown and pink curls, which were draped over my bare shoulders. I walked to the front of the car.

I'd never noticed how eerie the dark, empty house looked at night. I couldn't remember a time I'd come home not to find at least one light on waiting for me.

Coop stood at my side. "Parents still out?" he asked.

I nodded. "Until tomorrow night. Yours gone too?" His house sat a hundred feet away, as dark and still as mine.

"Yeah. Now that they're getting divorced there's no reason for either of them to be here."

Oh Coop. I couldn't imagine how lonely living in that house must be for him. I took in his wrinkled T-shirt and baggy jeans, the dirty blond scruff covering his jaw. I imagined him like this before my call, sitting in front of the TV in his big, vacant house, his only company the characters up on the screen, and my heart ached for him.

"Well," he said, looking down at his tennis shoes, "you should probably get some rest."

"Do you feel like watching a movie?" I asked, trying to mask the desperation in my voice. His frown filled with concern told me I'd failed. "I don't really want to be alone right now," I said quietly.

Coop nodded. Without a word, he lowered his hand and grasped mine. He led the way across the lawn, up the steps to his front door and into the warm, dark foyer, with me following close behind. He flipped a switch, and the room lit up.

"I'll go get some of Caitlyn's old clothes you can change into."

I took in my wrinkled blue dress in the light of the foyer. I'd spent hours picking this thing out, and now I wanted nothing more than to get out of it. "Thanks."

Coop disappeared upstairs, coming back down a minute later with an old T-shirt and navy-blue sweatpants in his hand. I changed in the guest bathroom, grateful Caitlyn was almost the same size as I was. The sweatpants were a little higher on my ankles than they were supposed to be, but they were warm and comfy, perfect after so many hours in that dress.

The TV in the living room was already set up and Coop sat patiently in his spot on the couch. I settled into my usual spot, several inches between us. We said nothing as Coop started playing what was titled *The Philadelphia Story*.

The opening credits played as names popped up on the screen, one after the other. We hadn't gotten through half of them when I found myself sliding across the couch, scooting closer to him until my back was against his arm. He shifted in his seat, and without hesitating, he wrapped his arm around my waist while I leaned into him. With my head resting on his shoulder and my back nestled into his side, I could feel the rise and fall of his chest as he breathed, his exhales fluttering through my curls when he rested his chin gently on top of my head.

I let out a deep breath as the last of my tense muscles finally relaxed. It went against everything I'd been telling myself the last two weeks. But after everything that'd happened tonight, all I wanted was to feel safe.

I could think of no safer place than right here in Cooper's arms.

Chapter 23

Slowly, I opened my eyes to a dark room only faintly lit by moonlight. The coffee table was reflected dully off the wide TV hanging on the wall, surrounded by several rows of built-in shelves full of countless movies in various shades of gray.

I'd fallen asleep in Cooper's living room. I couldn't remember exactly how far I'd made it into *The Philadelphia Story* before my eyes grew unbearably heavy, and I'd given in to my overwhelming exhaustion. Now the TV was black and dormant.

I stretched my legs and felt the weight of a blanket covering me from the waist down. I grinned as I imagined Coop grabbing it and placing it over me, not wanting to wake me before he climbed the stairs to his bed.

It had to be early, maybe two or three in the morning. I blinked, fighting the powerful desire to close my eyes again and drift back to sleep, trying to prepare myself to make the walk to my house in the dark.

I should probably leave Coop a note to thank him and tell him I was going—

Something shifted behind me.

My lungs froze midbreath, and it took everything I had not to move. The stirring ceased, and then a moment later, a gentle snore broke the silence.

With the utmost caution, I turned enough to make out Coop's sleeping face over my head. Only then I saw his arms, one under my head acting as a pillow, the other wrapped around my waist and holding me tight.

We were so close, his entire body warming mine everywhere we touched. How had I spent who knows how many hours snuggled up with Cooper Bradshaw and not noticed?

Oh so gently, I lifted Coop's arm from my waist and slowly started to roll over. After painstaking effort and what felt like several minutes, I'd turned myself completely around, bringing myself chest to chest with him. Gingerly, I set his arm back down over my waist, probably enjoying too much the comfort and security accompanying it.

He breathed softly, his chest rising and falling and barely brushing against mine. I barely could make out the shape of his hard shoulder, and I couldn't help imagining the defined muscles I knew lay beneath his dark T-shirt. It took every ounce of restraint I possessed not to run my hands over them.

I followed the curve of his neck up to his face, studying every line and angle of his features in the moonlight. He looked so peaceful, almost like he was still that carefree little boy in all those photos hanging in the hallway. Except for that scruff, evidence he hadn't shaved since Friday morning. Ten-year-old Cooper couldn't have pulled this look off, but it suited seventeen-year-old Cooper so well.

With a mixed surge of curiosity and courage, I ran my fingers gently over the short, blond hairs on his jaw.

"Mmm…"

Cooper's sleepy moan filled the dark silence of the room and rumbled through my insides like thunder. His arm draped over my midsection came up between us, and his hand touched mine where it lightly touched his jaw. He nuzzled into my hand, and my heart raced. Then, with his eyes still closed, he pulled my hand from his jaw and brought it to his lips to kiss my open palm.

He had to be dreaming. My chest tightened for a split second as I thought of the girls in Columbia. Was he dreaming about one of them?

"Bentley."

My breath caught and my chest nearly exploded with quiet joy at the loving sound of my name on his lips. His blond lashes fluttered, then his eyes opened only slightly.

"Bentley," he croaked again.

Not dreaming, then, which meant he couldn't've been dreaming of me. The fire in my chest fizzled, but only a little. "Yeah?"

His eyes slid closed and he bent his head forward the two inches it took to place his lips on my forehead. "Go back to sleep."

"Okay."

He didn't let go of my hand, and brought our joined fingers to rest in the narrow space between us. I shifted once or twice, settling in before I let my eyes drift closed, all thoughts of going back to my house and my bed gone.

***

The next time I woke, the sun had already crept through the windows and filled the room with the bright light of the late morning. It didn't take me near as long to get my bearings this time, but that probably had something to do with the steady beat of Cooper's heart under my ear.

We'd shifted at some point in the night, and instead of sleeping on our sides and facing each other, Coop lay flat on his back with me half on top of him. I raised my head from his chest, noting the way my arm had wrapped around him and my hand rested on the tiny sliver of exposed skin at his hip. I yanked my hand away, blood rushing to my cheeks as he began to stretch beneath me.

His eyes drifted open, and I pushed myself off him, putting some space between us. It was one thing to be cuddled up next to him in the darkness of the night, but another to be caught in the light of day.

I sat on the far end of the couch and ran my hands through my hair. Coming to himself, he searched the couch until he found me huddled in the corner. His messy hair stuck up at odd angles, and I could only imagine what kind of train wreck I'd turned into overnight. But when his eyes settled on me, he smiled and muttered, "Hey."

"Hey."

He sat up, threw the blanket off himself as he stood, and raised his arms over his head in a full-body stretch. I caught another glimpse of the skin around his hips and looked away.

I stood from the couch and adjusted my borrowed shirt and sweatpants, not looking at him. "So, um, thanks…um, for coming to get me last night and, um, for letting me hang out here." I hazarded a glance and found him watching me with a grin.

"I should get going." I grabbed my blue dress from where it was draped over the couch, then I grabbed my heels and the clutch I'd left on the floor.

"Are you hungry?" he asked, taking a step toward me. "We could go get some breakfast, or I could make you something here." I could've pointed out his fridge was bare aside from the boxes and boxes of takeout, but I was too caught up in his hopeful smile.

I brushed some hair behind my ear, shaking myself out of my daze. "I would. I mean I want to, but I promised Aubrey I'd meet her at her house to work on our English projects. I should go home and clean up first."

He nodded, the smile fading. "Yeah, sure. No problem."

I smiled apologetically and turned to go. He followed me silently down the hall and out onto the front the porch. "I guess I'll see y—"

"What about tonight?"

"Tonight?"

He took a deep breath and shoved his hands deep in his pockets. "Dinner, tonight. Say, seven?"

The fluttering in my stomach rushed back with a vengeance, but I managed to keep my voice from shaking. "I'd really like that."

"Great." The smile was back and was a thousand watts brighter. "I'll see you tonight, then."

"Great." I turned and walked slowly down the porch steps and across the lawn, waiting until I was in the privacy of my own home before I let out a giddy shriek.

***

I practically floated up to Aubrey's front door less than two hours later. I rang the bell and waited as the sound of her heavy footfall came closer. She opened the door, took one look at me, and narrowed her eyes suspiciously.

"Sorry I'm late," I said. I made a show of ignoring her inquisitive glare and stepped inside.

"It's fine. Mom and Dad left to take lunch to a sick church member."

"That was nice of them." We headed down the narrow hall to her bedroom where she spent most of her time, even when her parents weren't home.

I plopped down on the mattress like a child, jostling the notebook and laptop sitting open at the head of the bed.

Aubrey stood at the door her arms folded. "Okay, what gives?"

"Hmm?"

She laughed. "You're acting like a complete loon. Does this mean the date with Liam went well?"

That happy feeling I'd been floating on all morning dissipated, and I crashed into the memory of last night. Aubrey winced. "So maybe not."

"I don't want to talk about Liam."

"That bad?"

I sat up and crossed my legs. "If you consider him taking me to a cheap motel, trying to convince me to sleep with him, and then leaving me there as *that bad*."

Her mouth fell open. "Holy shit. Are you okay?"

I nodded. "Suffice to say, Liam and I are officially done."

"Ouch. I guess that explains this." She pulled her phone from her pocket. A moment later I was faced with a picture of Liam making out with a girl who was obviously not me. "Ally Carter sent me that while she was at a party last night. I tried to give him the benefit of the doubt, like maybe it wasn't him or you dyed your hair, or he was performing some new version of the Heimlich."

I closed out the photo and handed her phone over as she sat on the bed next to me. "Nope on all three counts."

"You don't seem too upset about it."

I shrugged. "I'm not, really. I think I knew it was wrong for a while, and I was waiting for him to be the one to end it. Now, mostly, I'm relieved."

She considered that for a minute. "Okay, tell me exactly what happened."

I took a deep breath. "It all started with dinner." I went through the whole story, and gave her every single detail. When I got to the part about the motel and Liam not wanting to take no for an answer, she looked about ready to punch somebody. Then I told her about the slap, and she looked like a mother whose kid had made the honor roll.

"So, Bradshaw came to the rescue," she said once I'd finished. "What then?"

"Well, after I convinced him not to go murder Liam, he took me back to his place and we watched a movie."

"And?"

"And…" I said, drawing out the word as the smile from before came creeping back to my lips. "I slept over at his house."

Her hand shot up. "Hold on. When you say slept, do you mean like slept or *slept*?"

"I mean we put on a movie and I literally fell asleep in the middle of it."

Her hand and face fell. "Oh."

"But when I woke up, he was lying on the couch with me with his arm around me."

"Now we're talking. What was it like? Did he snore? Did he get handsy in his sleep?"

I laughed. "No. It was perfect. He was sweet and comforting, and there was something there. I think you were right. We're not only friends. Or at least, I don't want to be." I shook my head and sighed, looking down where my hands sat in my lap. "Does that sound awful after Liam dumped me last night?"

"Nah. You said things with him were off for a while, and this thing with you and Coop has been there for a while too. Even if you couldn't see it."

"So, I'm not a horrible human being?"

She patted my leg. "Nope. A normal teenage girl as far as I can tell. Now tell me what else happened at this co-ed sleepover?"

"Nothing really," I lied. I could've told her how he'd moaned in pleasure from my touch, and how he'd kissed my hand and then my forehead before holding me close the rest of the night. But they were such beautiful, simple moments I wanted to keep them to myself. "He asked if I wanted to have dinner with him tonight."

"Wow, that Bradshaw sure is smooth, huh? Well, good for him. Team Cooper for the win."

"You have a team?" I asked, half laughing and half amazed. "Since when?"

"Since I saw you two at the movies together three weeks ago. Beth is totally team Cooper too, if it helps."

"You've been discussing my love life with your girlfriend?"

"Extensively. Now, what are you going to wear tonight?"

I frowned. "I honestly have no idea."

"Then what are we doing sitting here? We've got an outfit to plan."

"We're supposed to be working on our English projects," I pointed out.

Her shoulders slumped as she glanced over at the notebooks and laptop sitting open on her bed. "Oh yeah.

"But after that we are in serious date preparation mode."

Chapter 24

I checked the clock on my nightstand one more time, confirmed I still had ten minutes until seven, and studied myself in the mirror. Again. Aubrey had done a great job. After picking out my casual yellow sundress and comfortable flats, she'd worked my hair into a simple braid over my left shoulder and painstakingly applied my makeup with only the most natural-looking tints and shades.

In a way, I felt more confident like this than I had any of the times I'd been trying to impress Liam. Mostly because I didn't feel the need to impress anyone tonight. This was me, and so far it seemed to be enough for Cooper.

My stomach danced. I'd been so anxious all day, constantly checking the clock and calculating how many more hours I had to wait before I would see him again. It was the ultimate prize after a dramatic and unexpected weekend.

I smoothed my hands over the dress again, fighting off any wrinkles that might try to pop up. Then I looked at the clock again. *6:51.*

Screw this. I couldn't wait any longer. I grabbed my jean jacket from my closet, the one Aubrey had already confirmed would go great with the dress. Next, I grabbed my phone, my keys, and my wallet and put them in my jacket pockets. I had no idea what Cooper had planned. Aside from dinner, he'd given me no clues as to what to expect. Were we going out somewhere nice or just down the road to the nearest burger place? Or were we even going out at all? With Coop's tendency to order takeout, I couldn't dismiss the possibility that he'd have something delivered.

Surely, he wasn't planning to cook something himself.

With all these possibilities running through my head, I took the stairs two at a time and resolved to wait out on the front porch. Lucky for me, I didn't have to wait long.

Coop stood at the bottom of my porch steps, and every nerve ending in my body tingled as I took in his khaki slacks and light blue button-up shirt. In true Cooper fashion, the sleeves were rolled up casually and the first two buttons of his shirt were undone.

Not a suit and tie ensemble—which meant I could exclude any ridiculously fancy restaurants—but a notable step above faded jeans or sweatpants—so hopefully not another movie night either. Which put this night somewhere in between.

"Hey. Sorry, I think I'm a little early." He climbed the steps and put his hands in his pockets.

"That's okay." I closed the door behind me and locked it.

The sun was setting behind him, casting an orange glow over us. He took a moment to soak in my appearance. "You look…wow."

"Thanks." *Score one for Aubrey.* I swallowed. My mouth was suddenly dry. "Are we going out to eat or having something at your place?"

The left side of his mouth hooked up in a crooked grin. "Neither. I've got a surprise for you."

"Oh?"

He nodded and removed his hand from his pocket, holding it out for me to take. "Come on. I'll show you."

I tried desperately not to let him see the way my hand shook as I reached for his. He started down the steps, gently pulling me with him. I didn't know where I expected him to take me, but it certainly wasn't around the back of my house.

"The woods?" Unfortunately, in all of Aubrey's amazing date preparation, we hadn't once thought to use bug spray.

"Trust me."

We passed through the edge of the tree line and onto a familiar trail. I hadn't been back here since we were kids, searching the woods for lost treasure or clues to a mystery. We walked silently, the only sound coming from the various small life forms around us— birds chirping, toads croaking, gnats and mosquitos buzzing in our ears—and the leaves and twigs crunching beneath our feet. The ground was uneven, and I made a mental note to thank Aubrey for the sensible footwear.

Score two.

Another minute of walking, and I could make out the sounds of the babbling creek we used to play in. I looked around, starting to register where we were. The trail, the creek. If I didn't know any better, I'd think we were—

"Here we are." We stepped through the line of trees and into a small clearing. My mouth fell open.

The grass was much shorter than I'd remembered. So short, in fact, I half wondered if he'd come all the way out here and cut it himself. A green blanket had been laid out over the ground, and on top of it sat a basket I recognized as one his mom used to take to the park with us for afternoon picnics. Four tiny little lanterns surrounded the blanket at the corners, already working to illuminate the small clearing since the sun was setting behind the trees. I took a step closer, pleased to find that they were citronella lanterns, used to keep the gnats and mosquitos at bay.

"Coop, this is beautiful."

Still holding my hand in his, he pulled me over to the blanket. "You remember this place?"

"Of course I do." Like it was yesterday, the two of us running around the clearing as we played superheroes, detectives, and house. I looked away, my cheeks heating at the memory of me and Coop playing Mommy and Daddy to whatever imaginary children we had that day. How long had it been since I thought of that game?

Coop let go of my hand and sat down on the blanket in front of the basket. I did my best to situate myself in my knee-length sundress beside him.

"Let me prepare you by saying I've put a lot of thought and hard work into this meal. That being said, are you ready for the first course?"

"As in there are multiple?"

"Naturally."

I smiled. "Then, yes, please."

"All right. Drinks and appetizer, coming right up." Coop flipped the top of the basket open and pulled out two Cokes and a small Tupperware container. He carefully removed the lid and offered me its contents. I peeked in, then grinned before I reached inside.

"Cheese crackers," I said, pulling one out and examining the cheesy, yellow spread sandwiched between two small round crackers.

He shrugged. "Only the best."

"So how long has it been since you've been out here?" I asked through a mouthful of cracker.

"Couple weeks?" he said, sounding unsure. "I like to run on the trail sometimes when I get bored with the neighborhood. You?"

"Oh man, it's been years." Almost three, to be exact. "I think the last time was when Liam and his mom went to go visit his grandma in the hospital, and you and I came out here to go fishing in the creek."

"I can't believe we managed to hide it from him all those years."

I shrugged and grabbed another cracker. "I didn't really see it that way. To me, this was our spot. It wasn't we purposefully hid it from him. We knew that some things meant more if we kept them between us."

He chuckled. "Well, maybe *you* didn't hide it on purpose." He picked up a cracker, chewed it, and swallowed before he spoke. "Why haven't you been back here since then?"

"Well, you stopped talking to me or wanting anything to do with me. It wouldn't've been the same without you, so I stopped coming." The sun was almost completely gone now, but the lanterns were bright enough for me to make out Cooper's subtle grimace. "Are you ever going to tell me what happened?"

"I don't want to get into all that right now." He sealed the lid on the cracker container and placed it back into the basket. "Let's talk about something else."

I wanted to talk about it, but after all the effort he'd put into tonight, I couldn't bring myself to force the issue. Then my stomach gurgled, distracting me altogether. "Like maybe the second course?" I suggested. I popped the top of my soda can and took a sip.

"Ah yes, the main course." Coop reached into the basket again, then handed me what looked like two slices of bread inside a sandwich baggie.

"Is that..." I tore the bag open, took the sandwich out, and looked between the two slices. "Oh my god. It's a fluffer-nutter."

"You used to beg my mom to make you one every day after school."

"If it wasn't for your mom, I probably never would've tried one in the first place." I took a huge bite, moaning in ecstasy. "If my mom knew I was eating a sandwich made from peanut butter and marshmallow fluff, I would never hear the end of it."

"Your secret is safe with me." He took his first bite, having almost the same reaction I did. Neither of us said anything as we devoured the sticky, sweet goodness. Once the sandwich was gone, I took several sips from my soda, trying to wash the globs of peanut butter and fluff down my throat.

"That was so good. I forgot how much I love those things."

"You're lucky I happened to find this stuff in my pantry. Mom must've had a craving the last time she was home."

"Totally lucky. That was better than I remembered." I wiped my fingers on my dress, kicked my legs out straight in front of me, and leaned back on my hands. "How's your mom?"

"Doing all right, I think. From what little I've heard, she'll get some type of allowance from Dad for the next few years. My aunt's been trying to talk her into seeing a financial advisor when everything gets settled. She won't get to live like she's used to, but I think she'll be comfortable."

"How about Caitlyn? How's she been taking the divorce?"

"Not too bad, but not great either. After being in Greenville for so many years, she didn't see how bad things are between them lately. I think she was in denial."

"I'm sorry. I hope it hasn't ruined her wedding plans."

He took a sip from his Coke. "Nah. If anything, she's more determined to get married. She's set a date for this October."

"That's ambitious." It was already the beginning of April, which meant she had less than seven months to plan her perfect wedding.

"If anyone can pull it off, she can. Now, could I interest you in dessert?" he asked, overly formal.

"You could."

The crickets chirped like soft thunder around us. Cooper dipped into the basket one last time and pulled out two chocolate Little Debbie cakes. I grinned. "You really did go all out for this meal, didn't you?" I teased.

"Hey. I took these out of the box and unwrapped them myself. For me, that's about as close to homemade as it gets."

I shook my head. "I'm not complaining. This is delicious."

We ate the packaged cakes, my gaze constantly meeting his and darting away. I hoped the lanterns were dim enough so he couldn't see the red coloring my cheeks. He finished his cake first and drained the last of his Coke. He set the basket aside and laid out flat on the soft, green blanket, one arm behind his head and the other resting on his abdomen. He stared up at the clear night sky.

I followed his lead as I finished my cake, setting my drink aside and scooching over next to him. Our arms brushed against each other as I lay back on the blanket.

The best part about living in a neighborhood so many miles from the center of the city was the unsullied view of the stars. There was only one cloud I could see, hovering far over on the edge of the trees, but otherwise it was a crystal-clear night. I could see every star from here to eternity. And there were so many. All sparkling in the sky like one of Addie's messy glitter projects.

I took a deep breath of the fresh, cool air and soaked it all in. The picnic, the sky, Coop. "This was amazing. Thank you."

He stared up at the sky, the barest smile on his face. "You really liked it?" he asked, then looked at me. "It wasn't too cheesy?"

I shook my head. "It was perfect. Easily the sweetest thing anyone has ever done for me."

His smile faded as he studied my face in the dim light. "I'm really glad you agreed to dinner with me."

"Did you think I'd say no?"

"I hoped you wouldn't. I've never been sure of anything when it comes to you."

I was about to tell him he should've given me more credit, but as I opened my mouth for the words to come out, the startling ping of a droplet hit my cheek. Then another. And another.

"What the—?" The cloud that had been skirting over the edge of the trees only minutes ago now sat directly overhead. So much for clear skies.

I shrieked as I jumped up to my feet, Coop following a second behind me. I pulled my jacket in tight around my shoulders, already soaked, and Cooper raced to gather the doused lanterns and the blanket, and shoved them in the basket. Then he snatched it up in one hand and grabbed mine with his other.

"Come on," he shouted over the deafening clatter of pouring rain hitting the trees. He took off with me following as best I could to the trail and through the trees. The ground was slippery. I'd never been a particularly stable runner, and I could tell he was going slow for my sake. My dress grew heavy as it soaked up the rain, and soon it was sticking to my chest and legs. The denim jacket was even heavier.

I clutched Cooper's hand like a lifeline, not wanting to lose him as we darted between trees and narrowly avoided rocks and roots. I held my free hand over my eyes to shield them from the water dripping down my face. I could barely see in front of me, and I had no idea how he was able to run so confidently on the dark path.

After the quickest quarter of a mile I'd ever run, we were finally through the trees and dashing over the wet, flooded grass between our two houses. Deep puddles drenched my shoes and splashed cold water up over my legs.

Coop pulled me around to the front of my house and up the front porch steps. I panted heavily, trying desperately to catch my breath. I let go of his hand and started wringing out my dress and then my hair. The porch light shone in the puddles forming beneath us on the light brown wood. I laughed and twisted my hair one last time before giving up. The braid was ruined, and the tiny bits of hair that'd come free while lying on the ground now stuck to my face and neck.

Coop stared down at me, his deep green eyes intense. His hair was soaked and dark and plastered to his forehead while his equally drenched shirt clung to his skin. He'd set the basket down and stood only inches from me. His chest rose and fell with quick breaths, though not as fast or as labored as mine.

"What is it?" I whispered. My heart pounding, only I couldn't tell if it was from the run or the way he looked at me.

He pushed back the wet strands hanging over my eyes. He brushed the hair behind my ear with gentle fingers where they lingered for a second before coming to rest on the back of my neck. My skin tingled where he touched it.

"There's something I've been dying to do for so long only I didn't know how you would take it. I didn't know if it would screw everything up." He stared at my lips.

"You should do it," I blurted out.

He leaned his head back a little, and his bright eyes widened before a crooked grin settled on his face. He rubbed his thumb over my jawline, and I nearly came undone. "Yeah?"

My breath hitched. A magnetic force like I'd never felt before drew me closer. "Definitely."

His gaze slid slowly down to my lips again, and I wet them with my tongue as I waited. He leaned down closer, stopping with only an inch between our lips. My insides buzzed, and he grinned. "You sure?"

I nodded. "Positive. I'd hate for you to have any regrets tomorrow, especially on my account."

His warm breath brushed my lips. *Just a little bit closer.*

He didn't move, and his grin grew wider. He was enjoying this, enjoying teasing me. "I don't know—"

I grabbed his neck and pulled him down the last inch. My lips crashed into his, and froze there for a second, neither of us moving while I waited for his reaction. But his shock wore off and his lips pressed hard into mine. His right hand stayed on my neck, pushing the kiss deeper while the other settled on the curve of my lower back and pulled me into him.

My entire body came to life like a sparkler on the Fourth of July. Heat and flame crackling from deep inside me. It wasn't like the kiss I'd tried and failed not to imagine fifty times in the last two weeks. It was a thousand times better. His touch was like an electric wire, burning my cold skin and warming me all over with a pleasurable pain. My tongue grazed his bottom lip, and he swiftly answered with a greediness of his own.

My subconscious laughed as I tried to compare this kiss to all my kisses with Liam. But there was no comparison. For the last three years, I'd thought it was Liam's kiss I wanted and needed, having no idea there was another I needed so much more.

My hands shook as they traveled from his neck to his waist to pull us closer together, and it was several minutes before our urgent kisses turned slow and gentle. When he finally drew his lips from mine, every inch of me felt wrecked.

He rested his forehead against mine and he wrapped his arms around my waist. "You're shivering," he said quietly. "You must be freezing."

"I'm not." It was the truth. My heart beat so fast, my skin tingled with so much of his warmth I didn't feel the wet cold of my clothes.

He chuckled. "You should go in and get warm, change into some dry clothes."

"No," I groaned pathetically. There was only one thing I wanted to do, even if it meant standing on this porch in Coop's arms until I got pneumonia. Or at least until my parents got home.

Which would be any minute now, the rational side of my brain reminded me. That would be a fun conversation, explaining to my parents why I—who for all they knew was still dating Liam—was caught locking lips with our next-door neighbor.

"Go." He lowered his head and brushed his lips over mine, sending one last jolt down to my toes, before pulling away completely. "I'll see you in the morning."

He let me go, and I waved reluctantly. "Good night," I whispered, afraid if I spoke too loudly the dream would come crashing down and I'd finally wake up.

"Night, Bent. Sweet dreams." He grabbed the picnic basket and took the stairs backwards in his wet and wrinkled clothes, his stare never leaving mine. Not until he'd reached the bottom step. Only then did he turn away and race to his front door.

I shivered again, this time unmistakably from the cold and a distinct lack of Cooper Bradshaw.

I took a ridiculously long shower, hoping in vain the heat would warm me enough to soothe my fried nerves.

But the cold lingered, even as I lay in bed that night, trying and failing to fall asleep for hours.

Chapter 25

I woke as if from a dream, scared to look at the events of the night before too closely for fear of learning not one of them was real.

Only they were real. And the object of that reality would be in my kitchen preparing coffee and breakfast in less than an hour.

I sprang from my bed, wasting no time as I brushed my teeth and jumped in the shower. Not wanting to look too eager to impress, I let my hair dry in seminatural-looking curls and I put on jeans and a simple shirt. Though admittedly they were my best-fitting pair of jeans, and the top I settled on made my eyes pop perfectly.

Between the rushing and the less extensive application of makeup I'd grown used to the last several weeks, I managed to get done a whole ten minutes earlier than usual. I grabbed my phone and my wallet, then darted into the hallway and down the stairs. I froze at the bottom step, took a deep breath, and walked casually the rest of the way to the kitchen. I rounded the corner of the open doorway, and my heart stuttered erratically.

Cooper stood at the island, pouring fresh coffee into the two travel mugs we used every morning. He looked up and saw me, and his eyes lit and his face shifted into a heart-stopping grin, further proof the night before—the picnic, the stars, the kiss on the porch— was not a dream.

I had no choice but to smile back.

"There you are, sweetie."

I jumped. Standing at the kitchen table, so quiet I hadn't realized he was there, Dad stuck a handful papers into his work bag.

"Dad," I said a little breathlessly. "What are you still doing here? I thought you left with the kids."

He smiled as he zipped up his bag. "I did, but we had to turn back around when I realized I forgot all of the new plays I was working on this weekend. Imagine my surprise to come in and find Cooper here raiding my fridge and stuffing his face with Danish."

Coop shook his head and started pouring spoonfuls of sugar into one of the mugs. "I swear I was only taking a few bites."

"I'm messing with you, son. You know you're more than welcome to anything in this house." Cooper's eyes flashed to me and then away. My whole body heated.

Dad, oblivious, checked his watch. "Damn, the boys are going to be late." He grabbed his bag and placed a kiss on my cheek. "I'll see you tonight, sweetie. Try to keep this one out of trouble," he whispered conspiratorially, pointing at Cooper over his shoulder. "Love you."

"Love you too." I turned, watching him until he was out the door. When I spun around, Cooper had already crossed the kitchen.

"Oh my god, that was close. You didn't tell him anything, did you?"

Cooper gaped. "You think I'm going to be the one to tell him his daughter practically attacked me on his front porch last night?"

"Attacked? Is that really what you th—" His lips hit mine, and I lost my train of thought as I got caught up in the maelstrom of sensations of his kiss. My hands settled against his chest, and my body melted into his. He secured one hand in my hair, the other tracing a line down my spine. Just like last night, this kiss had me shivering in his arms.

He pulled away a few inches, and reluctantly, I let him. My short, quick breaths mingled with his.

"What would you call that?"

"Attacking," I conceded before grinning. "But in a good way."

He nodded. "A *very* good way."

"So…no regrets?"

He beamed at me: his eyes brighter than I'd ever seen them. "About last night? Not in the slightest."

While I was glad not to have added to his list, it also reminded me of the two regrets he still hadn't told me about. Maybe I'd convince him to tell me one day, but I was too caught up in this moment to bring it up now.

He glanced over his shoulder at the clock above the oven. "We should get to school."

I moved my hand resting on his chest up to his jawline and over his smooth skin. He'd shaved this morning. "Maybe we should play hooky."

"Did you really suggest we skip school?"

"Come on. WWFBD?" He stared at me, clueless. "What would Ferris Bueller do?"

He laughed. "You did not bring Bueller into this." He shook his head, then brought his lips to my forehead. "As much as I would love to spend the entire day sneaking off somewhere with you, I don't intend to be the guy caught aiding your truancy. Coach would never forgive me. Not to mention, we have a test in chemistry today. Unless you're willing to risk that GPA of yours…"

"Damn," I muttered, admitting defeat. No matter how badly I wanted to hide out from the rest of the world with him, I was far too competitive to risk letting my GPA fall below his. "Fine. We'll do it your way."

He started to turn away, but I wrapped my arms around his waist. "No skipping," I muttered as he turned back to me. "But can we at least be a little tardy?"

He laughed. "Who knew you were such a bad influence?"

Before I could answer, his lips landed on mine again.

***

Despite our delicious ten-minute delay, we were able to make it to school before the bell. Without the detour to Liam's that morning, we made great time through town.

"You want to watch a movie tonight?" Coop asked once I'd put the car in park. "I'm thinking it's time to finally introduce you to *The Godfather*."

"That sounds great. Maybe I'll even whip up some of my famous chocolate chip cookies for the occasion."

"Perfect. But you should know, if you fall asleep like last time, I may have to reassess what it is I see in you," he teased.

Had that really only been two nights ago? Me waking in Cooper's living room, the TV screen dark and his arm securely wrapped around me as he held me close? It felt as much like a dream as the front porch kiss last night. A magical, life-altering dream.

My face grew hot for about the tenth time that morning.

"I love when you do that."

I focused on him grinning in the passenger seat. "Do what?"

He rubbed his thumb over my cheek. "When you blush like that. I'm always dying to know what you're thinking."

"Maybe it's best you don't know." *For my pride if nothing else.*

He went into a brief breakdown of *The Godfather,* complete with several quotes, which sounded vaguely familiar but meant nothing to me, as we traversed the parking lot. I debated reaching for his hand, but before I could make up my mind, he froze.

"What's wrong?"

His jaw clenched, his eyes zeroed in on something across the lot. A small group of guys had gathered beside a blue pickup truck. A mess of shaggy blond hair stood out among the others.

Liam.

I hadn't seen him since he stormed out of the motel. In all that'd happened with Cooper the last two days, I'd hardly spared Liam a second thought. But facing him after the way he'd treated me that night…

My stomach churned, and I thought I might actually be sick.

I saw a blur of movement at my side, and then Cooper was gone, storming over to the group. He dropped his bag in his wake, and I chased after him. "Don't, Coop. Let it go."

He didn't hear me. Or didn't care. He broke his way into the small circle and shoved Liam hard into the back of the truck. "*What the f*—" Liam shouted upon impact.

Cooper's gripped Liam's shirt. "You *asshole.* You really thought you could do that and then leave her there?" The other members of Liam's group, including Thomas and Will Benson from the soccer team, stood back and looked at each other, trying to figure out what was going on.

I ran up behind Cooper. "Please, Coop. Let's go inside."

"You think I'm going to let you hurt her and get away with it?" he yelled.

Liam straightened and pushed Cooper off. "I don't see how it's any of your business. Then again, I shouldn't be surprised you'd come running in like her little white knight. Especially after all your hard work trying to screw up our relationship."

"You did that all on your own."

"Stop, Cooper. It's not worth it," I told him.

Liam sneered. "And the second she called, you went running." He looked at me over Coop's shoulder. "Still got him wrapped around your little finger, don't you?"

"Don't you fucking talk to her," Cooper warned him.

He laughed. "You hoping if you act tough she won't figure out what a coward you are? I don't know, Coop, should we tell her how brave you really are? Or better yet, maybe we should tell her the truth about why I'm staying in a shack while you're still living it up in that million-dollar house of y—"

Crunch. Cooper's fist slammed into Liam's nose before he could even finish his sentence.

"*Coop*," I screamed.

The guys reacted, two of them grabbing Cooper and hauling him back while one got ready to restrain Liam. But he stayed where he was, throwing his hand over his nose to staunch the blood pouring down his face and neck.

Several feet away, Coop threw his hands up in submission. "I'm good," he told Will and Thomas. His voice had calmed, but only by the smallest margin. Both boys hesitated before letting him go. Without another word, Cooper snatched his bag up from where he'd dropped it and headed for the main doors.

Once again, I ran after him. "What the hell was that?" I asked breathlessly when I caught up.

"I wasn't going to let him stand there as if he'd done nothing wrong."

"You could get in serious trouble. I told you it wasn't worth it."

He grabbed my hand and pulled it up to his lips with surprising gentleness. "It was worth it."

"What did he mean about telling me the truth and you were a coward?"

"Nothing."

I stopped short outside the doors, pulling him to a stop as well. "Is it about your regrets?"

"Let it go, Bent."

I held his hand more firmly when he tried to walk away. "Please, Cooper. Talk to me."

"No, Bentley," he nearly shouted. "Not here, not now." He shook his head, pulling his hand from mine. "Look, I'm not a coward. I just—" He glanced back at the parking lot, where I guessed Liam and the rest of the team still stood, and his shoulders slumped. "I *will* tell you, but I need a little time. When you find out…it could change everything. All I'm asking is you give me time to come to terms with what all that means. Please."

I swallowed any further protest at the tenderness in his eyes as he gazed down at me. I could see part of him did want to tell me, and he would tell me when he was ready.

"Okay."

***

"Dr. Richards will see you now."

I nodded and stood. I shouldn't't've been surprised when my second period English teacher told me I was needed in the vice principal's office. After Cooper punched Liam in the face on school grounds, I knew it wouldn't be long before he was called to the office. Seeing as I hadn't done anything, I had hoped my name wouldn't get dragged into it. But clearly it had, which made me wonder how much Dr. Richards knew of my involvement in the incident.

I smoothed down the wrinkles in my shirt and stood in front of the vice principal's door. I knocked lightly.

"Come in."

I'd never been in his office before, never having had a reason to be here. Dr. Richards was a middle-aged black man wearing a pastel pink dress shirt, and he sat behind a large, mahogany desk. "Please take a seat, Miss Erikson," he said, his attention on his computer screen while he clicked his mouse a few times.

I sat in one of the two available chairs in front of his desk. The light green walls held various pictures and diplomas. Two large bookcases sat on either side of the door I'd come through. And in the left corner—

I froze. Dad stood in the back corner of the office, watching me patiently with his arms crossed over his chest.

"Bentley," he said stoically. That was twice he'd surprised me this morning. Only this time he didn't look happy about it.

He came around the back of my chair and leaned against the filing cabinet behind Dr. Richards's desk.

"Don't worry," Dr. Richards said, his attention fully on me. "You're not in any trouble. I've been told you were a witness to an altercation between Mr. Bradshaw and Mr. Haynes in the parking lot this morning. Because one of the students involved is a player on your father's soccer team, I thought it important to have him here for this process."

Dad nodded at the vice principal, who then looked back at me. "If you don't mind, I'd like to hear your account of the altercation."

Crap. "Um, sure." I put my hands together in my lap and started fidgeting. There was nothing to do but tell the truth. Especially with my dad here. "Well, Cooper and I arrived at school and were walking to the door when we saw Liam standing with some friends in the middle of the parking lot. And then Coop…"

Dr. Richards asked when I hesitated, "And then he what?"

I glanced at my dad and sighed. "And then Coop got really angry. He walked over to Liam and shoved him. Then they started yelling at each other, and Coop hit Liam in the nose. Thomas and Will went to hold him back, but he was ready to walk away."

Dr. Richards's lips pursed, and I refused to look at my dad. "Mr. Bradshaw was unprovoked?"

I laughed humorlessly. "I wouldn't call it unprovoked. Cooper was pissed after what happened Saturday night. Sorry," I muttered after realizing my word choice.

"What happened Saturday night?"

"He…" I stopped again. I didn't see how this part was the vice principal's business, and I really didn't want to rehash the weekend's events in front of my dad. But I needed them to understand this wasn't completely Coop's fault. Or at least, his actions were understandable.

"Liam and I were on a date Saturday night, getting dinner in Greenville. I thought he was taking me home, but he…" I silently begged my dad not to get upset. "He took me to a motel."

Dad's entire body went rigid, his jaw clenched, and I could see the fury and disbelief in his eyes. His mouth twitched, and he looked on the verge of losing his calm exterior. I rushed on. "But I told him I wasn't ready for that kind of step, and he got really upset. I'm fine, I swear. But we got in this huge fight, and then he left me there. Coop was the one who came to pick me up and take me home."

Dr. Richards ignored my dad, who'd started pacing silently in the small space between the filing cabinet and the back wall. "So, you're saying the incident this morning was a direct result of what happened between you and Mr. Haynes this weekend?"

"Yes," I said firmly. At least, it'd started out that way. *Maybe we should tell her the truth about why I'm staying in a shack while you're still living it up in that million-dollar house.*

"Please don't blame Cooper. He was trying to defend me. He was so angry when I told him what Liam had done. You could hardly hold it against him."

Dr. Richards frowned, looking like he wasn't happy about what he was going to say. "I'm afraid it doesn't work like that. You are free to return to class, Miss Erikson."

I nodded, stood, and walked out the door, not looking back at my dad. I was closing the door, but then made a split-second decision when I saw the office assistant wasn't at her desk. I left the door cracked and stepped aside, hoping no one would notice.

"Well?" my dad asked.

"I won't pretend not to know Cooper's reputation, but based on what your daughter said, and the fact that his school record is immaculate, I'm loath to go so far as expulsion or even out-of-school suspension."

Dad said nothing.

"But it was a physical altercation on school property, so I can't do nothing. After hearing theirs and Bentley's stories, I think a week of in-school suspension would be sufficient."

"And Liam?" Dad asked stiffly.

"Technically speaking, he did nothing wrong. At least, not on school grounds. As far as what he did to your girl, I think you and Bentley should discuss it more thoroughly at home. How you choose to handle it, I caution you to remember to draw the line between your professional role and your personal one. And take it easy on Bentley. She seems like a really good kid.

"If it helps," Dr. Richards went on, "I've got a friend of a friend from grad school who could take care of Liam for you for a couple hundred bucks."

My eyes widened, but Dad laughed. "Thanks, Ken," he said. "I don't have to ask you to keep Bentley's part in this quiet."

"Nah. Trust me, if it was my Emily—"

I left then to avoid getting caught before his assistant returned to her desk. The hall was quiet when I left the front office. The bell to end second period wasn't due to ring for another ten minutes, which meant the halls were pretty much empty.

Except for the lone figure leaning against my locker.

Liam looked up as I came near, but I deliberately ignored him and kept walking.

"I saw you pass Señora Wallace's door and figured they must've called you to the office too," he said, falling into step next to me.

"Go away."

"Look, I know what I did was awful, and I'm sorry. I'm a total jackass."

"Yes, you are."

"I'm so sorry. I shouldn't've tried to push you to do something you weren't ready for. I should've been more patient, and I definitely shouldn't've left you like that."

"No, you really shouldn't have," I snapped. "You also shouldn't be talking to me. In case it wasn't already clear, the two of us are done."

He sped up, successfully planting himself in front of me so I was forced to stop. With disturbing satisfaction, I saw for the first time the red and swollen skin around his eyes and nose. "Look, I'm not trying to win you back. I'm not even asking you to forgive me because I know I don't deserve it."

"Then what do you want?"

"I'm trying to make sure you know what you're getting into."

"And what's that?"

"This thing with Cooper. It isn't going to end well for you," he said, running his hands through his hair.

I rolled my eyes. I should've known this would be about Cooper. "You have no idea what you're talking about."

"That's where you're wrong. I know Cooper better than anyone. I've seen the way he treats the girls he gets involved with. It's not pretty."

Part of me wanted to deny there was anything between me and Cooper, but I was too tired to pretend. Even for Liam. "It's not like that. I'm not like those other girls."

He shook his head, lowering his voice. "Maybe you're not right now. But the moment you give him what he really wants, you'll be exactly like all the rest of them."

I flinched away as if he'd slapped me. "I don't know what you mean."

"Don't play stupid. We both know you're too smart for that." While his words were harsh, his voice was gentle. He actually had the nerve to look at me with pity after everything he'd done. "He's going to get bored with you like he does with all the rest of them. And when he does, you're going to be the one who ends up getting hurt."

I stared, my breaths coming short and fast as I struggled to come up with any kind of response.

Liam placed his hand on my shoulder, and I was too shocked to pull away. "Think about what I said. Decide if it's really worth it." He turned and made his way down the hall before rounding the corner.

I tried not to let what he said bother me, to let it wash over me. But it was impossible.

Because a big part of me was almost certain he was right.

By the time the bell rang, I was still standing frozen in the middle of the hall.

Chapter 26

I didn't see Cooper again until after fourth period, giving me two hours to marinate on Liam's warning. While I should've pushed everything he said out of my mind, I couldn't help but see the merits of his argument. Mostly because they were the exact same points I'd made to myself over the last several weeks.

I hadn't paid attention in either of my two classes, too caught up in my thoughts, feelings, and doubts. I was so out of it when class ended, I didn't even see Cooper standing at my locker until I was right there. I didn't say anything as I switched my books out for my next few classes. He waited patiently while leaning against the locker next to mine, much like he had that day back in January when he first asked me for a ride to school. Only now he wore a frown.

He didn't speak as I went through my locker, and I assumed he thought I was mad about this morning. If he only knew what I was really thinking.

It wasn't until most of the students cleared the hall to head for the cafeteria that he said, "I'm sorry."

"For what?"

"A lot of things. For losing control this morning. For not protecting you from him."

"Protecting me?"

"I knew he could be an asshole, but I had no idea he was capable of that. What he did to you." He took my hand in his. "Still, I should've done something."

I sighed, looking down at our hands, amazed at how his touch was almost enough to ease my anxieties completely. Almost. "There's no way you could've known."

"And I'm sorry about constantly brushing you off when you try to talk to me like you did this morning. I can see it's hurting you, and I hate that. But it's also...there are things about me...if you knew, I don't think you'd ever look at me the same."

The sincerity in his voice made the skin on the back of my neck prickle. I couldn't imagine anything worse than his history of unbridled promiscuity, worse than Maya and all the other faceless girls from Cooper's past. Girls he'd had his fun with before moving on to the next one. Would I become one of those forgotten girls?

I was wrong.

There was something far worse.

I pulled my hand from his. "I think we need to slow this thing down."

"Hey." Coop lifted my chin with his finger until I looked at him. "I'm ready to go as slow as you want. I don't want to rush this either."

"That's not what I'm saying."

His brow creased, and the corners of his lips turned down. "Then what are you saying?"

I sighed, still fidgeting. "I mean, Liam and I broke up two days ago, and now this thing with me and you... It's all happening so fast."

"This thing with you and me has been happening a lot longer than two days."

"I know, but I think we need to take some time to figure out what we really want."

His mouth slid into a crooked half-smile. "You think I don't know what I want?" He stepped closer, placing his hands on my waist as he lowered his lips to mine in a quick, chaste kiss. His half-grin doubled in size when he pulled away. "In case that wasn't clear enough, I want you. However I can have you, as long and slow as it takes."

His voice was so gentle, and his words caused my heart to stumble. I felt myself falling even further for this guy than I had already. Which meant the impact when I inevitably hit that rocky bottom would be all the more painful.

"You're all I want."

I pulled out of his arms, ignoring the way my body protested the loss. "But for how long?"

He took a step back, his smile gone. "What does that mean?"

"It means, as much as I hate saying it, Liam has a point."

"Liam? When did you talk to Liam?"

"He was waiting at my locker when I left Dr. Richards's office."

Cooper scowled at the door of my locker before looking back at me, his eyes as sharp and cold as a steel blade. "What the hell could he possibly have to say to you? Actually, no. I don't care what he said because I can guarantee whatever it was, he's using it as an excuse to manipulate you somehow. And the worst part is you're letting him."

"Excuse me? I'm not letting anyone manipulate me."

"Look. I know you've been under the illusion that Liam is some kind of saint, but you don't know him like I do," he said, repeating Liam's words earlier and making me even angrier. Why was it that everyone felt the need to question my judgment?

"Really? You think I don't know the kind of guy he is after everything that happened this week?"

Coop put his hands on my shoulders, forcing me to meet his eyes. "It's more. He's using you," he said, taking a calming breath. "This *whole* time he's been using you to—"

"You mean like how you use people? Like how you used whatever girl you were with at Jay's after the movie? It took one fight between us for you to go off with some random girl at a party."

"What?" His hands fell away from my shoulders, and his stunned silence and the way he looked at me like he had no idea what I was talking about was enough to bring my anger to the edge. Before I knew it, it was spilling over.

"You're such a hypocrite. You call Liam manipulative, accuse him of using people when that's exactly what you've done every weekend for the last two years."

Coop shook his head. "Don't do that. Don't pull that bullshit into this."

"How can I not? It's who you are. You use girls to get what you want, and then you move on. But I won't be one of them. Sure, you may like me now, but you'll get bored with me like all the others. As soon as you do, you're going to be right back in Columbia every weekend."

Cooper took another step back, adding to the growing chasm between us. His jaw clenched as he ran his hands through his hair. He shook his head and released a humorless laugh. "You know," he said with surprising calm, "I never cared what anyone else thought, but I really thought—hoped—that you of all people would see through it."

I had no idea what he meant, and when he turned away from me, I knew he wasn't going to elaborate.

With his back facing me, he stormed down the hall, slamming a locker someone left open as he passed. I flinched, the sound of the metal crashing together echoed through the hall and filled the gaping hole in the middle of my chest. I realized for the first time there were several people staring at me. Only I didn't care. I couldn't care. Not when I was so busy trying to hold myself together.

***

The next morning, Coop wasn't standing by my car and he wasn't in my kitchen barking orders for me to hurry up. Or the following morning. Or any of the ones after.

Not that I'd expected him to be. But still, it was alarming how sharp the pain of disappointment hit me with his continuing absence. It was excruciating and terrifying to realize how badly I needed another person to feel whole. Not like I was missing half my body. More like I was still me, but somehow he'd become the life, blood, and energy keeping me filled and keeping me going. Without him I was drained and lifeless. A shell.

I tried not to let people see how empty I felt, but judging by the pitying looks on my classmates' faces and the constant chatter of whispered gossip every time I walked into a room, I suspected I wasn't hiding it as well as I thought.

My parents saw it too, only they probably assumed it was because of the way things ended with Liam. They'd been waiting at the table when I got home from the twins' house that night, much like they had a few weeks earlier. They sat patiently while I explained what'd happened between me and Liam that weekend, how he brought me to a motel and then left me stranded when I wouldn't give him what he wanted. They didn't ask about Cooper, and I couldn't bring myself to say his name.

Mom was proud, but clearly concerned about my emotional state and well-being. Dad swore if Liam ever touched me again, he would "beat the living shit out of him." Which, given his usually calm exterior, I would've found terrifying and mildly funny if I'd been capable of caring at that point.

I cried myself to sleep that night, the first time I'd allowed the torrent of tears threatening all day since Cooper turned his back on me in that hallway. I'd thought the pain of losing my best friend three years ago was unbearable. I'd had no idea how much harder it is to lose the person I'd fallen in love with.

That was the worst part, realizing what love felt like as I was losing it. I'd pulled away from him hoping to spare myself the pain of falling for him even more before it all inevitably blew up in my face. Only I hadn't realized I had nowhere left to fall. I hadn't recognized it before, but now it stared me in the face.

I loved him, really loved him. Something I'd never felt before and couldn't imagine ever feeling for anyone else. But that was exactly why I couldn't be with him.

"Hello...Earth to Bentley."

My attention snapped to Aubrey sitting on the other side of our lunch table. Then my gaze went to the half-eaten plate of food in front of her. "When did you get here?"

"Seriously? I've been talking to you nonstop for the last five minutes."

I glanced at the table of soccer players where Cooper sat, staring down at his untouched food, pointedly and successfully ignoring my existence while his friends laughed and talked around him.

Aubrey looked over her shoulder at the table across the cafeteria and then back at me. "Oh."

"I'm sorry. I'm a horrible friend."

She smiled, but it was tainted by half-lidded eyes and the same look of pity I'd been getting all week. "Don't worry about it. It's not your fault. You probably don't want to hear about Beth's grandma's collection of grotesquely too-small string bikinis anyway." She giggled. I tried to mimic the sound, but it fell flat in the space between us.

"I'd ask if you've talked to him any, but the mopey face and constant stream of not-so-subtle glances are answer enough."

Okay, so I definitely wasn't hiding it well.

"Look, it's obvious this whole thing is killing you, and it takes only one look at Cooper to see how miserable he is." She glanced over her shoulder. "Though even I can admit heartbreak looks good on him. He's sexy as hell when he's brooding and depressed."

"It's the scruff," I muttered. The scruff I secretly loved. Why hadn't I told him how much I liked it that night on Thomas's porch?

Aubrey nodded her agreement as she faced me. "Why don't you tell him how you feel so you two can make up already?"

"We can't go back to being just friends. He and I know it would end badly if we tried a relationship. He won't open up and talk to me."

Aubrey pointed over her shoulder at a gloomy, unshaven Cooper. "Is this supposed to be it ending *well*?"

"Can we please stop talking about this?" Not knowing what was in it, I picked up the sandwich I'd randomly chosen for lunch, took a bite, and swallowed without tasting it.

"Fine. How much longer are Xander and Theo home for?"

"A couple more days. Mom asked them to help out around the house until I got through midterms, but they're not planning to head back until Sunday night."

"Two college guys, when given a week to party their asses off at a warm, bikini-babe-filled beach, chose to spend their spring break at home with their mommy and daddy? That's so cute."

"Seeing as they go to school on the coast, they're not really that excited by the beach. Not to mention they are both hopeless with laundry and in desperate need of clean underwear."

"Still, I'd take the beach over watching a bunch of kids any day. Which reminds me, what souvenir do you want me to bring you back from Daytona? Snow globe? Key chain? One of those T-shirts that make you look like you have a Barbie waist and gigantic, tan bikini boobs?"

I offered her a tiny grin. "I'll leave it to your better judgment. When are you leaving?"

"Tonight. Beth's dad wants to try to beat the weekend traffic." She watched me closely, and I forced myself to take another bite of sandwich. "You sure you don't want to come with us? It'll be fun."

"No, it's all right. I've made plans with Maya to go visit the campus with her early next week."

"Really? That won't be too awkward given her history with *he who must not be named*?"

"Voldemort?" She glared at me. "It'll be fine. It's not her fault I fell for the one guy who's slept with her and half the other girls on campus."

"That's a mature way to look at it, I guess. If it were me, I'd be ready to knock the shit out of any girl boasting to the whole world about her history with Beth."

"Well, seeing as I've never been in a catfight, I don't imagine I'd do well in one now, so it's probably best I avoid them."

"That's why you're the smart one." She took a sip from her drink, her gaze never leaving me. I took another bite of the tasteless sandwich. "You going to be okay this week? Maybe I can talk to Beth's dad and see if we could put off leaving until tomorrow morning. We could do a girls' night, watch one of those old movies you've been hounding me to see."

My stomach twisted. I wasn't in the mood for a girls' night, and especially not one that included watching one of the movies Cooper and I had seen together. "Thanks, but I'll be fine. I swear."

"You sure? We could buy a bunch of toilet paper in bulk and TP Liam's house."

This time my laugh came naturally. "Tempting. But yeah, I'm sure."

"I hate the thought of you all alone over spring break when you're down like this."

"I'm not alone, remember? I've got a house full of kids to distract me, not to mention Theo and Xander and all that laundry. I'll be too busy to even think about Coo—" The name stuck in my throat like a bite of food refusing to go down. I swallowed and cleared my throat. "About Cooper."

Aubrey's eyebrow rose an inch.

"I'm fine, I swear," I said, sitting up taller. "Please, promise you won't worry about me all week."

Her lips pursed. "Fine, but on one condition."

"What?"

"You have to convince Theo and Xander to TP Liam's house with you in my place."

My lips curled into their first real smile in days. "Trust me, that can easily be arranged."

Chapter 27

I stood at the kitchen island transferring warm, gooey chocolate squares from the pan to a plate. Theo, Xander, Noah, and Caden all shouted at each other over the PlayStation in the den where they'd been going nonstop for the last hour.

"Brownies are ready," I shouted.

The dissonance ceased, replaced by the sound of bare feet stampeding over wooden floorboards.

Noah and Caden rounded the corner first, each racing in and snatching a handful of brownies from the plate I still held. They bolted to leave but stopped short when Theo filled the doorway in basketball shorts and a T-shirt, his hulking figure blocking the way out. He scowled down at them. "What do you say to Bent?"

Noah and Caden glanced back at me. "Fank ooh," they muttered with mouths full of brownie.

"You're welcome."

Theo stepped aside and the boys retreated back to the den. Theo rolled his eyes. "It's like they were raised in a barn or something."

"Did they get 'em all?" Xander ran in, only an inch shorter than Theo, wearing sweatpants and a muscle tank. His eyes lit up when he saw the plate of brownies in my hand. "Yes."

He reached over the island counter, plucked a brownie from the plate, and shoved it into his mouth. "Mmm, ah ma gaw dat's guh."

Theo shook his head.

I held a brownie out to him. "Here, try one."

He took a bite and grinned. "Okay, that really is good."

"Yeah?"

"Even better than the hundred or so cookies you made yesterday, and the dozens of cupcakes the day before." He nodded toward the kitchen counters behind me where containers of baked goods had taken over.

Okay, so maybe I'd gone a little overboard lately. It turned out, despite what I'd assured Aubrey, bags of laundry and five siblings were not enough of a distraction to stop me from thinking about Cooper.

"It is a bit much, isn't it?"

"I'm not complaining," Xander said after he swallowed. He grabbed a second brownie. "Though Coach is going to be pissed when we get back to school twenty pounds heavier."

Theo pulled out a stool on the other side of the island and sat. "This all because of your breakup with Liam?"

"No," I assured him, but his eyes narrowed. "Honest, it's not about him."

"Good. I don't like that guy."

"You don't even know him," I said, moving more squares from the pan to the plate. "At least not anymore."

"Doesn't matter. I've got a built-in douchebag radar." He put a finger to his temple.

Xander grabbed one of the containers of peanut butter cookies and settled onto the stool beside Theo. "What about Coop? We thought something was going on between you two."

My hand froze halfway to the plate. "Where'd you hear that?"

"We have our sources," Theo answered cryptically.

"Addie told us," Xander said at the same time. Theo frowned, then smacked Xander on the back of the head.

"Addie? She's three."

"True, but her mind is like a sponge. She absorbs *everything* she hears. Like, say, a private phone call between Benny and her best friend about a certain next-door neighbor."

"That little weasel." Nothing in this house was sacred. "Well, for your information, there's nothing going on between me and Cooper."

Xander shook his head. "That's too bad. He's a good guy. I thought maybe he finally got up the nerve to tell you."

"Tell me what?"

"Oh sweet, naïve Bentley." Theo sighed as he picked a brownie from the top of the stack. "He's been in love with you since the day we moved in."

I gasped to nearly choking. "He has not," I managed to get out.

"It's true," Xander muttered after snatching the brownie out of Theo's hand and shoving the whole thing in his mouth. He chewed several seconds before swallowing. "Liam used to tease him about it all the time. Then he went and kissed you that day to piss off Cooper."

"What are you talking about?"

"The day he and his mom left—"

"I remember the kiss," I said, my cheeks warm. "I mean, why would Liam want to piss off Coop? They were best friends."

"Probably trying to get back at him." Theo shrugged. "They'd been acting weird for days, but we thought they were upset about Liam's move. Then we overheard Liam yelling at Coop about something right before he left. Sounded pretty intense."

"Do you know what it was about?"

He shook his head. "Not sure. Something about what was happening with Liam's dad, I think. Whatever it was, it must've been bad. We all knew how Coop felt about you, and Liam kissing you was like an open declaration of war."

I stared back at my two older brothers, speechless.

Were they right? Was my first kiss—the one I'd spent years looking back at and fantasized over—really nothing more than revenge against Cooper? I hadn't noticed anything strange about the two of them in those last few days, but then I hadn't really thought about much beyond I was losing one of my two closest friends. Little had I known I would end up losing both.

"But that doesn't make sense. If Coop liked me that way, why would he spend the next three years barely acknowledging my existence?"

Xander tilted his head. "How do you think you'd feel if you were fourteen years old and you watched your best friend kiss the girl of your dreams?"

I didn't have to think about it, not when I'd felt it every time I imagined Cooper with Maya or any other of the hundred or so girls he'd slept with. My stomach twisted, and for a moment I thought I might be sick. Was that how Coop felt? Had the fallout between the two of us really started all because of that kiss?

I almost forgot you had a huge crush on him before he left.

He'd said it the first day I gave him a ride home, but I hadn't thought he actually believed it. He had no idea before that kiss I'd never once thought about Liam as anything more than a friend.

"I can't believe it."

"Yeah well, believe it." Theo grabbed another brownie, and Xander reached to take this one as well. Theo smacked his hand away. "Or better yet, why don't you ask him yourself?"

***

"Everything okay?" Maya asked gently.

Having finished a food-truck lunch, we decided to do a walking tour through the campus, the leaves overhead shading us from the blazing afternoon sun. She'd pointed out various buildings while I tried my best to look like my brain wasn't a hundred miles away. Clearly, I'd failed.

"You seem a little down. Like someone trying to have fun but who really wants to lie on the couch in their pajamas eating ice cream and binge-watching *Gilmore Girls*."

"I'm sorry. I'm really glad to be here. I have a lot on my mind."

She nodded. "Bad breakup? Lots of drama?"

"Something like that."

It wasn't fair. I'd been counting down the days to my campus visit, but the closer I got to Columbia, the heavier my chest felt. Maybe Aubrey was right. Maybe coming to this place and meeting Maya wasn't such a great idea. When she stepped out of her car, and I knew I'd made a huge mistake.

She turned out to be even more gorgeous than her profile picture. Her flawless dark skin and long, shining black hair, her legs looking a mile long in her jean skirt beneath a relaxed button-up blouse. As if that weren't enough, she turned out to be sweeter than a chocolate-covered strawberry. So sweet I couldn't hate her for getting Cooper's attention because really, what guy wouldn't notice her?

She'd greeted me like an old friend, hugging me and relaying all the nice things Beth had said about me. I tried hold a smile as Maya drove us around campus, telling me about some of the amazing experiences she'd had in her two years of college so far. But no matter how hard I tried to stay in the moment, my brain circled back to one thing.

She drove us by Stone Stadium after I told her my dad was the high school soccer coach, and all I could think about was if Coop had ever been to a match while he was in town. She took us by the Nickelodeon Theatre, and I wondered if he'd ever been to see one of the classics on the big screen. We stopped by her sorority house in Greek Village to meet some of her sisters, and I tried not to think about how many of them "knew" Cooper the way she did.

It was pointless. No matter what I did, no matter where we went, there was no getting away from him.

"You know what the best part about coming to school out here is? You get to start over. Back home, I'd been in this really long relationship. I thought we'd be together forever, and I became so dependent on him I didn't know who I was without him. When he graduated and broke up with me, I spent my entire senior year as the pathetic girl who was nothing without her boyfriend. That's how everyone saw me, including me.

"But then I left for school, and I realized I had a fresh start. No one knows who you are, and the ones who do are lost in a sea of thousands of people you'll never see—unless you want to, of course. In college, you get to reinvent yourself. Now I'm the girl who doesn't need a serious relationship to have fun and feel good about myself." She smiled, put an arm around my shoulders, and squeezed. "You can be whoever you want here and no one's going to call you out on it. In another year, this guy will be nothing more than a blip on the screen."

I smiled back at her, wishing her words were more comforting. For anyone else, it'd probably be true. But not for me. Not when the person I needed to escape had already made his mark over this entire campus. I didn't know if I could handle it. If I could face four years of wondering if Coop had been here or if he'd slept with that girl. If his weekends in Columbia continued, would there always be a chance of running into him?

Maya stopped beside me. "I've got a class in an hour, so I should probably take you back to your car soon."

"Sure." I checked the time on my phone. How was it already almost two in the afternoon? "Thanks again for showing me around. Sorry I've been so out of it all day."

"Don't worry about it. You need a little cheering up is all. In fact..." She held out her hand. "Here, give me your phone."

"Why?"

She giggled. "Relax. I'm going to put my number in. Anytime you want to hang out and blow off some steam, you can give me a call."

I doubted I'd ever take her up on the offer, but I handed her my phone anyway. She quickly navigated to my contacts and typed in her number. Then she opened the camera and took several silly-faced selfies. She scrolled through them, trying to decide on the best one for her contact photo, and her eyes doubled in size.

"No *freaking* way."

"What?"

A grin spread across her face. "You know Cooper Bradshaw?"

"Oh." I cringed. I'd really been hoping to avoid discussing him, but it seemed Fate was against me. "Yeah. He's a friend of mine."

Her eyebrow rose. "I'd say he's a bit more than a friend. Oh my god. Is he the ex-boyfriend?"

"What?" I took the phone from Maya and stared at the screen. It was a picture Liam had taken weeks ago. The two of us were on his bed, our lips locked together and my fingers tangled in his hair.

"That's not Cooper."

Maya took the phone back and studied it. "Sure, it is. His hair's a bit longer than the last time I saw him, but that's definitely Cooper. He and his friend used to come to campus every weekend to party." Her head tilted. "How do you know him?"

"He goes to my high school," I said as I snatched the phone again.

"High school? He said he went to Central Carolina Tech."

Barely listening, I swiped through photos until I found a candid shot I'd taken of Cooper during one of our movie nights. I held it up for Maya to see, my hands shaking and my lungs tight. "Is this the friend?"

She had to look at it only for a second before she nodded. "Yeah. That's his friend Liam. He's hot, but he's not really much of a party guy. He usually sits around and keeps an eye on Cooper. Makes sure he doesn't get into trouble, has a safe ride, that kind of stuff."

"You're sure?" I swiped to another picture of me and Liam. This time he looked directly at the camera. "You're sure *this* is Cooper Bradshaw?"

"Yeah. I don't forget the guys I've slept with." She winced. "Sorry. It was a long time ago. I haven't seen him in months."

"It's fine," I muttered, not really listening. How was this possible? If Maya thought Liam was Cooper, did that mean the entire school did?

You can be whoever you want here, and no one's going to call you out on it.

They must have switched places, switched names. In Columbia, Liam became Cooper and Cooper became Liam. But how did no one in Oakcrest notice? All it took was one look on social media…

Except that neither of them had it. No TikTok, no Instagram, no Twitter. Nothing. As far as the Internet was concerned, those two hardly existed. Without profiles or photos to tag, there was no way to know what either of them looked like.

That's why Coop had never been interested in the high school parties and why he said he didn't drink. And it explained why Liam went to every party and always got wasted.

People see what they want to see, Bent.

When gossip spread from Columbia to Oakcrest, all anyone in town heard was "Cooper" had slept with this or that girl. But it wasn't Cooper. It was Liam. Everyone had believed the lie. Including me.

I thought you of all people would see through it.

My phone fell to my side. I closed my eyes and ran a hand over my face. "I'm such an idiot."

"What?"

I shook my head and looked at Maya. "He tried to tell me it wasn't real, but I didn't see it." I didn't *want* to see it.

"Who did?"

"Cooper…the real Cooper."

Her eyes scrunched. "The real Cooper?" She shook her head, then grabbed me and pulled me over to a bench on the edge of the walkway. "Okay, I'm going to need you to start from the beginning."

"What about your class?"

"Believe me, this is much more important than anything I'd be learning in Western Civ."

Chapter 28

I ran over to Cooper's house the moment I got home, taking the steps two at a time and throwing the front door open without bothering to knock. I had to find Cooper and get answers.

He wasn't anything like I'd thought he was. At least, not who I thought he used to be. He was still the amazing friend who'd sacrificed his future for Liam's. Who'd helped me get the boy of my dreams even if it meant giving up the girl of his. Who proved to be a better friend and a better man than Liam could ever hope to be.

I saw it now. I saw exactly who he was, and I needed him to know it.

"Coop," I shouted as I ran inside. I left the door open behind me, racing down the hall toward the den. "Cooper."

I froze. His tall, broad-shouldered father stood behind the kitchen counter, much like he had the last time I'd run into him. He wore slacks and a white dress shirt, a glass tumbler in his hand. He took a sip as he eyed me up and down.

"Still walking in, I see," Mr. Bradshaw grumbled.

"Where's Cooper?"

He shifted, the gel in his combed hair shining under the soft kitchen lights. "He's spending the break in Greenville with his sister."

"What?"

"I'm as shocked as you are. The minute I bought him that new Jeep, I expected him to head straight for Columbia. But it would seem he's finally putting all that garbage behind him." His eyebrows rose, and he looked down at his glass. "I think I have you to thank for that."

"Me?"

He nodded. "I also owe you an apology. I wasn't in the best form last I saw you. I accused you of things. Regardless of whether they're true, it's clear you've made a positive impression on Cooper these last few months."

I waited for the ground to swallow me up, for my alarm clock to go off and tear me from this crazy dream. But Mr. Bradshaw continued to stand in front of me, waiting for a reply.

"Part of me wishes I could take the credit, but I can't. Your son didn't need anybody to change him."

He nodded and took another sip from his glass, and I realized with some relief it was filled with water. "I'm sorry for how I acted, all the same."

I started to turn away but stopped myself. "Can I ask you something?"

His eyes narrowed. "I suppose."

"All those stories you heard about Cooper, about what he was doing in Columbia. Did you ever ask him if they were true?"

"I...I'm not—" He stumbled over his words.

"I know you didn't. Neither did I. Because we see what we want to see." I took a step forward, squaring my shoulders. "You saw someone whose sins made you feel better about your own, and I saw someone who couldn't hurt me because I believed he'd never really want me in the first place. But we were both wrong. Cooper is better than either of us could've anticipated.

"If you knew the things he's done, the things he's given up for someone who as far as I can tell doesn't deserve even a fraction of his loyalty. If you knew, you would see him for who he really is. Someone who puts us both to shame." Mr. Bradshaw blinked. "Anyway, you don't have to take my word for it. Do me a favor. Next time you see him, ask him what he was really doing in Columbia all those times."

Mr. Bradshaw said nothing as I turned and left. I closed the front door gently behind me and stood motionless on the porch. My eyes had watered as I told Cooper's dad every wonderful thing about his son I'd realized too late.

Tears began to fall and I collapsed onto the porch's top step. I'd been so stupid thinking I could save myself from future pain by pushing Cooper away. Pushing my best friend away. But it'd all been for nothing. No matter what would've happened between me and Coop, there was no way it could compare to this moment.

Knowing I'd had everything I ever wanted in the palm of my hand and I'd let it go.

I wanted him so badly. I needed him. I didn't want to know whatever fresh start waited for me without his sweet smiles and the way he always made me laugh. Without our silly made-up games and his grumpy rants about technology and modern movies. The way it felt when he held me close and pressed his lips against mine.

I'd screwed up. We both had—me by not seeing who he was through all the rumors, and him by not trusting me with his secrets—and maybe it was too late to fix it. But if there was even the smallest chance I could, any chance I could get all of that back, I had to try.

But it would take more than a quick call or text. I had to do this right. I had to show him how important this was, how important *he* was to *me*. I had to do something big.

And thanks to Coop, I'd seen about a million movies filled with over-the-top romantic apologies. All it took was one amazing idea.

I knew the perfect one. The only problem was I had no idea how I was supposed to pull it off. It would take time, money, not to mention someone who could help me find everything I needed.

I wiped away the last of my tears, pulled out my phone, and found the number I needed. It rang in my ear twice before she answered.

"Southern Charm Designs. How can I help you?"

"Caitlyn? It's Bentley."

She gasped. "Oh my god, Bentley. How are you?"

"Not great," I admitted, running a finger over the hem of my shorts. "I'm calling about Cooper."

"Does this have something to do with why he's spending his school break lying around my house and watching movies all day like a miserable mope?"

"He is?" Hope flooded my chest. Maybe I wasn't too late.

"What's going on? I've never seen him like this. He won't eat. He won't talk to me or Owen. I don't think he's showered in three days."

"It's all my fault. I screwed up. But I've got a plan. I need your help, please."

"What do I need to do?"

"Really? You'll help me just like that?"

"Days, Bentley. He hasn't showered in *days*. I'll do whatever you want me to."

"You're the best. A total life-saver."

"This is true." She giggled. "Now tell me what you've got in mind."

***

I stared at myself in the full-length mirror, forcing in a deep breath to help settle the frazzled nerves running beneath my skin. I'd devoted nearly half an hour on the perfectly styled brown and pink curls falling over my bare shoulders. The red dress I wore was tight and revealed more of my chest and legs than I was used to.

It was perfect.

The hotel outside of Oakcrest wasn't extravagant by any means, but this room was a thousand times better than the stained and smelly motel in Greenville. White, fluffy sheets covered the king-size mattress. On the dresser opposite the giant bed a bottle of champagne I'd taken from my parents' stash and sneaked in my backpack sat chilling in a bucket of ice next to two empty champagne flutes.

Knock, knock, knock. I checked the clock on my phone and grinned.

Right on time.

"Just a second." I scanned the room once more, making sure everything was in place, before opening the door with a smile. "You came."

Liam frowned at me. "Mom's got the car today, which means I had to take a bus here. I almost didn't come at all." His gaze slid down over my short red dress before lingering at my chest, and his brow furrowed. "I'll admit, though, my interest was piqued when you told me you wanted to meet here of all places."

I stepped aside to let him in.

"You said you wanted to talk about something important." He stopped in front of the bed, spinning slowly until he faced the mahogany dresser. "Is that champagne?"

"I thought it might help ease some of the tension from the last few weeks. You want some?"

His eyes narrowed, but then he shrugged. "Sure." I grabbed the open bottle, poured a heaping glass, then offered it to him before he took the flute and downed it in one go. "That's good stuff."

"My mom always has some on hand for when she's got something to celebrate."

Liam sat on the edge of the bed and looked me up and down. "What are we doing here, Bentley?"

I lowered myself next to him, angling my body to face his. "First, I wanted to say thank you."

"Really?" His eyes squinted to slits. "What for?"

"For talking some sense into me about Cooper. You're right. He's not the guy I thought he was. If you hadn't reminded me, I would've ended up getting hurt. So thank you for looking out for me like that."

The side of his mouth turned up. "Of course. No matter what happened between us, I do care about you. That's why it drove me so crazy seeing you two together. I could see him looking at you like another notch on his belt, and I got so jealous and angry I took it out on you that night. I'm really sorry."

He placed a gentle hand on my knee. I covered it with my own and bit my lip. "That's the other thing I wanted to talk to you about. I think I may have overreacted that night. I know I made such a big deal about the first time being perfect, but I think I've been putting too much pressure on it. Maybe you were right. Maybe it would be easier to get it out of the way."

"Is that why we're here in a hotel room?"

I nodded. "I want to do this now, before I lose my nerve and talk myself out of it."

"You're serious? Why me?"

"You were honest with me about Cooper. You were looking out for me even after we broke up. I realize you wouldn't have hurt me that night. I can trust you, and that makes you the person I want to do this with." I bit my lip again. "I mean, unless you're not interested."

"Oh I am." Liam lifted his hand to the nape of my neck. "Very, very interested." He leaned forward, pressing our lips together in a soft kiss, then another. His other hand slid up my leg.

"Wait." I sat back, putting several inches between us. My breath shook. "Sorry. I *know* it's just sex, but I guess I'm still a little nervous anyway. Can you give me a couple minutes? Maybe once the champagne kicks in…"

"Sure."

I grabbed the other flute from the dresser and poured, then held the bottle out to Liam. "More?"

"Please."

I filled his glass to the brim before taking a sip from my own. He drained half the flute, then patted the bed next to him until I returned to my spot by his side.

Gripping my leg again, he leaned in closer, bringing his lips within an inch of mine.

"Can I ask you something?" I whispered before our lips touched.

He sighed and downed the other half of his refilled glass. "Don't see why not."

"Why did you kiss me?"

He chuckled. "It's called foreplay. But if you'd rather jump right in—"

"No, I mean the first time, right before you and your mom left town. Why did you kiss me?"

"Oh, that. Wow, I totally forgot about that."

My stomach tightened. "So, it wasn't because you liked me?"

He didn't answer, his gaze falling to the empty glass in his hand. I traded it out with mine, and he emptied it as easily as the first two.

"It's only a question. It's not like you have to worry about my feelings getting hurt. We're not dating anymore."

When he still didn't answer, I eased closer to him. I slid the champagne glass from his hand and set them on the bed behind us before placing my hand on his cheek. Slowly, I trailed it down his neck to his chest, his heartbeat strong and fast beneath my fingertips. "I want to know the truth. But if you can't give it to me, maybe you're not the right person for this after all." I pulled away.

"Wait." He gripped my hand resting on his chest. "You and Cooper are done? For real?"

I tried to swallow, but my throat felt too thick. "We haven't spoken since the day he attacked you at school," I admitted. Then I leaned in, brushing his ear with my lip. "Why did you kiss me, Liam?"

His jaw clenched, his breaths becoming short. "T-to piss him off."

"See, that wasn't so hard." I pressed a light kiss to his cheek. "Thank you for being honest. It means a lot."

He turned, his nose less than an inch from mine. He'd looked surprised by my reaction at first, by how coolly I'd handled his answer. Now his gaze burned into mine. I wasn't the same girl who'd pushed him away and cried in a dirty motel room, and he liked it. Wanted me.

Now.

"Does it?" His voice had turned to gravel, and he caressed my shoulder with the back of his hand.

I nodded.

"How much?"

This time I kissed his lips and let them linger. What started out soft and sweet quickly turned hard and dominating as Liam snaked his fingers into my hair and pulled me even closer to him. His other hand slid down my arm and settled firmly on my hip.

I ripped my mouth away from his and pushed him back on the bed, leaning over him. "I have one more question."

He blinked up at me multiple times, panting hard. "Do you have to ask me *now*?" He tried to pull me down on top of him, but I held strong.

"It's only one question, I swear. And it's important."

I could practically see the steam coming off of him, but I leaned in closer. "I promise it'll be worth it." I trailed my hand over his chest and abdomen, inching closer to the button of his jeans.

His eyelids fluttered and his breath hitched. "Fine. Ask."

"It's about your issues with Beth."

"This again? How many times do I have to tell you? I'm not homophobic." He tried to sit up, but I shook my head.

"I know, I know. I believe you."

"You do?"

I nodded.

"Good." He pushed himself up to meet me in a hot kiss, the force of his lips like granite, first against my own, then lower as he trailed kisses down over my neck.

"But still, I can't figure out why you keep avoiding her. Is it because she's too nice? Or is it her voice is too soft for your liking? Or, maybe," I shoved him hard down to the bed, "it's because you had sex with her cousin under a false name."

He stared up at me blankly for several seconds, then somehow managed to reel back farther into the mattress. "What? I never—"

"Don't play stupid," I said, standing from the end of the bed to adjust my dress. "We both know you're too smart for that."

He propped himself up on his elbows, his mouth hanging open. "How did you—? Did Cooper—?"

"Not Cooper. Though he could've spared all of us a lot of time and grief if he had. No, that juicy tidbit came straight from the source."

"*Maya?*"

I shrugged. "Turns out the two of us had a lot more to talk about than the school campus I toured with her. You, for example. And once we got talking, it didn't take long for us to figure out your whole operation."

He shook his head as if he could wake himself from this awful nightmare. If only he were so lucky.

I grabbed the champagne flutes from the other end of the bed and placed them on the dresser. Then I pulled my phone from my dress pocket and leaned it against the ice bucket. "The only thing I still can't figure out is why. Why pretend to be Cooper? Why make him go along with it?"

His lips curved into a smirk, but there was zero trace of humor in it. "So that's what this was for? All so you can get me to spill the beans? Fine." He sat up and leaned back into his hands as they dipped into the fluffy duvet. "You want honesty, Bentley? I did it because I wanted him to know how it feels."

I crossed my arms and leaned against the dresser. "How what feels?"

"How it feels to lose everything."

"Why?"

"Because I did. I lost my money, my house, my dad. I wanted him to know how it felt, and I didn't stop at taking his name. I took his dream girl. I took his spot on the soccer team. I took his car—"

"His car?"

"I was the one who wrecked his fancy little Maserati on New Year's. I got drunk, stole his keys, and ran it into a telephone pole. Coop showed up before the cops and took the blame."

Of course he had. Because taking the blame for something he didn't do was exactly Cooper's style. Just like getting wasted and making stupid decisions was Liam's.

God, how could I have been so clueless?

"Well, it all stops here," I said, my voice strong and steady. "You're never going to use Cooper like that again. And you're definitely not going to keep on *stealing* his identity to get girls."

He shrugged. "I prefer to call it borrowing."

"*And* you're going to tell all those girls the truth about who you really are."

"Right. So, what? You expect me to pop over to Columbia, go up to every person I've had sex with, and say 'Actually, I'm not Cooper Bradshaw. I'm really Liam Haynes, a poor little high school student parading as a rich college kid to get laid every weekend.' Sorry, not going to happen."

"That's okay," I said, offering him a slow, knowing grin. "You've said all you needed to."

His brow creased. "What do you mean?"

I snatched up my phone where it had been propped against the ice bucket. "I've got your entire confession right here."

"You were recording that?" He jumped to his feet.

"Uh-uh-uh." I held one hand up to stop him, tapping away at my screen with the other. "It's too late to make any fuss about it now. It's already sent off and out of my hands."

His jaw clenched. "Who'd you send it to?"

"Does it matter? Soon it'll be in the hands of every girl at the Columbia campus. All you need to know is your little weekend scam is over. No more taking advantage of Coop's kindness."

"His kindness? You think he's been playing my friend all these years out of *kindness?*"

"What else would it be?"

"Try guilt. Shame. Either of those would work."

For the first time since Liam had entered the room, I felt unsure about what was coming. It was what Cooper had said all along. There were things in his past, actions he'd regretted. "Guilt over what?"

"For ruining my life. My dad's life."

"Your dad?"

He watched me for several moments before he scoffed, "You really have no idea. Can't say I'm surprised he's still too scared to admit what he did."

There are things about me, if you knew, I don't think you'd ever look at me the same.

"What did he do?"

Liam shook his head. "No. You want to know so bad? Go ask him yourself. I want him to have to look you in the eye when you find out. To see exactly what you think of him then."

A shiver ran up my spine. What could possibly have been so bad Liam would give up the satisfaction of telling me all so Cooper would be forced to?

I pulled my shoulders back, regaining my composure. "Fine, I will ask him. In the meantime…" I grabbed my bag from a chair in the corner of the hotel room and tossed a key card at him. "The room is paid for. Why don't you stay here until you figure out how not to be such a dick?"

I reached for the door handle. "Oh, and by the way? I *hate The Fast and the Furious*." The heavy door thudded behind me. On my way to the elevator, I half expected Liam to race out after me, but he never came. Probably couldn't turn down the chance to down another half a bottle of champagne.

The load on my chest grew lighter with each floor the elevator descended, and it wasn't until I reached my car that I checked my phone for Maya's response.

Got the video. Let you know when it's done.

I grinned, feeling the full weight of what exactly I'd done. Phase One of the plan was complete. Now it was time for Phase Two.

Chapter 29

Everything was perfect. I didn't know how Caitlyn had pulled it off, but she had. In only four days, she'd somehow turned my Oakcrest backyard into the Moroccan piano bar from *Casablanca*.

Wide, curved arches had been placed around the perimeter. Tables draped in white linen carefully arranged around the yard, and planted palm trees were scattered throughout. Paper lanterns matching chandeliers hung above along with a giant neon sign Caitlyn had somehow found that said *Rick's Café Américain*.

And my favorite part, in the very center of it all, a small, wooden upright piano, much like the one Sam played every night in the bar. I had no idea how Caitlyn managed to get any of this on such short notice, but it was even better than I could've dreamed. She and her crew had finished setting it up hours ago, and I'd nearly cried when it had all come together.

"Thank you so much," I'd told her as we stood in the foyer. "There's no way I could've done this without you."

She wrapped her arms around me. "Anytime. But maybe try to give me more than a few days' notice next time."

"You got it."

She released me and smiled. "We'll be back in the morning to pick it all up," she said as she turned toward the door. "Oh, and I almost forgot." She hurried over to the stairs and grabbed a garment bag I hadn't noticed draped over the wooden banister. "This is for you. The finishing touch."

I unzipped the bag, and my smile grew. "This is perfect. Thank you."

"You're welcome. And good luck."

Now, standing amidst the trees and arches and lights, it really was perfect. I ran a hand over the puffy sleeves and thin, gossamer lilac fabric of the dress Caitlyn had found for me— like the one Ilsa wore in the Paris flashback—and I hoped it would all be enough. If it wasn't…

I couldn't think about it. I was so nervous, and my anxiety grew when I heard a car pull up in the driveway at the front of the house. I raced over to the record player on top of the piano and turned it on. The sounds of "It Had to Be You" filled the air.

"*Bent,*" Coop shouted from inside the house. "Bentley, where are you?"

"I'm out back."

The French doors flew open, and he rushed out onto the back porch. "What's wrong? What's the emergency?" He stopped at the top of the porch steps, his gaze traveling around the yard. He took in the lanterns, the wooden arches, the piano. And then me.

I shook my head. "Of all the gin joints in all the towns in all the world…"

"What is all this?"

"This is what we in showbiz like to call the Grand Romantic Gesture."

He looked around again as he slowly came down the porch steps. "How did you do this?"

"I may've had some help from your sister."

"Caitlyn? You were her big important client this week?"

"Pretty sneaky, huh? You never saw it coming." I grinned, but it died quickly. "I'm so sorry, Coop. I never should've said those things to you. I was so scared you would hurt me if I let you get too close."

He ran a hand through his hair. He took a few slow steps toward me. "It's not your fault. I've been thinking about it a lot the last few days and I realized you had no reason not to think that after everything you'd heard. I should've told you a lot sooner, but I need you to believe you're the only girl I've ever cared about my entire life." He stopped in front of me, cradling my face in his warm hands.

My shoulders tensed and relaxed simultaneously.

He took a deep breath. "I love you, Bentley. No other girl has or will ever come close to how I feel about you."

"I know. I know everything."

His eyes flashed. "You do?"

"I know you and Liam have been switching places in Columbia."

"How?"

"I went to see Beth's cousin and figured it out. I should've known it wasn't you. Everything I've learned about you since New Year's, the way I feel about you, I should've realized you couldn't be that person. You are so much better than the guy everyone thinks you are. And I love you for that."

His smile was radiant in the dimly lit yard. He bent his head to place his lips against mine, soft and sweet, sending a rush of electric current over my skin.

The music segued into the familiar melody of "As Time Goes By." He reached for my hand. "Do you want to dance?"

I smiled. "I did get all dressed up and everything. It would be a shame to waste it."

He chuckled as he pulled me close, and we swayed to the music. "You look gorgeous."

My heart fluttered like there was a nest of hummingbirds living inside my chest. "Thank you."

"You've always been the most beautiful girl I've ever known. Even when we were kids. I told you I have only two real regrets in my life. One of them was that I never got up the courage to tell you how I felt."

"Is the other one about Liam?" He hesitated before nodding. "I know he blamed you for something."

"How do you know?"

"He told me. After I talked to Maya, I confronted him to get some answers. I seduced him—"

"You what?"

"—and he told me all about it. That he lost so much because of you. He said he wanted you to know how it felt, so he took everything from you. The only thing I don't get is why you let him. Why let him use you like for all these years?"

"He hated his life because of something I did, the least I could do was let him pretend to be someone else for a couple days a week. Even if that someone is me. Besides, it was only a name."

I rested my head on his shoulder. "But it's not only your name you've given up. You quit the soccer team for him. You took the rap for your car because he'd been drinking when he crashed it. You agreed to be my wingman and helped me get a date with him even though it killed you."

"I didn't do that for him." He wrapped his arms around my waist, pulling me tight to his chest. "I did it because you asked me to and because it was the only way I could think of to get to talk to you every day." He brushed his lips over my hair. "Not to mention I *really* didn't want to ride that bus."

I shook my head, smiling despite myself. "You gave up so much of your life for him."

"After what I did, I owed it to him."

"You can tell me. I know you're afraid of what I'll think, but I promise it's not going to scare me away."

He stopped dancing. He looked down at me and swallowed hard. "It's my fault Liam's dad is in prison."

"What do you mean? How could that be your fault?"

"We were at his house one day. I don't remember what we were doing, but I grabbed some paper from his dad's office to write something down. When I brought it home, my dad saw a list of numbers on the back. They were off-shore accounts where Liam's father had been hiding the money he embezzled from his company. The cops had been looking into him, and when my dad gave the list to them, it was the proof they needed to put him away."

"Cooper," I said softly. "That's not your fault."

"If it wasn't for me, Liam would still have his dad. He'd still have his home, and his money. He'd be able to afford any college he wanted. I ruined his life the day I brought that list home."

"You're not responsible for his father's actions. Liam's dad stole from his company. He's the one who put money over his family, over his son's future. He was the one stupid enough to leave a list of his secret account numbers lying around for anyone to find. If you hadn't found them, someone else would've and he would've gone to jail." I placed my hand on his cheek. "You're not the reason Liam's life is the way it is. You are not the bad guy here. That's on his dad. I bet Liam knows it too, but it's easier to blame you."

Cooper set his hand over mine and nuzzled into my palm. "You make it sound so simple when you say it like that."

"Well, I do have the highest GPA in our class."

"Second highest."

"Fine, I'm *tied* for the highest GPA." I wrapped my arms around him, and he began to sway to the music again.

"I guess I should tell Liam it's all over. No more trips to Columbia pretending to be me."

My lips curled. "Yeah, about that. I don't think it'll be a problem anymore."

"What do you mean?"

"You remember how I told you I got Liam to tell me everything?"

"When you breezed right over the part where you seduced him?"

"Nothing happened." I turned and grabbed my phone from the top of the piano. "But I got him to tell me the truth, and I happened to record the whole thing."

After a few swipes of my screen and I handed the phone over to Cooper. He stared blankly for a moment and blinked a bunch of times. Then he stared at a video of Liam sitting on the edge of a bed, the words *Not Cooper Bradshaw* filling the bottom of the shot.

"I'm not Cooper Bradshaw. I'm really Liam Haynes, a poor little high school student parading as a rich college kid to get laid on the weekends," Liam said.

"Does that hashtag say *Free Cooper Bradshaw*?"

"Clever, huh? Turns out Maya is a wiz with social media. She had this vid trending at South Carolina in less than a couple of hours. I'm pretty sure every girl on campus has seen this by now."

"That's—" He squinted at the screen. "Is that a hotel room?"

I snatched the phone away. "The details aren't important. What matters is Liam will never be able to sully your good name again."

"I'm not sure how good it is at this point, but thank you." He kissed me gently, then harder as I leaned into him. His fingers tangled in my hair, his other hand at the small of my back pulling me tighter against him. I wrapped my arms around his neck, and heat radiated through my body.

When I reluctantly tore my lips away from his, we were both panting.

"Where's your family?"

"The kids are staying with my aunt while my mom and dad are in New York for a book event. They won't be back until the day after tomorrow," I said between quick breaths. "But my dad made me swear not to let any guys inside while they're gone."

"My dad probably left a few hours ago for his next flight. He won't be back until Monday."

"So you're saying your house is completely empty for the next few days?"

Cooper nodded and rested his forehead against mine. "You thinking what I'm thinking?"

"If you're thinking chocolate chip cookies and a *Godfather* marathon, then yes."

He laughed. "I must be the luckiest wingman ever."

ABOUT THE AUTHOR

A small-town Georgia girl, Shannon finds no greater joy than stepping into the lives and worlds created by the written word. Despite a severe aversion to reading as a child, she has since found a passion for literature she's nurtured with incessant reading and a Bachelor's degree in English from the University of Georgia. It's this passion that helps her bring her imagination to life.

Currently living in Athens, Georgia with her sister and their four-legged furry friends, Shannon is almost always in the middle of a book, working on her own stories, or traveling to seek inspiration in the world around her.

Connect with SHANNON.:

website: shannonstults.com

facebook: facebook.com/ShannonStultsAuthor

instagram: instagram.com/shannonstultsauthor

pinterest: pinterest.com/shannonstults

www.BOROUGHSPUBLISHINGGROUP.com

If you enjoyed this book, please write a review. Our authors appreciate the feedback, and it helps future readers find books they love. We welcome your comments and invite you to send them to info@boroughspublishinggroup.com.

Follow us on Facebook, Twitter and Instagram, and be sure to sign up for our newsletter for surprises and new releases from your favorite authors.

Are you an aspiring writer? Check out www.boroughspublishinggroup.com/submit and see if we can help you make your dreams come true.

Love podcasts? Enjoy ours at www.boroughspublishinggroup.com/podcast